# An English Airman

# Foresees

# His Death

*An English Airman Foresees His Death*

by

David Milnes

First Edition

First published by what tradition books in 2021

Contents © David Hartley Milnes

British Library Cataloguing in Publication Data available

ISBN 9781916183247

This is a work of fiction: any similarities to persons living or dead is coincidental.

Also from what tradition books:

*The Ghost of Neil Diamond* by David Milnes
*The Whores of Coxcomb Hall* by Egg Taylor
*To Have Nothing* by David Milnes
*The Pathology of Graphology* by David Milnes
*Way of the Infidel* by David Milnes

# An Irish Airman Foresees His Death

## W. B. Yeats

I know that I shall meet my fate
Somewhere among the clouds above;
Those that I fight I do not hate
Those that I guard I do not love;
My country is Kiltartan Cross,
My countrymen Kiltartan's poor,
No likely end could bring them loss
Or leave them happier than before.
Nor law, nor duty bade me fight,
Nor public man, nor cheering crowds,
A lonely impulse of delight
Drove to this tumult in the clouds;
I balanced all, brought all to mind,
The years to come seemed waste of breath,
A waste of breath the years behind
In balance with this life, this death.

# An English Airman

# Foresees

# His Death

## by

## David Milnes

www.whattraditiion.co.uk

infowhattradition@gmail.com

These days it's commonplace to say taboo things and here's mine: I do not love my son. I do not even like him much. I hide it, of course, as everyone hides or disguises such feelings. When he provokes me I show nothing, not even mild irritation. I raise my eyebrows as if to say, You could have a point there, or Have it your own way, but inside I shout at him, I rail at him.

A few Sundays back he came here alone. His wife sometimes sends him over to keep him out of harm's way. I wonder why, Alex? Hmmn? . . . Well, never mind that. I took the chance to broach something I've been meaning to raise for some time.

"I want you to take the dog," I told him. "Take Mason away. Give him a new home, a new life."

He guffawed at the very idea.

"I don't want your *Mason*! . . ." Quite ribald laughter. "Really, Dad. Whatever next!"

I never wanted animals. Laura brought them into my

life, then left them chained up, caged up, expected someone else to look after them. Who? Me? Don't be ridiculous. This is the way people carry on – assuming something on a whim of sentiment then slipping away, sloping off.

"I'm weary of responsibility," I explained. "I don't want any more responsibility."

He shut his eyes and kept them shut.

"Leave it, Dad . . . Mason is your dog. Unto his dying day. Poor animal."

"Your mother – "

"Dispute it no further, Dad! Please!"

He shouted at me. Blindly. Completely lost patience with me.

"It's pointless! What's the matter with you?"

"Your mother owned all the dogs," I continued, speaking to the blank television in front of us; the screen seemed awfully dark and dusty and far off that afternoon. "You know that. I understand nothing about them. Never went to the vet. Not once. Never wanted animals." Then I looked down at him, sitting beneath me in his mother's chair. More softly, I said, "Now, little Joe would love a dog. Rachael said so . . ."

At the mention of his family he stood and went to the bay window beyond my card table. He stared hard at the garden. He was on edge. I could tell he hadn't slept. Another lousy weekend. He's always moaning about his 'lousy' or 'rotten' weekends. No money. Never had any. And his happy marriage, of course.

"A cuddly puppy, Dad. Not an abused and neglected brute like Mason, gnawing at his entrails."

Come to think of it, that was the Sunday for 'the great rapprochement': Rachael's mother was visiting for the first time in twenty bloody-minded years. It was a state occasion but neither of us was invited. She may as well have been coming back from the dead, as far as I'm concerned. Never even met her, never seen a photograph. Widowed again is all I know. Take no notice – family soaps, intrigues, step-relations and so on. I like my mysteries in Len Deighton and Eric Ambler, not in life.

The Sunday Times was spread out flat on my card table, on my freshly brushed baize – genuine baize, not felt – open at the crossword. I caught him glancing down at it. Crossword is complete. Doubtful here and there maybe, but complete. He raised his chin, stroked his neck, averted his gaze.

"Can the old man fake an education doing crossword puzzles?"

He cast a backward glance at my shelves, lined with book club giveaways, of which I'm actually rather proud: Whitaker's Almanac (several years' worth), Jackson's FactFinder, Hartrampf's Vocab-Builder, Harry Lorayne's How to Develop a Super-Power Memory . . .

"One across. Two letters."

Thanks, son.

I'll swear he thought that jibe up in his ugly little Nissan Micra on the way over. Middle-age is bringing this on. A pettiness, a bitterness. Nothing to declare for twenty years of adulthood. Married life adds a drop of bile as well, I should say. Just a drop or two.

More long stares out the window. I waited for another sigh. There was nothing to see out there. Sunday weather, Norfolk weather, dull as dyke water, dull as fenland skies, dull as obligatory family visits.

"Aren't you gardening any more?"

"No."

"It's a mess."

"I don't care."

He looked back at me, smiling. "Should we put you in a home, then?"

Funny how he'd never have said that with his wife around.

"Hah," I replied.

But he's right. It's true. I am a deeply lazy man. Ceylon taught me that. While waiting for the *Athene* I watched the tribes out there, the Coast Veddas, doing nothing all day, every day, week in, week out. I spied on them through the mangroves, smoking endless Navy Cut. They sat around in their coastal settlements, no shame or guilt about it. They had their food and drink from the sea, the rain, the trees, and that was it. Religion took care of the rest. Hinduism, I think. Ritualistic. Infantile.

Oh, but Alex thinks my laziness is awful. It's sinful, in a very British way. The less you do the less you do until you're just a parasite, a scrounger. He thinks in these earnest Christian circles. If you ever want something done, give it to a busy person, he says. But that always turns out to be him. He can't see it's a game: someone else is always knocking off at his expense. Laziness is as instinctive as sex or jealousy. It's irreversible as water. Workers like him are precious to the rest of us, and watched over all their busy, fretting, pointless lives, and then dumped, expelled, when they've nothing left to give. We drones run the show.

So in the morning I read the papers, do my crosswords, read my thrillers, listen to my stereo – Bach and Chopin are current favourites – and from early afternoon I watch tv – news, cricket, golf – or listen to quizzes on the radio. If there's nothing on I play patience to while away the hours. And he loathes it, can't stand it, my sweet tooth for sloth. The sheer mass of hours and days whittled away like this into a heap of waste. But he can't say as much and that fires up his resentment too. What he really wants to tell me is that I have always been a lazy scrounger, for as long as he's understood the difference between work and play. And he's right. Again. But he can't quite say it. Not yet. Though he has tried. He hasn't got the power, the money, to say that yet, and he never will have, so there's an end to it.

But that Sunday, after the gardening bit, he plucked up some courage. He asked:

"Why didn't you work, Dad?"

"Why didn't I work? I did work! From age fourteen, thank you very much. Nearly went down the bloody mines!"

"After your commission, I mean."

"The war, Alex. Try to remember. Keep up."

A pause while he regrouped.

"Your pension wasn't enough to live on, though, was it?"

He wanted to add: *'So you lived off your wife, didn't you?'*

I raised my lovely eyebrows and slid a look down and away at the same time, as if surprised he could stoop so low, but actually, I was surprised he could be so bold. He is a gutless son.

"You'd have to dig pretty deep to get to the bottom of that."

Which was enough to make him back off.

I don't understand where his assurance comes from to say such things, to challenge me in his mealy-mouthed way. I don't know where his smugness comes from at all. He's no longer young. He's not handsome. He's not clever. He's not funny. He's certainly not rich and never will be. Nor does he have that ghastly sexual confidence that lends some men their insufferable self-belief. So where does it come from, his assurance; his pomposity, almost. Certainly not from me. I've none myself, never believed in myself, never believed in him either. I never thought either of us would amount to anything, and we haven't.

The way he stretched his neck by the window – I can see him now – and stroked himself there, around the Adam's apple, that preening gesture, while staring at the derelict garden. He always does that. Stands and stares out the bay window at the garden, and preens himself in that way. Something proprietorial about it. Then smooths his hair – that's some of it too, the preening business. His hairstyle hasn't changed in thirty years. The same low-browed, pressed parting from left to right, with a wayward and awkward forelock, once lightly brilliantined but now curled up into a dry, crisp cone. He cups it in his hand, smoothing his hair, protecting it, that dry and greying cone, so unbecoming for a man his age. This is the hairstyle they gave him at his precious school, for being captain of rugger, or senior prefect, or for singing bass in Iolanthe or some such nonsense. Though middle-aged now his face is still open and naïve, with his hanging, fleshy lower lip – from his mother, that. Like the flesh of a pomegranate, I always thought, but dried up. What's happened to his body Lord only knows. The upper chest still has its prop-forward bulk, then his torso shrinks in unnaturally to the waist above his stocky legs. It's as if he wears a corset. It's a horrible, unnatural shape. Like that of a comic book hero, at the point where he enters the page top left, in full flight and colour, everything tapering away from the chest. He wears lambs' wool pullovers from Marks & Spencers all year round. Bottle green or beige. Or rather, bottle green and beige, because the armpits of the bottle green ones are stained beige. Whatever did Rachael see in him? She isn't ageing like him. She isn't giving up. Not her! She's just had her hair permed into the sweetest, darkest, slipperiest ringlets. I love them. I want to touch them, feel them, to drape their waxy softness over the back of my ancient, speckled hands.

So why on earth is he so assured? Apart from his wife, it's the only thing I envy him. This is something I always thought I would take for granted by now, but no, not a bit of it: extinction beckons – I hate it, I can see it, feel it, I know it's here, all around my chair, my recliner, I sense it everywhere – and I feel less and less assured about who or what I am, about what I've done and what it's worth, about anything at all, yet I still have to pretend the exact opposite. The calm, the serenity one is meant to assume, to possess almost as a right – Hah! Some feelings quieten down, subside, some you can't be bothered with any more, but some never go away. Not for men.

Anyway, he left shortly after that.

During the war I did what I was told and the war was good to me. This is something Alex knows but never raises, for some scruple of his own. He knows I enjoyed myself. I had a good war. I flew through it and saw the world on the way. Of course there was terror at times, but mainly it was exhilarating, thrilling. It was as Alex says – roller-coasting in the sky. On the ground there was the real thing, the bayonet, the shrapnel, the mud and rats everywhere, but up in the sky there was just a red button on the joystick, and the man you killed or burned or maimed was wrapped up in a fancy, decorated, pretty machine, often tarted up with paintings, for goodness' sake – graffiti and cartoons! Even if you caught a glance of his face you couldn't really see it because of the goggles. This is all exposed now, of course, the truth of this, because it's what the computers simulate for boys like Joe, for the joy of millions of real boys and Peter Pans – *Fighter Pilot, WW2 Ace, Dogfight* etc. I haven't just given these to Joe at Christmas, I've bought them myself. Alex helped me get started, to load things up, sort out the bugs and so on. He loves computers. He thinks knowing about them, sending things whizzing about the screen, makes him intelligent. With a modicum of knowledge you can be so helpful, show off so much. Actually, his wife's overtaken him. But let that pass. The games themselves are not bad, but details are wrong. Instruments in the wrong place or things that simply didn't exist then. The Hurricane's stick was articulated, there just wasn't room for it not to be, but in the games it's a rigid shaft. Perhaps the real Hurricane cockpit is too stark and primitive and boring, and must be upgraded for today's child. What they don't give is any impression of the sheer confinement, of course, and the noise, or the heavy yaw when taking off, rudder locked over – or the terror, when that came, even while taking off, a few times. But the confinement. I'm not tall and lanky so I fitted in like a nut in its shell. Hawker might have designed the plane for me alone. My feet sat on the pedals as if I were in a shoe shop. But anyone over six foot had an awful time of it. Some talked about that more than combat. The cramps. Unable to move the limb to stop the cramp, to stop the muscle tearing from the ligament, and too distracted by it to defend yourself. I suspect some died on account of that. The battle on my ageing IBM – and how about an upgrade this Christmas, Alex? – is roughly the same if you take away the noise, vibration, the smell and the cold at 20,000 feet. What I mean is the battle was just that quick – kill or be killed, burn or be burned – and the game captures that. Except you have ridiculous amounts of ammunition. The Brownings carried thirteen hundred rounds in each wing. A couple of minute's worth if you were lucky, though you only used it in two or three second bursts. You can't make much of a game out of that.

And yet there are the pictures on my wall, here, today, on display, and they've been there for forty odd years, on the opposite wall to the bookshelves, photographs from more than half a century ago, of me standing in line to shake Churchill's hand, when thousands who had a real war, infantrymen in their thirties or forties – fathers and uncles, poor sods! – on the western front, or teenage conscripts in ships sunk by U-boats, lie nameless under the mud or snow or sea, and have no recognition like that at all, no photo with the war-leader, the most recognized Briton in all history. Then to come back afterwards to the same old snobberies and mean-spiritedness, the same cousinhood or cozenhood owning 90% of everything – Private Property! Keep Out! Police Notice! By Order! – and have to pretend that you had done it all for king and country, just so that you could fit in somewhere and draw some paltry pay-cheque – I couldn't do it. Not after all that. What was life for? Pretend all over again? I hid in the R.A.F. until they grounded me, then scurried off into the countryside. Deserter, if you will.

Still they come, the enthusiasts of The Few, the idolizers and hero-seekers, and I have to keep up the old pretences. *This is what I mean!* I cannot escape these people, these stories, without disgracing or mutilating my life, yet, retold, the stories themselves disgrace and mutilate my life. What can I say to them? Some weeks I mutter just a few words to the butcher, the baker, the candlestick maker, and even then can hardly muster the tritest pleasantries. Most days pass saying nothing whatever. Not a word. Not that I would have it otherwise. I don't want to meet people. Any of them. They sicken me. What a thing to say! So melodramatic! But it's a perfectly true and fitting thing to say. What can I tell these hero-seekers, anyway? I can't tell them my fellows were children, boys – the average age was twenty for the Battle of Britain! – I can't say they were not men at all because the men who come here are all Peter Pans too! You can see it in their eyes. They would have given anything to have had a war like mine. They think they missed out. With me they have to pretend to be doing some weighty historical research for their silly books. They never touch on the pleasures, the thrill of the thing. Wouldn't dream of being so indiscreet. Of course they want to know who I remember – Bader, Lacey – anecdotes of prangs or pranks, but they box that up as something different, peripheral, when actually it's at the heart of every question they ask. Then the material bit: the movements, strategies, the Jap at Singapore, which aircraft carrier etc., getting the details right – but again that's so boyish. The way boys play at war on their own, colouring in maps or marshalling armies and weapons, making it all into a board game. We tread carefully round the Jap, though: we'll get to that, or maybe not.

But still they come. Men of Alex's age, Alex's generation. The sons. Only the sons. Never the daughters, worse luck. Not interested. It's a Boy's Own world.

Mechanized violence – lovely phrase, exactly right; or I should say 'the mechanizers of violence', because someone actually did it; men, always men, designed and made these things – had developed for us a new and unique form of fencing, a test of wits and guts, a new sport, with both combatants masked, unknown, loosed from the old code of knightly conduct. There was a dash of relief, perhaps, if I saw a parachute, but then gain height, gain gain gain and get above them, get away from the danger and the reality of it. They ask, Did the Germans shoot pilots in parachutes? Well, I never saw it but I can quite believe it happened. Makes sense. How can I bring these things together? Running out of fuel, bailing out over the English Channel, knocking the side panel loose and tumbling out above the dull sea, with land in sight, Kent in sight, and the flat grey sheet of metal sea below, freezing, waiting for me – how can I bring that together with my life as it is now? There's no guiding intelligence behind it at all. Nothing adds up. The ends don't meet anywhere.

Perhaps I should say this to the would-be historians and archivists manqué. After all, what do I care about their piffling books? Must they write them? There can't be any money in it. Why bother? Why glamorize yet another life? The endless glamorizing of things, the endless graffiti over the fuselage and the writing on the wall. They irritate me so, again and again, every bloody time, with their half-apologetic questions about the Spitfire, with that glint coming into their eye, or rather behind their bifocals – while I still don't wear glasses, except for very small print – when it comes to comparing British fighters. They'll even bring in Mosquitoes, given half the chance. But I give them no quarter, stop them in their tracks, because nothing could turn like the Hurricane, and that was at the heart of the business. I mean nothing in the air at that time could equal it because that aeroplane was so *strong*. We drew Zeroes into a spin because we knew they would break up – it was actually a tactic. The Jap couldn't pull out without his wings folding, without falling to pieces. Hurricane pulled out every time. Even when you had to heave on the stick as if it were a pickaxe. In the Battle of France the Spitfire never used the grass strips we used. The undercarriage just wasn't strong enough. It buckled, failed, busted. Strong, stronger, strongest – those are the only words to use about the Hurricane. No others do it justice. No others respect the facts as I knew them, first hand.

*The News, Tomorrow's World, The Two Ronnies* – while Laura was sick upstairs I sat tight in my study. Alex came down and asked me for the newspaper. She wanted to read the local paper. I couldn't find it and flew into a rage. "I don't know where the bloody paper is!" Alex was shocked. He thought it was the welling anxiety, the prescient grief. But at that particular moment it was not. It was simply his interruption, his piercing of the tv bubble and my reaction inside – Why should I feel? Why are you making me feel something I don't feel, or don't want to feel?

When she became very ill the stench in the bathroom was like a fire, a living scream from within a fire. If you're burned at the stake, your legs kick out as the muscle burns, then your gut blows out with your gas expanding until it pops like a balloon. I know screams, what they are. I've heard screams, the screams of full-blooded, deep-lunged young men who screamed on and on like that because the pain had nowhere else to go. They were burned at the stake. With a feeder tank of 100 octane in front of the cockpit, what did anyone expect? But hers was the curdled, gurgling, visceral scream coming up from the bowels themselves, expanding, blowing up, the scream of mortality inside. For God's sake do something, Antony! But I carried on, and she carried on. She still did all the cooking, and I let her. She brought in supper on a tray, or the milky Nescafé in the morning. I found her in the kitchen sitting on a high stool at the sink, peeling potatoes. She needed to sit because she was so weak by then, and because of the weight inside her bowel. Peeling potatoes. King Edwards. Heavy lumps of food outside, heavy lumps of knobbly, undigested food inside. I stood there, holding open the kitchen door. When Alex was a boy I fixed a closer on the door to stop him slamming it all the time, cracking the plaster all around the architrave, creating more work – *'That's right, Alex! Go on! Give it a bloody good slam!'* – I stood holding the door wide against its spring without saying anything, and she didn't turn from her potatoes at the sink. She knew I was there because of the whine from the door-closer and the draught, but she did not turn. She reached for another potato from the bowl, her elbow pivoted on the side of the sink. A huge, dirty King Edward. I could feel the pressure of the door-closer against my hand. I could feel the weight of the potato. I could feel the pressure in her bowel.

Until I stood back, let the door shut, and returned to my study.

Sitting on a stool. Her belly distended as if six months pregnant, at sixty. Finally she couldn't get out the bath. She called out to me – "Antony! You'll have to help me now! I can't get out the bloody bath!" Her exact words. Unforgettable. She never swore. So I took her to the hospital. You must admit my wife, I told them. Immediately. No further delays. No procrastination, no waiting lists. Call the surgeon. Now. I don't care where he is, what golf course he's on – I'm not leaving here until you bring him. Get him here! After the houseman examined her there was no more trouble. They put her in a private room and the operation was set for the next morning – a Sunday – first thing. Emergency. But when I came back the houseman had gone off duty and they hadn't done it. They'd moved her into a mixed ward and delayed again. Again. That Sunday afternoon her gut burst, flooding her with excrement from within.

I could not sue. I turned it over and over in my mind, but I could not. Because I couldn't pretend, or if I did pretend, some clever lawyer would find a way through my pretences. With her collusion I had let things happen, take their course. But nothing any good ever happens unless you make it happen, unless you push push push against the inertia. Maybe she had given up completely by then, I sometimes think. In fact, I can hardly doubt it. At sixty. Just sixty. The burden of her sickness, from which she must have sensed there could be no real reprieve, and the burden of her disappointment with the way things had turned out, with me, with Alex – it had all become insupportable. Too little left to live for, too little that side of the scales. She had her faith to help her out: long talks with Alex about all that, tidying up mortality, making sense of it all. Shortly after retirement she'd started attending church again, when she felt the first symptoms, I suspect.

Of course my simpleton, priggish son came back at me. Not immediately. He left a decent interval, but then it must have got too much for his precious Christian soul. It all came tumbling out in blundering double-negatives.

"You are the only one who doesn't feel he didn't do enough, Dad. Didn't do his bit. No one else doesn't feel he didn't do enough. Just you."

I said nothing. I was actually playing patience when he arrived. I heard his horrible Jap car on the gravel. He burst in on me, quite upset, tearful, out of control. I remained at the card table, laying out the cards in their lines, but very slowly.

"We all knew what you were like, but I told myself

it's too unfair to you not to trust you to do the right thing. Not to trust you to judge it for yourself."

I turned a royal card, a Jack, tapped it on the baize.

"You expected me to confront the doctors. The consultants. Challenge the experts."

"You handed her over to the experts. That's what you did." He was still at the door, holding it open, very distressed, letting out all the warm air from my fan heaters. I have no central heating whatever. Conked out ages ago. "Then you waited. You sat back and waited. You didn't push them and you didn't push her to help herself. That's what you didn't do, and what you should have done, Dad. And you know it."

"I can't take these people on. You know that. GPs. Consultants. Specialists. Medical people. For goodness' sake, Alex – I haven't your confidence, your assurance, your education. You know that. For your mother, you know perfectly well – "

"Then you could have asked for help, Dad."

That 'Dad' again did it for me. I put aside the deck and looked up at him:

"So what was it, then? Your pride? You wouldn't help unless I asked?"

"No. I got it wrong. I admit that. But you don't admit it."

"No, Alex. I don't admit it. I don't admit I got it wrong, in your ghastly phrase. Stew in your own guilt, Alex. I want no more of this, do you hear? You don't know what you're talking about!"

"You're going to be a very lonely old man soon, you know."

"That's my business."

"Well – "

"Shut up, Alex. Just go away. You've said enough. Leave me in peace. You've done enough. Go away. Please! For goodness' sake."

Oh, they all said, Don't hold on. Let go and get on with life. Some youngsters actually said that. Some horrible grand-second-step-nephews and nieces or something I'd never seen before. Sympathetic adolescents. Could anything be worse? All cock-eyed make-up, bulging bodies and undeveloped sensibility. *Get on with life, grandpa!* What did they think I was going to do? Emigrate? Make my fortune in the colonies? In my late sixties? As if life were somewhere out there to be grasped hold of, taken properly in hand and managed and moved along, like a career. The rubbish you have to listen to when your wife dies.

The warmth in the study from my fan heater and the Belling convector ends at the bay window, facing east. Those heaters cannot penetrate here. Standing in the bay, looking up the overgrown bank to the belt of trees and the church wall, you feel the full force of the cold the other side of the glass, from three fronts. You feel its mighty opposition to life, just beyond the frail and rotten sash windows. The mortal cold. Extinction everywhere. Its pressure, its draughts, squeezing out my tiny, ancient pulse of warmth. In the morbid silence I can actually hear my own pulse. This is the latest thing. I can hear it behind my right ear in the silence of the countryside, which is why I have the radio on all the time now, and a transistor radio in the kitchen, both set to Radio 3, so I can't hear this pulse, the tattoo of my blood, my heart, building up to aneurysm, stroke, disability.

It had to be cremation. She said untended graves were

the most pitiful sight in the world. But was she right? Given my laziness, and our feelings for each other towards the end, of course she was right. But was she *right*? I'm not sure. Sometimes I think that I would have been more attentive than either of us could have foreseen. In a way she robbed me. I could have had a place to go. It makes a difference, knowing that the body is actually there, still exists, under the sod, rather than knowing it has been burned to boiler dust and mingled with the corpses of a thousand unknowns. Had there been a grave I would have had somewhere to go and talk things out. Alex put the dust under a tree he planted on the drive, a special pine of some sort, inexpensive and very slow growing. I cannot talk to a tree. I could have talked to a grave, and keeping it tended would have been a way of showing something, saying something.

What she had to put up with, even at the very end, in the hospital. When I'd gone they moved her out of that private room – without informing me – onto the mixed ward. She woke during the night in great pain, despite the drips. She woke in the small hours of that dreadful Sunday morning, at some godforsaken hour, to hear, and then see, and then smell, an old man in his pyjamas masturbating by her bedside.

When I visited that morning I shouted at the ward sister in her prim little office, with its brand new, shiny white coffee-maker. Never give these people offices. Keep them walking up and down the bed ends. Shouted at her. Bloody nurses! Bloody doctors! Bloody National Health! Bloody *indignity*!

The day outside is dull and brimful of stillborn English melancholy. When those chirpy adolescents, whoever they were, who'd had a little too much of my dry sherry after the service, because sherry was all I had, and they'd probably never drunk it before, when they said, Get on with life, they meant, of course, get on with it on their terms. Get on with the good times. Look to the future. 'You can make it to the millennium, grandpa!' Someone actually said that, or something very like it. And he received some grinning, cheerful, brace-toothed support from the others too. There was a chorus of them by then. To whom, on all of God's green earth, did they think they were talking? Alex cut across to help out but he was clumsy and no use, the worse for wear himself by then. He does like his tipple these days, our Alex.

To me it is beneath contempt – this modern drunkenness. Shameless, in-broad-daylight drunkenness. Any drunkenness disgusts me. Always has. I despise it. On their monthly visits, Rachael and Alex cook the Sunday lunch together. In the shopping bags, along with the beef and veg, there's always a bottle of Sainsbury's plonk he's sneaked in. Minervois or Corbieres. £3.99. He drinks most of it, rendering himself pretty much unfit for the afternoon's fatherly duties. In the garden last Sunday (we had a touch of Indian summer) I told him, "Go and play with your son, Alex. Dry out a bit." I omitted Joe's name. Your son, Alex. Duty calls, Alex. Dry out, Alex. He looked awkward, vexed, but he was too befuddled with the wine and the sunshine to work out how to get out of it, so he stumbled off to push Joe on the rope swing, leaving me free to chat to Rachael on her own.

Oh, rare and delicious treat!

Recently my head has started to nod if a conversation is slightly nervous and endures beyond the opening skirmishes or pleasantries. Nothing too serious, but noticeable. Such an agreeable old chap, don't you know! Well, the stress and agitation of being alone with Rachael in the sun set it off immediately. Charitable as always, she said nothing about this nodding, which I know full well is perfectly visible and must look very odd, very ancient indeed. But, good Christian that she is, she said nothing. Actually, I can't believe in her as a serious church person. She's too damn *sensual*. I suspect a deeper life, a troubled, double life, maybe. Alex got her too young and no mistake, which is what caused the rift with her mother. On that thought, I asked how the reunion had gone, 'the great rapprochement', even though Alex had warned me not to. "Don't go there, Dad." But I don't like mysteries and I've got more guts than him.

She looked away, to Alex pushing Joe on the rope swing, but she wasn't really watching them.

"Not so well, I'm afraid." She was speaking to no one. "Long gaps aren't good for family relationships, I discovered."

"Bit hard," I prompted. "Bearing a grudge against your own daughter for twenty bloody years!"

"They kind of die out."

"Twenty bloody years! I ask you!"

"It's not quite like that."

"Oh? Why did she visit, then? What's up? Is she broke?" Always my first suspicion.

Still without looking at me, she said, "She's rich as Croesus, Antony."

"Hah!" I laughed. "Sounds like the kind of old bird I'd like to meet!"

Now she did look at me. "Maybe you will some day," she said, with that knowing, teasing smile she has, that suggests secret plans, schemes, duplicities. An actress's smile. "But you better watch out if she comes here, sees this place," she warned, still teasing. "Stay sharp." She turned back to look at Joe, who was shrieking on the rope swing now. Alex was pushing him wildly, with drunken abandon. Then she looked at me again, frowning and smiling at the same time, about to add some jibe she knew she shouldn't but just couldn't resist. "She's a gold-digger, though, Antony, not a grave-digger, so I don't think you'd get on."

Tee hee hee. I shrugged. Part of that shrug was a sadness to think that if the old girl really was rich, Alex didn't seem to be in line for a penny of it. Really, the way people's feelings interfere with what matters in life, with the hard arithmetic.

So I invited her to see my whisky advertisement. It's in a cupboard in my study. She'd pricked my vanity with that jibe about not getting on with her mysterious mother, not being rich enough or sharp enough for her.

When I retired, in between making notes for the great testament, one of the few ads for employment I took seriously was by Whyte & Mackay, for a screen test. Change of direction, one might say. It so happened I was exactly what they needed for their billboards, and for a few weeks of the winter of 1969 I was on watch all across the nation, beaming down on the snow and slush from decrepit corners in derelict northern towns, bearing down on the mink-stoled shoppers on Oxford Street and Piccadilly Circus, keeping an eye on city gnomes from across the tracks of Moorgate underground . . . What success the image had I do not know. Probably none at all because there was no offer of any further work. I was handsome enough, I suppose, but perhaps the military look was out of fashion by then to the right quarters of whisky-drunks. Be that as it may, a dozen of us had posed, and I was chosen. In a corner of a studio in Maida Vale, I sat in a buttoned leather club chair, wearing an army Captain's uniform (the common touch), surrounded by bookshelves, panelled walls and lighting apparatus. There was a barley-twist standard lamp by a rosewood table, on which sat the bottle of Whyte & Mackay. The oaky light of a gentlemen's club, or regimental mess, fell from the lamp onto a cut crystal tumbler in my hand, and onto my swept back, brilliantined hair and sober smile. I keep the photo in a backed envelope on the top shelf of my gramophone cupboard. To get to the upper shelves I have a miniature step-ladder in there, which gave me the height to stare down Rachael's summer dress. Couldn't help myself. Couldn't miss a chance like that. Then I stood next to her in the cupboard while she looked at the photo. Her dark ringlets were so close to me, to my face, a thousand dark and mischievous silken ringlets. In the dimness of the cupboard she could have been a decade younger too, in her late twenties even.

"So that's what your study's all about," she said.

I took the photo back and looked at it myself.

"Quite the part, weren't you?" she added.

She was right to mock me. My study is panelled, but not with beautiful seasoned oak. I did it with contiboard. And the shelves around my recliner are all lined with the wrong books, of course – Whitaker's Almanac, Jackson's Factfinder, Hartrampf's Vocab-Builder, Harry Lorayne's How to Develop a Super-Power Memory . . .

"I wanted you to know how famous I once was, you see."

"Is that all?" she asked, raising her eyebrows, her arms folded lightly under her lovely breasts.

Oh, you're far too sharp for Alex, I thought. You must bring him some earthly misery, all right. Oh yes.

Muttering something about Joe, she slipped out the cupboard and away from my study, back to the cool hallway and the garden and her family.

I went to the kitchen and made them tea and cut up the Madeira cake. I always buy a Madeira for their visits: Alex needs something sweet and spongy to soak up the wine before the drive back, though she drives more often than not these days. He kips in the front seat like an old man in a deck chair. I brought the tea and cake out on a tray and we sat in the last of the sunshine. She came round and poured the tea. Alex followed. Joe stayed still as a stopped clock on his rope swing, holding on for attention that he wasn't going to get, for once.

"I wish my wife were still alive," I said to Rachael, watching her pour for her husband, for me, "to see how you've brought Alex such happiness."

She glanced at me, then looked quickly down at the teacups, as if she'd given something away by meeting my pilot's eyes just then.

Which she had.

Not long after they'd gone, forty minutes or so, still plenty of light (they arrived late and left early, as usual) a Datsun Cherry, very red and ugly, came up the drive, with a middle-aged couple inside, the man driving. He took a long sweep, far too long, around my gravel and parked to face back down the drive. After switching off the engine he sat there a moment, staring ahead. He'd seen me watching from the kitchen window, sitting at the head of the refectory table. I hadn't moved since Rachael's indicator light gave its farewell wink through the trees at the end of the drive.

The hatchback door of the Datsun was rusty beneath the number plate. D reg. All these Jap cars have me surrounded.

No one got out. He said something to his wife, or companion, nodding at the windscreen as he spoke, as if repeating something he'd said to her many times and which he now said yet again with spelled-out patience and irritation, as if what he was about to do was something that had to be done, gone through, endured, yet again, and there was no choice in the matter.

Who was it? A salesman? Insurance? But with his wife? Or some long forgotten relative come to seek me out. Driven all the way from the East Midlands, bearing momentous or portentous family news. Stories of the imminent bankruptcy of my millionaire nephews! Could I help? Could I see my way clear to . . .?

Awful sorry, and all that.

He opened the door and set foot on my gravel, my drive. Brown, polished slip-ons with elasticated sides, and beige socks with a blue diamond pattern. Ah, my airman's eyes! He got out the car and stood there a moment, in his suede jacket and open shirt, hitching his trousers, cavalry twill, and taking in my house, my trees, the caw of my crows, the whole of my three acres. Then he turned, resolved, and shut the door. A short man, mid-fifties, with a puffy chest and narrow waist. An older version of Alex's body shape – this was a connection I did well to make, as it happened.

Missus stayed in the Datsun.

I went out to the porch and closed the kitchen door behind me before opening the back door. I stood waiting on the porch step. A couple of paces before he reached the step, he stopped and smiled and stretched out his hand, and for some reason he also set his head on one side, actually cocked his head at me, like a bird.

"Antony Rose?"

His hair was soft and brushed forward. It should have all been grey but instead it had a faded, nicotine tinge, as if he were an inveterate chain-smoker. His forelock didn't lie flat but curled inward and underward. Maybe his wife did that for him, curled his nicotine fringe. No sooner had I thought this than I knew it was true. She did that for him. Lucky fellow.

I had a tea towel over my arm.

"Can't shake hands," I said. "Doing the dishes. Are you lost?" I said 'lawst'. It just slipped out. "Are you selling something? If so, not today, thanks."

He just smiled at all that and his crow's-feet wrinkled up around his nondescript brown eyes, and at the same time all these bird notions took flight. Suddenly I was a boy again, at the seaside, poking anemones with a bamboo cane I'd found on the beach.

"Group Captain Antony Rose, if I'm not mistaken, sir."

She has done this, I thought. I know what this is about, all right. Oh yes. This is her work, and this is why they were late today; not what she said. This fellow was no autograph hunter in search of the last of The Few, even though the promotion to senior commissioned officer was just the kind of flattery I was accustomed to from those people.

He came forward the last two paces and took from his suede jacket a plastic box of business cards. He opened the box and removed one for me. I took it and looked at it. I stared at it so long I heard his slip-ons shift on the gravel.

The card was magnolia and luxuriously thick. On it was a sketch of a long, bleak building, reminiscent of a Victorian workhouse, but the lines of the building were broken up by trees in full green leaf. The trunks of the trees were shaped unnaturally with supple curves, and there was something about these curves that drew the eye. They made the trees sway in the breeze, like dancers. They were actually women's curves. The female form. A quite unbelievable crassitude.

The Grosvenor.

"Is this a hotel?"

"No, sir."

Proprietors: Frank and Jane Simmonds.

"Looks a bit shabby to me. I don't need a hotel anyway."

"The Grosvenor is a rest home, sir."

"Is it now?" I asked, stropping the card. Then I told him: "You'd better come in."

Extraordinary. Superhuman, the effrontery.

Little wonder Frank had to suppress his wife's doubts in the car.

Must get to the bottom of this, I thought. Sort this out, once and for all.

The Grosvenor, indeed. Always there has to be that idea of the upper classes, the idle rich. The Grosvenor, The Beaumont, The Windsor, The Mayfair, as if you were going to end your days strolling around private art galleries, racing enclosures, billiard rooms, tropical hot-houses . . .

Pretending that I hadn't noticed his wife, I closed the porch door behind him and ushered him through the kitchen door. I gestured to him – no words – to sit down at the refectory table. He did so, his back to the window. I remained standing.

"Well?"

He knitted his hands and held them in front of him on the table. He looked at his knitted hands, touched thumbs before speaking again. I moved closer, to the opposite side of the table, the tea towel still over my arm.

"Just an enquiry, sir. Jane and I have been running The Grosvenor for thirteen years, which is long enough to know what our clients want, and how to provide it for them with the highest levels of comfort and security."

"Who told you to come here?"

"Your reaction is understandable, and not uncommon, Mr Rose. No one told us to come here. No one at all. Your son and daughter-in-law – a delightful couple, if I may say so, and a great credit to you – came to look round The Grosvenor. That is all."

"My son told you to come here? Or was it her?"

"No. He did not. They did not. Emphatically, they did not, sir. I took it upon myself." He looked up, all earnestness and deep concern. "What we offer is best described first hand, and in a friendly, non-threatening and open way, prior to any visit."

"Any visit? Any *visit*?" But I had to block my anger. Had to think. Get to the bottom of it. "Well, now. Are you expensive?"

"We're at the top of the market, sir."

"Because I haven't any money. Did he tell you that?"

"It wouldn't be a problem."

"No?"

"We would handle all that – valuation, solicitors, everything."

"Ah . . . I understand," I said. "At least, I think I do."

The nodding had started. I was nodding at him as if I agreed with him. The excitement was too much for the old pipes and wires, despite my tiresome walks around the three acres, my attempts to keep fit, stay strong, stay sharp, on guard, for this kind of thing; defend oneself to the last from the plots and schemes and machinations, the bloody enemy, the traitors all around.

"From what I understand, sir, with your pensions – "

I raised a hand to stop him – couldn't bear it – but I had to find some other movement to channel the excitement away. I took the tea towel from over my arm and folded it neatly and set it over the back of the kitchen chair, opposite Frank Simmonds. I smoothed the tea towel over the back of the chair.

"What I have to do," I said, looking down, smoothing the tea towel along its blue stripes, as if it were some precious flag, "is speak to my son about this." I sounded a little faint and cleared my throat. "About this visit. Your visit. Not mine. Not my visit to you, to the Grosvenor. Your visit to me, to the rectory. Because it is most unwelcome, you see. Your visit. Most unwelcome. Do you understand?"

He got up immediately, but not in any hurry or panic. "I do understand, sir, and I am very sorry."

He'd queered the pitch and he knew it.

I stood back and let him open the door himself, then followed him into the porch. The porch was full of cobwebs and leaves, I noticed, seeing it with my guest's eyes. I let him open the porch door as well.

But his car was empty.

She was having a stroll around the grounds!

"That's funny!" he said, embarrassed.

We heard a crunch of gravel as she came round from the front of the house.

He laughed. "There you are!"

"Lovely place you have here, Group Captain!" she

declared, very brazen, looking up at me. I hadn't moved from the porch step above her.

Every pore of her face had been filled in. It was as if her hair had been tied back from her head while her face was dipped, like an animal's butt, in some chemical slime. The grease of it was all over her neck too. Her hair was raven black and far too long – the wild gypsy look. She was not a woman yet, just an adolescent in her early fifties. Everything garish, pubescent. She wore bulbous, sea shell earrings that looked far too heavy to be comfortable, and fistfuls of sunken treasure barnacled her fingers. She looked away from me and down the sweep of the drive. It's a two hundred yard curve to the gate and the lane beyond. Two hundred yards minimum. Quite magnificent. These people, these gypsies, do not belong here, not to my slice of Norfolk, my slice of England. They have no right to be here. No right to listen to my crows cawing, my pigeons cooing. No more right than Rachael has to sell it from under my feet.

"Take the guts out of a million," said Simmonds. He glanced up at me and nodded, appraising, respectful. Ah, the stupendous power of money.

I withdrew and closed the porch door without another word for either of them. But I stayed in the porch, watching, until they'd both turned and walked back to the Datsun with whatever dignity they could muster, opened the doors, climbed in and started it up. That rusty tailgate. D reg. He waved out the window before putting on his seat belt, and then she lowered the window and waved her coral rings halfway down the drive.

Well. It has begun.

The new Leisure Pool is a large, black-timbered bungalow on the edge of town, sunk fifty yards from the ring road on a concrete plinth. The PVC windows are not the usual aching white but a soft shade of burgundy, which in the rain gives the whole place a red-rimmed and rather tearful aspect. You park round the back. Beyond the new galvanized fence, always dripping with dew for some reason, are open, shiny, slimy fields, on all sides. At the moment the soil is freshly ploughed and black, and the fields are empty. Autumn. No movement anywhere. Under a grey sky *The Leisure Pool, off the Ring Road in Wet Fields*, is a study in oils from my private collection: Rural Life, Circa 2000.

In bathing trunks I am what I am: foul hollows, hairy tufts, unsightly folds. But for someone in his late-seventies, any doctor would tell you I'm in good shape. Fairly lithe and supple. Work hasn't flogged the life out of me, and I'm not fat or sick from its compensatory ills – too much drink, food, self-indulgence. Gave up smoking decades ago. I've always looked after myself, kept reasonably fit. Hence this new venture, The Leisure Pool, which is free on Mondays and Wednesdays for gentlemen of a certain age, between 8.00 a.m. and 10.00 a.m. I have Male Changing (such crass signage) entirely to myself.

For my first dip I dug out a pair of navy blue trunks that I hadn't used for twenty years. They were exposing, repulsive. For my second I swapped them for some colourful baggy shorts – the things teenagers wear. My legs stick out, knobbly-kneed and spiky, in exactly the way men's legs stick out on those lewd seaside postcards. I am the living inspiration for those ageless cartoons.

That first dip, however, in the twenty-year old

trunks, didn't go entirely as foreseen. I executed a graceful swallow dive, very pleasing – but felt the tepid water rush over me like a premonition. After just a few strokes, as the blue base of the pool began to lighten below, I felt my lower half falling, failing, then slowing me down, pulling me under. I didn't look – I couldn't – but I knew the lifeguard was watching from his elevated seat. I stopped moving and let my feet carry on to the bottom. But there was no bottom. Before I could really believe what was happening I was beneath the surface without any air inside me. I pushed up and snatched a wild gasp.

"Take hold!"

Then there was just the blue, and the heavy black lines on the bottom, and the sense that I must not breathe, *must* not breathe, though my chest felt crushed by fifty fathoms. Arms and legs started an automatic, useless floundering against the thickening blue. Then the red ring pushed at me, under me, nudged my flank, a hard red ring on a wooden pole. I took it and in a moment I had surfaced, and the drama was over. Air! Sweet, warm, chlorinated air! Crouched at the poolside, the lifeguard was drawing in the pole very cautiously, just a few inches at a time.

"Don't move. Hold. Tight as you can."

Oh, the soft, tepid, chlorinated air!

At the side I reached instinctively for the guttering.

"No. The ring. Keep hold of the ring. I've got you."

He trapped the pole under his knee, reached under my shoulders and clamped me there, then drew me out the pool as if I were a child. He set me on the tiles and clasped my hands about my knees and made me rest with my head forward, on my knees, while he held me steady. After a minute he must have been assured there would be no need for an ambulance and he took his hands away.

"Shallow end for you, matey."

"Yes," I muttered between my legs. "Oh yes . . . Thank you . . . Thank you . . ."

I was acutely aware of my ancient blue swimming trunks at that moment. Their perished elastic and bobbled fabric.

"Might get yourself a new cozzie, too."

Just three weeks ago this young man saved my life, yet now we are sworn enemies. There you have the fickleness of the human heart! Who'd go to war over what people feel or think? Ridiculous. I now see this lifeguard as a lout, a lump, an idiot; and to him, I am – what? Just a pain in the arse. I can hear him say it. Pain in the arse. Or, 'that old shit'. Something excremental, of course. I am the new irritant in his life, the spoiler of Monday's and Wednesday's precious rites.

The sauna too is available free of charge to us ancients on Mondays and Wednesdays, between 8 a.m. and 10 a.m. It's tucked around the corner from the second row of showers. No signs anywhere. And pinned to the door, along with the manufacturer's official warnings and disclaimers, is a long laminated list of forbidding, misspelled rules in blue felt-tip. The lifeguards' work.

When I discovered the sauna the second lifeguard was already in there. They should both be at the poolside, of course, but for my swim they take it in turns. The other is always in the sauna. Until I came along I suppose they were accustomed to sharing a sauna together, and a swim and shower afterwards, perhaps, before they took breakfast in the cafeteria. Full English, on the house, whipped up on Mondays and Wednesdays by the flirty, frumpy mum behind the counter. The lifeguards are her 'lads'. The pool doesn't reopen to the public until 10.30, so in effect they begin work no less than two and a half hours late, after a sauna, dip and free breakfast, all at the local burghers' expense.

My arrival has changed all that. I like the sauna too. Worse still, I might tell my friends about the empty pool and the empty sauna. I might bring along a coachload of elderly, unsightly, sinking, stinking bodies for them to deal with. I have interfered with their laziness, their peace of mind, their withdrawal from work and responsibility, and they hate me for that. Yet three weeks ago one of them saved my life.

If I sauna before I swim, which guard will be in there when I open the door, and will he be naked? The one who didn't save me – Aaron – tries to embarrass me away by appearing stretched out like a pornography item on a lower shelf. Or sitting hams on hands, glistening with sweat, stony-faced and overbearing. It doesn't work. I like the sauna. I take it twice a week. It's free. It keeps the colds away.

My rescuer was Mark. I've picked up their names from echoey shouts in the changing rooms and across the pool, and from flirty mumsy in the empty café. How can we get used to living together, to intersecting here twice a week, we three? And now things are complicated by the arrival of a pretty, Mediterranean looking school-leaver, on trial as the new cashier/receptionist. She smiles perpetually at everyone. Mummy and Daddy must have told her she has a nice smile and that she should use it, profit by it, until someone wipes it from her face. So she sits in her glass booth smiling, in her best skirt and blouse, white and navy, not much more than a school uniform, which also smiles in its own way, safe, warm, snug, a lump of sex-bait in a keepnet for the long-jawed pike – Mark and Aaron. The whole bungalow's hot as a hospital, paid for by the bourgeois burghers who never use the pool or sauna, who don't even know about it yet or want to know about it. Every day, at stroke of eight, she enters her cashier's booth, takes off her red-riding-hood winter coat, and her lambs' wool scarf, and organizes her belongings – handbag, packed lunch, magazine – and then what? She deals with me. And then what? She deals with some lewd approaches from Mark or Aaron, or the pair of them together. (Since her arrival, I've heard them laugh and brag in the changing rooms of Aaron's prowess as a "virgin-buster".) And then what? She checks her face in her compact. She reads her magazine. She eats an egg sandwich at elevenses. She silently breaks wind but the smell is trapped safely in her booth. She serves a young mother and her children. She checks the time. She checks the rolls of tickets, the neat silver rows of brand new locker keys. A large family comes in and she checks the ages of everyone. Some enter free, some don't.

There are those, like Alex – pacifists of course – who deride my years in uniform as too easy and protected, a withdrawal from the challenges of civilian life, shut away in camps and compounds, everything found, clinging to the breast of the state. But I'd have it all over again, every day of it, not change a minute of it, up to this very moment, stuck in my grand, freezing, rural slum with my bills and isolation, I'd play every game of patience out at two or three a.m., rather than have what this girl has now. Youth in a booth. Life suspended from the hands of a swimming pool clock. And the long hours drag round to what? To the astrology chart in her magazine, to tonight's video, to the better life in the new millennium.

When I leave, my unsightly tracksuit covered up by my charcoal Crombie, my towel and costume in a bright orange roll under my arm, my wet hair scraped from my shiny, protuberant brows, and my face a touch raw and blotchy from the sauna, when I leave I knock on the glass of her booth with my car keys. She's deep in her magazine. Startled, she looks up into my dentured smile.

"Bye!" I say loudly, still smiling. "Have a nice day!"

"Bye for now," she says, flustered, smiling back. She gives a short wave, from the wrist only. " . . . See you later."

Have a nice day!

See you later!

Enjoy!

The Leisure Pool doors open automatically. I pass through but stop under the phoney black eves of the bungalow as if it were raining, but it is not raining. The doors shut behind me. The car park lies empty before me like a runway, under the low dead belly of the autumn sky.

Where to? Where to now?

Nowhere. Nowhere. Nowhere.

Only Home, and no one.

More than a hundred empty spaces.

Mine the only car. A lozenge. A metallic oyster Austin Allegro, set square in the new white lines like some piece on a board game, pointing this way, pointing to me, waiting for me. What a picture this is – another study in oils. Paint the Battle of Britain pilot, still sprightly, still dapper in his old-fashioned way, exiting The Leisure Pool in his charcoal Crombie, over navy blue tracksuit, in his ancient, balding, suede Hush Puppies, with his stub of orange towel rolled under his arm, walking across the empty car park, catch him mid-step, under the louring sky, ten feet from his oyster Austin Allegro. My existence is full of these studies in oils. Every day brings a new masterpiece. Paint a fat young Dad coming out the automatic doors of B&Q, Sunday morning, with a sheet of orange melamine on his shoulders, hurrying across the car park in the rain. Paint the hairdresser knocking off early Friday lunchtime, hastily locking his door behind him, setting out at brisk pace for orange scampi-in-a-basket at The Boar's Head . . . Such delights! Such joys!

But the prize – the Turner prize – goes to Youth in a Booth, to the schoolgirl's face, looking up so startled and anxious from her magazine, that fleeting guilt and panic in her eyes at the sharp rap of my car keys on the glass, and then her relieved and grateful smile, and her eyes glazing over as she's drawn back by the impulses in her lap beneath the soft folds of her navy skirt, and her marigold magazine. She's grateful to me for being only what I am, not her boss or Mark or Aaron, with their predatory demands, but just me, a set of smiling dentures in an elderly, pink and lonely face, leering into her teenage soul.

What flesh. So soft, unwrinkled, full-lipped. Her wonderfully dark and stupid eyes. A well-loved face. A girl much cherished by her father, no doubt. Some Latin lover who brought the genes for those doey eyes to these hard, cold, dirty shores, which I defended with my life more than half a century ago.

Fifty-nine years ago this year. There was another fuss, but I ignored it, as usual. There'll be a fuss every year now, as we die out, one by one.

And so there bloody well should be.

"These damn bills!"
"What about them?"
"Can't pay! Won't pay!"

"Oh, come on, Dad. They're your bills. Not mine."

"You're falling at the first fence, Alex!"

"We'll talk next month . . ."

I'm leaving the other business – the Grosvenor business, Mr & Mrs Simmonds business – until the next visit. Make it count. Might leave it until they're actually getting back in the Micra and I'm about to wave goodbye – surprise attack, show a little forethought. *"Will you be dropping by The Grosvenor on your way home?"* Too messy, though, perhaps. Too bloody. Less chance of control than on the phone.

Which is in a broom cupboard in the freezing hallway. All year round it's cold and damp in there. From early autumn your breath actually condenses on the wallpaper. The skirting is coming off the wall. It's a horrible place to communicate. I lined it with the same wallpaper – thick, red, embossed in gold – that I'd used in the dining room. Some tarty idea of class I had in the sixties. Lack of background showing through again. To her credit, Laura said nothing at the time. I'd put weeks of work into the dining room and I'd kept it locked and hidden throughout, till I was ready to show her. A true labour of love. She could be sensitive when she wanted to be. But I can't remember what inspired this phone booth. Why did I make it? It was an ample cupboard, of the kind found in plentiful supply in rectories, halls, manses and so on, and very useful. Why couldn't I just leave it alone? Why this doll's house idea of converting it into a telephone booth? To imagine the younger self in here with scrapers, brushes, knives, a bucket of wallpaper paste, hanging that saloon bar wallpaper with such loving care . . . Ridiculous. Just the waste of it all, the small sad waste of time.

I closed the door and retreated to my study. There

are only two rooms I keep warm downstairs – kitchen and study. Upstairs I move my bed into the bathroom as soon as the evenings draw in. It's heated, after a fashion, by the immersion tank in the airing cupboard. Downstairs the kitchen and study are warmed by my fan heaters and our ancient Belling tower convectors. Each of these rooms is at the opposite ends of the house, connected by the hallway, the no-man's-land. Even at the height of summer you never stop in the hallway, unless summoned by the phone. There's a multifuel burner I installed thirty years ago in the study, but in one's seventy-ninth year coal has little charm. I bought a lorry load of logs last autumn and swore to keep the fire in day and night from mid-October, but I was conned: the logs were damp and green and fly-tipped on the gravel before I'd a chance to protest. Some burly peasant woke me up banging at the study window.

"Logs!"

I stayed still when he woke me, face of stone, and stared at him from my recliner. Stared at his gestures, his invasion, his red, weathered, unshaven, trollish, peasant face, his shiny stubble in the afternoon light.

"Logs!"

His yellow teeth. His dirty knitted hat, navy blue, like a trawler fisherman.

"Logs!"

In the end I gave them all away to a family in the village who had storage to dry them out.

So I went to Alex with my electricity bills. I know he can't pay them from his churchmouse salary, but he could come to some arrangement with the bank, as I keep telling him. The house is his. Laura left everything to him. I can't sell a stick of the contents either. That's how bad things were at the end. The house was in her name, bought with her inheritance, and she made Alex her executor. She wrote in the will that I could live here as long as I wished, but that's granted under the law anyway, thanks very much, dear wife of mine. Not something you could ever bequeath me, my love. She left me nothing. Absolutely nothing. So I say to Alex – go to the bank and borrow on the house, use the cash to pay the bills and do some maintenance, keep the place weatherproof. Fix the central heating. I want to be free of these things, these responsibilities. He won't have it. Stalwart Christian that he is, he'd rather I froze to death out here than put himself in hock to the bank.

But these days I suspect there's more to it, some other strategy, hatched by his lovely wife. Some secret plan. If my existence here becomes not only too uncomfortable but plain damn unaffordable, I may be more inclined to move out. Well, I've made my offer: buy me a bungalow by the shops. Or build me one. Still time. Not some rented dump full of third-hand furniture – *buy* me something decent outright, off-plan, gas-central heating, and do it out nicely. New television. Lovely bathroom suite. Show-home kitchen. You'll have the cash from the house, I tell Alex, and the bungalow to sell when I'm dead, and I'll be warm all year round for the first time in my bloody life. I'd sign a contract leaving everything to him. An irrevocable contract. Everything, dear boy. Dear son of mine. But he won't do it. He says this is not the time to sell a rectory in three acres. Best hang on, he says. We have to wait for the right 'window', he says. Meanwhile all my windows are rotten and I'm freezing to death in here! I've been hanging on by myself for twelve bloody years! I need warmth and shelter now, Alex – not when you can make a killing on the property market. Then he says, What about my attachment to the place? Where would I put all Laura's stuff in a bungalow?

She has some valuable pieces, heirlooms: the card table, the dining table, the piano. Where would I put these things? He says his house is too small to take the dining table, let alone the piano – well, I don't know because I've never been there, to where they live, but this stuff is worthless junk anyway, nothing to worry about. He won't let me sell the piano for a hundred quid to pay a damn electricity bill. The house must stay as it is, he says. You cannot live in empty rooms, he says. Besides, he's attached to the piano. Why? You could never play the bloody thing, I tell him. I chafe him now as I chafed him as a schoolboy.

One winter exeat, which I hadn't been looking forward to for some reason – we'd begun to live beyond our means and I was irritable the whole time – I told him I'd cancelled his piano lessons. They weren't worth it, I told him. He'd taken to working out Beatles tunes in the treble clef and improvising pop numbers of his own. He played a lot of rubbish and I told him so. He burst into tears, ran from the dining table. I'd ruined the Sunday lunch. Laura was upset too, of course. Sunday lunch (we didn't bother with it on our own) was his last treat, she said, virtually in tears herself. Then she was quiet and sombre, and I wondered how I could make amends on the journey back to his school, just a couple of hours away.

But why did I never love my son?

The answer is simple, and I have known it all too long.

It is because I did not do the work. I did not change the nappies, I did not feed him, wash him, brush his hair, did not clean his teeth for him when they finally appeared, after all that sleepless, teething misery – I remember that well enough, of course – in fact, I hardly ever bathed him, the very least a dad is meant to do. But above all, and I know this is the worst, the very heart of it: I never played with him. I made things, did things, but that's not the same. I made him a desk to study at on his own, a tree house to get him out into the garden, an attic playroom to shove him upstairs. I put the train set on trestles, and made My First Science Lab safe under a foldaway hood. But no good, no good, My First Science Lab safe under a foldaway hood.

Once he was away at school some golden years followed. We spent my commuted pension on the central heating and a new bathroom. I did the decorating: humble origins coming into their own at last. It was my father's trade. I took great trouble and it became a source of pride, my thoroughness and the quality of my craftsmanship. She appreciated that. She came back from work and noted my progress from room to room, ceiling to ceiling. In the evenings we lit a fire and played Scrabble or read the papers, watched a programme or two, nothing much. We felt a vague unease about how peaceful life had become, how much less work it all was, without Alex around. So much less noise and mess and stress. No doors banging, no thumping up and down stairs, no jumpers and rubber boots all over the place. I could listen to my favourite musicals uninterrupted – *The Music Man, Fiddler on the Roof, Oklahoma, My Fair Lady, The Desert Song* . . . Funny how much I despise that stuff now, as we all do, as if it were the rubbish of childhood. Garish, tawdry sentimentality. The stuff of Radio 2. David Jacobs. These days I become obsessed for months with the classics. Gould's Goldberg Variations. Brigitte Engerer's Chopin nocturnes. Just these two have lasted me nearly a year. Never wear thin.

With Alex away there was peace at last and I could put the finishing touches to my study, my own nest.

Ah, by law, no man – No Man! – should be allowed

to build a study, a nest! Nests are not for humans. They are for mice and rats and birds. Yet you see them everywhere in England, and books are full of them, particularly English novels. Cosy studies, book-lined hideaways – shelves lined with books full of book-lined hideaways! – Sherlock Holmes' womb in Baker Street, Oxbridge college rooms with glowing fires – oh, so many lovely *dens!* There's no end to it. Such a regressive, infantile, English thing.

Life outside didn't count. The upheaval of the sixties was foreign news. We became too contented, I suppose, with each other's company: with talking about the garden, about decorating projects, about cooking and suchlike. A sense of progress, purpose. Rebuilding and reforming. The dates ringed on the calendar for Alex's exeats and holidays became for me (but never for Laura) like dental appointments or bills due.

Alex didn't mind his new life too much, not after the first year or so of bullying and finding his feet. The school was religious and he was game for that. He needed to believe in another Love by then, I should think. He shut up his feelings, in that boarding school way, and became altogether much less taxing when he came home. He became well-mannered, too. Self-contained, self-possessed. Nothing much seemed to surprise him, for good or ill. Yearly reports were average or mediocre but never poor.

He was good with his hands – something from me, and my own father, I suppose – sports and crafts, and that went down well at his place. When he was twelve they let him make a go-kart, a proper machine. The engine had to be specially ordered. A Clinton two-stroke, 50cc. I had to pay £40 for it in advance with a cheque to the bursar's office. One exeat in the spring, in May it must have been, when the thing was finished and they'd trialled it for safety, we brought it home on the old dinghy trailer, and as a surprise treat took a detour to a disused aerodrome in east Norfolk. Laura had planned the route for me and she'd made a picnic. I had a gallon of fuel prepared, two-stroke mix. Bardahl oil, only the best. And nothing went wrong. A military operation, all according to plan. We filled up the tank, I pushed him off and the engine burst into life straightaway. Wonderful smell of the two-stroke exhaust on the chilly aerodrome air. He went thrashing down the strip at top speed, about 25 m.p.h.

While he toured the aerodrome we sat and read the Saturday papers in the car, ate the picnic and drank coffee from the Thermos. Half an hour or so passed uneventfully. Then, after he'd buzzed by us for the umpteenth time, all went quiet. We looked down the aerodrome but he was out of sight. "Fuel," I said. "He's run out of fuel, that's all." Of course, Laura was worried and wanted to move the car, but the picnic stuff was still out and I was sure nothing serious could have happened at 25 m.p.h. "Stay here," I told her. "I want the walk anyway." I fetched the can and funnel from the boot and set off down the runway on my own.

But the real reason I walked off alone was that I didn't want Laura there when I found him. I wanted to have my son to myself for a moment. Maybe there was some mechanical problem we could talk about and sort out. I'd ask how the kart handled, how fast he thought it went, something like that.

Only then, walking down the runway with the can and funnel in hand, actually pacing the concrete, did I think of all the other aerodromes and airfields – the rough grass airfields, and the hastily pasted concrete aerodromes like this one – all over East Anglia, Lincolnshire, Humberside, Kent and the south east, that we'd flown from about thirty years before. Thirty years! Because this must have been 1970 or thereabouts. Just thirty years. I'd never been stationed near this one but I'd flown from strips just like it, and I'd maybe flown past this one, over this one, or damn near it, only thirty years before that day. My tyres coming down and hitting concrete just like this at Watnall or later Coltishall – now a prison, for goodness' sake. But it was at that moment, walking along the runway with the can and funnel in hand, staring down at the tufts of dandelions and wild oats in the shuttering cracks, that I realized the past, my past, was not what I'd always taken it to be. My life didn't exist as an unrolling record, a pilot's log – nothing like that. There was no accumulating biography, no epic account, as I'd always imagined, that could be set down as testament of some kind, though testament to what I've never really had much idea. Rather, my past only floated about, like spores, in other people's memories, and just the memories of those in the same narrative, same War and Peace. Like the dandelion spores across the concrete, but in other people's minds, across the mad, backyard junk of other people's minds. When a person forgot about me or died there was some shrinkage, until bit by bit the whole thing just disappeared, the story wasn't remembered by anyone, wasn't told any more, and then it ceased to exist, it was erased. It literally had never happened. The concrete felt solid beneath my feet and I knew well enough what I was doing and where I was heading, but this new sense of the story of my life to date, in which I'd taken some pride, and which I'd wanted to set down, record – this new sense that it was only a story, no matter how precious, or to whom so precious – had taken hold.

Ten years before my walk down that runway, in 1960, the American airman Joseph Kittinger was suspended by helium balloon in a basket more than nineteen miles up.

The glove of his pressure suit split during the ascent and his hand swelled to twice its size and his wrist began to bleed, but he didn't tell ground control and kept going. Beneath him he saw Earth as no one had ever seen it before, and no one has seen it since. Once his trip was done, it was for all time. He *felt* outer space behind him, actually there, behind him, over his shoulder – oblivion, blankness, nothingness, call it what you will, both at and on his very shoulder, behind his back. No abstractions. No artistic representation, no poetry, no philosophical or religious idea, for Joseph Kittinger this was a physical sensation, a first-hand physical experience. He felt it, the dark, the endless dark, at his shoulder, for fourteen minutes, the time it took before the basket aligned itself to the trajectory for his landing in the Mojave Desert, and he had to jump, from nineteen miles up. He understood in a way no one else can have understood before or since, suspended there in his broken suit, his wrist bleeding, that nothing at all exists outside our green envelope, our accidental planet. And he had the integrity to say as much, later, when he'd recovered and he was interviewed. Just on account of a technical enquiry into new parachute design, he became the only man in history, and a fit, strong, sane and mature man, to look down on the earth from the point of view of a descending angel, and to know with an absolute certainty in that moment, that all such speculation and wondrous imagery about angels, gods, or extra-terrestrial life of any kind, all philosophical or religious enquiry about the nature of what we really know and don't know, was just so much solipsism, the chatter of men and women down there in the forests, the streets, the deserts, or in the churches of suburbia or the magnificent cathedrals of our much vaunted cities. Nineteen miles up, with outer space pressing at his shoulder, bleeding lightly at the wrist, it was impossible for Kittinger not to understand that there is nothing but oblivion ahead, and behind. The rest is accompaniment, chatter, music, hope, prayers to nothing, and to no one. He could not help but understand the truth of that. The ineluctable fact of it.

Alex was sitting in the go-kart at the side of the strip next to a fresh hillock of de-icing grit. Norfolk County Council supplies for the winter. Such forward planning! He didn't turn as I approached. Funny that he should have felt the need to leave the road, as it were, when there was not another soul about. It also struck me that he hadn't got out of the kart, nor started back towards the car to fetch more fuel himself. Uneasiness returned, instinctive fear for my own flesh and blood. Of course, I knew Laura and I had been escaping something, sending our boy away and dedicating our lives to our home, ourselves, instead of to him, as was our duty. There was always this cumulative sense of things unpaid for beyond the school fees, whose dreadful burden distracted us from this other debt. Was he sitting there crying his heart out in his go-kart, sensing, on the soulless runway, under the grey and indifferent skies, under the shadow of next winter's de-icing grit, his own absolute aloneness in the universe, and our unforgivable neglect? A bit premature, such intimations of mortality, surely?

I became more worried when, as I approached, he yanked the steering wheel from side to side, as if he were bent upon destroying this thing on which he'd spent so much of his love, and so much of our money. The kart was a very bright, glossy, post-box red, and as solid and heavy and safe as a post-box too. On hearing my approach, without looking back at me, he lifted himself out, knelt down and undid the petrol tank cap.

"Out of gas?" I asked, mock-American.

He looked up, frowning. His forelock, flattened by the 25 m.p.h. headwind, was fanned low across his brow. His hair was mousy then, and his skin peppered with blackheads.

"You forgot the oil," he said.

I shook the can and smiled, kept up the American: "Ready-mixed, kid . . ."

"Oh."

He held his hand out for the can and funnel.

No, Well done, Dad. Or, Thanks, Dad. I so much wanted him to say something like that just then.

I dropped the funny voices, then dropped to my knees behind the kart.

"This is really well made, Alex. Zooms round, doesn't it?"

Good God, what words to choose! I could feel him wince. I touched the flanges of the cylinder, examined cables and welds, trying too hard, while he refilled the tank.

"A full tank lasts forty-six minutes," he said. "I timed it. I'll make sure I stop near the car next time."

"You weren't to know, Alex."

He looked at me. "Of course I wasn't!" He left the funnel in the jerry-can. "That's why I timed it!"

I stood up, gave up.

"I'll give you a push."

He ducked the thankyou by making a show of scrutinizing the carburettor, as if I didn't know what a carburettor was. Then he pulled the front of the kart round from the grit mountain to face into the runway again and climbed back in. I pushed him off without another word. Pull and push.

At fifty yards he gave a short wave, speeding away as fast he could.

Today I got rid of Mason, which took the best part of the morning. I covered the back seat of the Allegro with an old tartan travel rug, stained with picnic memories, and enticed him in there with some dog-biscuits and the scent of a ¼ pound scrag of lamb, the cheapest loose meat the butcher could offer. Once we were on our way, I stuffed that in the glove-box, safely wrapped in a polythene bag.

We drove north and west for an hour, Mason and I, deep into the fens, then headed onto B roads and finally a lonely farm track. My map reading skills remain impeccable. The journey could not be too long or he'd need to excrete, but it had to be long enough to establish a distance from which we could never meet again; about seventy miles, I reckoned. I got him out the car easily enough and he immediately urinated against the rear wheel; while he did so, I closed the door on him forever. The lamb was already in my pocket. I walked ten yards away, towards the gated entrance of a field. The spot was wonderfully remote and desolate for such a farewell. The engine of a faraway tractor turning in the headlands the only sound, and just a few inky trees and a solitary farm building sketched on the grey horizon. From the map I knew these belonged to the estate of East Winch Farm. Mason's soon-to-be-adopted home, perhaps. It sounded like the place for a hard life but no worse than what he was accustomed to. I hung the bag of meat on the gate handle and rent it to release the full force of its scent, and let nature take care of the rest. In the rear view mirror I saw him guzzling away as I drove off. After a moment's indecision, head dipping to and fro, he left the meat and gave chase. But I was already doing twenty miles an hour. After a few seconds he fell back exhausted by the sprint, and I carried on to the B road junction and headed south and east towards home sweet home.

On return, I made the call. In the mood for it.

"Why did you send him?"

"We didn't."

"So who did?"

I leant against the shelf in the freezing telephone cupboard and gripped it with my free hand till my speckled knuckles were white and bloodless.

"Dad, he came to see you of his own accord. We didn't tell him to come. Calm down. We didn't send him. Fact."

"I swim twice a week now, you know. I take saunas too. I use a computer every day. Physically and mentally I am perfectly fit. Did Rachael put you up to it? Hmmn? You should keep a more independent mind, Alex. Did she? Was it her? I'm getting a bit suspicious of your lovely wife."

"Shut up, Dad. You've got it all wrong. All wrong."

"Explain."

A pause, a sigh.

"We have to think long term. Someone has to. But

Simmonds was horrible. And his wife. The Grosvenor was horrible."

"There's nothing wrong with me, though, Alex. I promise you. Please don't worry yourself, dear boy."

The effrontery. And that impenetrable English assurance. That public school, installed-for-life English smugness.

"Hang around and I might outlive you, you know," I continued, raising my chin to the challenge in the freezing telephone booth. "Ever thought of that? Happens all the time these days, with the National Health." I tried to keep my tone light, but my head had started nodding with the excitement of all this. Nodding away in the freezing booth. "You're in the heart attack bracket yourself now, Alex. I might come to see *you* in hospital some day soon. Did you ever think of that? You're out of shape and you drink too much. I don't touch a drop. Best include me in your will for safety's sake, so there's no confusion over the house. Don't you think?"

"Shut up, Dad."

"People like me go on forever. You'll see. You'll see."

"I've got things to do. We'll talk about this next visit."

"No need to bring a basket for Mason, by the bye."

"Oh? . . . Good God, Dad! You haven't had him destroyed? . . . Have you? For heaven's sake! What's happening to you?"

"I've given him to a farm."

"Oh, well done. That's good. He'll make a good farm dog."

"That's what I thought."

"I'm glad you didn't have him put down. Would have been too cruel. I'll see you next month, Dad. Take care. Bye for now."

Take care, indeed.

It's his wife. I'm sure of it. Stay sharp, she warned.

She's agitating for change, with her incy wincy ringlets and her low-cut dresses. She's fed up with life as it is, years slipping by, heading for forty on their churchmouse salaries. Fed up with waiting for me to surrender, or for Alex to compromise. He's terrified that if he gives in and sells the price will surge and he'll lose hundreds of thousands, let alone the costs of buying me my bungalow somewhere. But Rachael is agitating *now*. Well, I'm game, Rachael. I'll deal. I've told Alex a hundred times. But he worries so about the sentimental bits and pieces too. Where would I put all Laura's lovely heirlooms? Agh! Sell them! Burn them! Chop them up for firewood! He can't get used to the idea that I simply do not *care*. They are things, that's all. Like this house. All this stuff is worn out, finished. Tear it down and start again. Build a block of flats for the proles. Throw it away like an old shoe. I just want to be warm for once, and well fed, like everybody bloody else in this first world country, and not to worry about my poor old pensions being outsped every month by gangs of bills, bills, bills. I don't want this enormous house any more, this pompous English dream of centuries past, with its wainscot rotting and the wind streaming through it like ice water. But Alex won't let go – I know he won't. "Dad, it's not just a beautiful place – it's our *home*!" He won't deal. It's that school we sent him to. It gave him unnatural airs and ideas, unnatural attachments to this place, rooted it in his psyche so he can't get rid of it. Something beyond sentimentality, more to do with identity and status. It's our fault for sending him away as a boy. Oh, we should never have done that. Irrecoverable for him, unpardonable for us.

It's her, though. She's the driving force, I'm sure of it.

She wants me *Out, Out, Out!*

She's had it with petit bourgeois mediocrity, life hemmed in by work and debt. No money to travel, to holiday, to spend on Joe's clothes and toys. Alex's salary must be pitiful. They only have a car because it comes with his job. He inspects Commissioners' properties, making assessments, advising on rents, grants, benefits, renovations. She does some minor secretarial stuff in the same offices. There are sizable swathes of Church properties in Peterborough and Leicester – his patch, he calls it. And once a year at least he's called to London to look at the portfolio there: offices, shops, blocks of flats on the Hyde Park Estate . . . Oh, he talks it all up when he's called to town. They stay at the Commissioners' own hotel, The Royal Lancaster. I never hear the end of it when he goes to advise in London. Yet he earns nothing. Peanuts. Two Christian saps grubbing for a pittance for a bunch of notorious hypocrites. "The Commissioners' portfolio is worth more than a billion," Alex brags. "And we have more than five billion under management, you know . . ." As if he ever saw a shiny penny of it! So where's their Christian sense of filial duty and selfless kindness? Where's their Christian guilt, for goodness' sake? Where's their Anglo-Saxon fair play? They should be coming every week to bring me presents and hampers and new games for my IBM, not trying to turf me out!

Rachael could have had a different life and she knows that now. In the sexual market place she was underbid for. He rushed her into it before they were twenty – First and only Love. Alex needed so much by then, even God was not enough.

Blustery July morning. I'd driven him to Lowestoft myself because I loved it down there, at the toy-town yacht club, or dinghy club. Norfolk jacket weather for me, but everyone on the jetty getting hot loading victuals onto the old Broads tubs. Chain gangs of tiny stevedores in bulbous yellow life-jackets, passing boxes down the jetty to six elderly yawls, complete with spars and booms, and ruffled wavelets lapping the bows. Specialist Broads Craft from Hoseasons Ltd. Same dirty old fleet every year. Alex and his Christian Union pirates relished all the damp and chilly, hair-shirted making-do. *Swallows and Amazons,* I fondly imagined. But in fact, the first time Alex went, when he was just thirteen and very shy, for a whole sunny fortnight he lazed the trip away in what they called the fo'c'sle, reading Agatha Christie novels. I'd given them to him just before he left the car. Last minute thought. "In case things get dull for you," I told him, hiding my guilt about packing him off like this during his summer holidays. He fanned the books in his lap and stared at them sceptically, not knowing how to refuse them. *Why Didn't They Ask Evans? Hickory Dickory Dock. Murder, she said.* And on the cover of *Death on the Nile,* a picture of Peter Ustinov as Hercule Poirot, looking very poised, grave and quite ridiculous - *"Now a major film starring Peter Ustinov!"* My instinct was sound, though, as it turned out. Alex enjoyed those detective stories, and that first trip was an immense all-round success. Maybe he loved me just a bit then too, because I'd done it all for him, down to that detail. All my idea. I'd seen the Chaplain's ad in the school magazine. Alex was so full of polite and earnest gratitude when we picked him up. Particularly he loved the evenings: barbecues, campfires, sing-alongs -

*Michael, row the boat ashore . . .*

Thanks, Dad.

During his voyage he sent us ancient watercolour postcards of sights and villages along the waterways. When I stared at those watercolours, so wistfully painted, which always arrived by afternoon post for some reason, and lay alone on the coconut doormat – *Reedham Ferry, The River Waveney, The River Yare, Staith High Street, Herringfleet Windmill* – I thought I'd sold my son downriver to a different era. Pre-war. The illusion of England we fought for.

*Welcome to The Norfolk Broads and Connecting Waterways!*

That fortnight became the highlight of his year. Better than Christmas by a mile, when he was too much the only child. He carried on with the trips after leaving school and took charge of everything: booking the faithful old tubs from Hoseasons, sorting out insurance, writing and sending invitation letters. Then he managed the whole business officially when the Chaplain retired. For at least three years that's how he and Rachael spent his annual leave. Cheap too, of course.

It was his first summer out of school, when he was still a virgin, I'm sure, that Rachael came along as the female in charge. He was standing on the jetty in his life-jacket, taking a roll call of the young crews, chatting with one or two old school friends, when she was dropped off with her gels from a smart navy minibus, the school's escutcheon on flanks and bonnet. Same boarding school background, same sexual inexperience, same unshakable faith.

I watched her on the jetty that July morning – alert to her even then – while I walked the pontoons, amid the sound of pennants flapping and sheets snapping on aluminium masts, and the wonderful cry of the gulls. She wore her hair pinned up because of the wind, and had to keep fastening it back or slipping it behind her ears. She was tending a boat further on from Alex, marshalling some of the smaller children into their crews according to Alex's lists on a clipboard. Her manner with the youngest was naturally amiable and confident, laughing and chivvying at the same time, reassuring siblings who'd been put in different boats. Very much the boarding school Head Girl, sent away for years, as Alex had been, but in her case there was some excuse – parents stuck in the Middle-East. There was not only that confidence about her but also an unspoken, sublime optimism, which they still share, and which I've always found mysterious and quite compelling. I remember the absurd feelings of envy I had when they announced their engagement. They *knew* their marriage was meant to be. Ordained. I envied them their excitement but I wanted it for them too, or rather for Alex, because we'd so short-changed him. Rachael might very well have been short-changed as well, which would explain their confluence of feelings just then. When she told her parents on the phone, they at first tried to counsel her out of it, then quietly hoped it would blow away as a late adolescent crush. But they were way out of touch. The banns were read and still they didn't come. Then mother wasn't even at the wedding. Step-father came alone to give Rachael away.

To me, a very memorable man. Tanned and aloof, a good deal older than I expected, in smoke-grey morning dress; overbearing, over-educated, and unmistakably disapproving of his step-daughter's union, which his wife felt too strongly about even to condone. Laura stood small and still beneath him, holding onto her wedding day hat in the late September breeze, listening to his excuse for his wife's absence, and trying to absorb her double disappointment at being snubbed in this way, at her son's wedding, and, by proxy, Alex's hurt that he should be so disapproved of. She tried to keep smiling, standing very upright, hand on blue hat, in her wedding finery, on what she thought should be the grandest day of her life. It had caused a family rift, step-dad let me know, hands behind his back, just before going into church. He didn't stay for the reception on my freshly mown rectory lawns. When I saw him back to his hire car, he whispered to me, half in half out the car, which was far too small for him:

"They're too damn *young!*"

But I didn't let him blight our big day. When you've glimpsed what I'd glimpsed that July morning, on the blustery jetty, first love unfolding before your very eyes for your one and only son, it's impossible not to wish him well, and her well, no matter what her family's presentiments, and with some purity of heart too, however much your own feelings underneath are eaten up with covetousness, desire and all the bloody rest of it.

The sun came out and Rachael stood there enjoying its warmth, still with her hair up, though the wind had died, and with her arms folded across her brand new, slim-fitting life-jacket. She was listening to Alex explaining a few details about the boats – toilet arrangements and so forth. He showed her the Elsan sachets and fluids, and they laughed about that. Of course she knew it all from different trips, similar boats. No hang-ups about bodily functions, then, I thought.

Lots of promise there, Alex.

A romantic scene, no two ways about it, and they were on the threshold of a great happiness. Brief, naturally, but bucketfuls to begin with. They must have felt the intimations of it too, on the warm timber jetty. You could see it among the children. Lighting up the smaller ones, disturbing the adolescents.

So many times of late I have had this unnatural, stupid urge to ask her about that first trip. Roughing it like that, with no escape from the body as it is. Not dressed up in uniform or ballroom buffoonery or discotheque sparkle. They skipped all those pretences. All that posturing, courtship nonsense, about which we've made such a fuss, built up and broken down and built up again, so many rites and rituals. Alex in his fisherman's smock and jeans, turning from her to deal with a clueless boy, helping him tie his life-jacket, blowing his safety whistle for him and making him laugh. "Helping others, Dad, you see?" Alex has said that to me so often, so sententiously. "Helping others is what it's all about, Dad. Not crossword puzzles and games of patience." Not the sty of contentment, he calls it, quoting someone or other. Ah, their faith in life and what it's for! "We're not here to indulge ourselves. We're here to help each other." So many times he's said that too. And never when he's drunk.

Even now, after all these years of having a son who was a boy of faith, then a man of faith, I cannot understand it. From the bay window of my study I look up to that churchyard where Laura should be buried, and all through the day the bells bong out their lonely Saxon chimes through centuries of moribund English mists, and that ancient faith means nothing whatever to me. It remains a perfectly explicable delusion, belonging to some earlier stage of human development. I love the music and the art and the churches – and who doesn't? I respect the principles and laws that have come out of it. But to believe in God Himself, even in my seventy-ninth year on the planet, when nothing could be more natural than a quick conversion – *Take away the fear, please! The oblivion! Kittinger's oblivion!* – well, I wouldn't know where to start.

For their honeymoon they found a giveaway flight to Morocco. *Dan Air*. Long gone now, of course. I took them to Gatwick. They flew to Tangiers, where they met some Americans on their way down to Fez and Marrakesh. They spent a month down there, then out to the coast, Casablanca, and a train back for the Algeciras ferry. Laura wanted every detail, became really quite indiscreet in her honeymoon interrogations. They hitch-hiked up through Spain and France, staying in youth hostels, visiting cathedrals and art galleries in Seville, Granada, Madrid, Segovia – How those names made me reel! And all the talk of Goya, Velásquez and so on. I wanted to burst out of the clouds and dive-bomb them all, like Guernica. But I sat tight at the head of the table, and smiled, and tried not to repeat any foreign names in my token questions. To Laura it was the adventure of a lifetime: she loved the medical bits, about how they'd looked after each other when things went wrong – stomach upsets, sand-fly bites, ankle sprains. She wanted to show them off while their tans lasted, but alas, thanks to me, I suppose, she had no one to show them off to. Alex looked quite appealing tanned, and so relaxed. His hair was longer, and bleached and loose. And that shamelessness I'd noted in July was much more confident. I remember meeting him on the landing early in the morning, outside the bathroom, and noticing his tanned, trim body and the lick of tumescence in his underwear.

"Hi, Dad."

Then Laura gave them the money to fly out to Israel and work on a kibbutz for a year.

They must have caught my envy when I was off-guard. The way it had all happened so naturally for them, whereas for me starting out was an anguish from which I never recovered. For the R.A.F. everything had to change: accent, haircut, manners, brand of cigarette. Instead of setting sail from that warm timber jetty in July, instead of mooring up at *Reedham Ferry* or *Herringfleet Windmill*, in my own nineteenth summer I became a poseur. But of what? Of some half crazed, celluloid idea of urbanity – forever tapping a fresh cigarette on my pilot's silver cigarette case. Worse, I was a poseur who had to ape those immediately around him too. The only place I was comfortable was in a Hawker Hurricane, where I was a perfect fit, and where I had reactions to match anyone and had to be given respect. But in the mess, or on leave in uniform, on the trains with fellow NCOs – well, it was hopeless. I didn't know what to do with myself when they asked me which school I'd been to. Today you take pride in my kind of background, there's a new inverted snobbery to it – there has to be snobbery of some kind: this is England, after all – but back then you had a chip on your shoulder, no matter what you said or did, and that was that.

But I had one great advantage over those who looked askance: I had known from early boyhood, and with a total certainty, what I wanted to do with my life, and nothing would deny me. It is a very enviable thing, that kind of certainty, the way it pulls you forward no matter what the yaw, no matter how you have to jam the rudder. At eighteen I'd passed my wireless operator's exam and won my licence, off my own bat. Not first time. Nothing was easy without an education.

Third time. Then the Luftwaffe came and anyone with a wireless ticket was drafted into the R.A.F. and trained up. It should have been such a triumph, but my joy was crushed by the new milieu. Crushed by it. From the start I felt more like an enemy spy than a fighter pilot. I had the uniform but there was nothing underneath. An elementary schooling to fourteen and an East Midlands accent doesn't give you much to go on with the fellows from Tunbridge Wells. Whereas for Alex, starting out was all so straightforward and genuine – the sun came out while he chatted about the Elsan sachets! – no sham to live with day in and day out, neither at work nor at home. The two great challenges of life, finding a mate and finding a job, he'd overcome by the age of twenty without even noticing, without a struggle of any kind, and he took it all as pre-ordained.

It made me more at ease, after their year in Israel, to see work and bills and a hefty mortgage fall upon them with all their satisfying, suffocating weight. Suddenly kibbutzes, suntans, art galleries and the rest were out of reach, even while youth dragged on. An old school tie got Alex his job with the Church Commissioners, guarding their fortunes for them, and he and Rachael bought their starter home on a new estate outside Peterborough, where they still live, and which I have never even visited, to this day, to my shame.

But now Alex bores me so. He doesn't talk on and on. If it were that, I could just tell him to shut up. He's become the kind of bore, a very English kind of bore, whom nothing can *surprise*. If something unsettles him or exposes his ignorance in any way, he raises his eyebrows – a trick he's filched from me – but then, instead of saying nothing, as I do, instead of staying above it all in lordly disdain and giving no one anything to get hold of, as I have learned to do during a lifetime's agonizing exposure of my ignorance, instead of like father like son, Alex cannot resist having his three-pennyworth. He has to try somehow to own, to consume what has unsettled him, to appropriate it and absorb it so that it can no longer harm, no longer expose. He'll give a bogus chuckle, put his head on one side, look to the ceiling, perhaps, or click his change in his pocket, and begin with something like, "Well, you know, I always say . . ." or "Well, despite all that, I still think . . ." or "You know, I suppose the next thing will be . . ." and that next thing is his attempt to extemporize, so that he makes the subject his own, appropriates it, as I say, so that it no longer makes him feel ignorant or stupid or out of date. He'll exaggerate his 'next thing' to make it funny, so that he can put the subject in his pocket and click it there with his small change, except his exaggerations are never funny, only predictable, tedious. And it doesn't matter how trivial or innocent the threat is, it must be *owned* in this way.

Last time they were here, over lunch, when conversation can be pretty hard going between the four of us, I told him I'd seen a red squirrel on the lawn, underneath the oak trees. I only mentioned it because the greys drove the reds out years ago.

"Well," says Alex, his glass of Sainsbury's Minervois in his hand, stroking his Adam's apple, "you would, wouldn't you, in this particular neck of the woods . . ."

In this particular neck of the woods, indeed. As if he'd just opened up his encyclopaedic understanding of natural history, that stretched from the oak trees of Norfolk to Kilimanjaro. This is another side of his boringness: this wanton, reckless pretentiousness. He thinks he's safe with an ignoramus like me, so he comes up with obscure words, and silly Latin tags from his schooldays that even I know – ad nauseam, ad infinitum, quod erat demonstrandum, de facto … Sometimes he gets stuck on a new word. The last one was 'detritus'. Before that it was 'quintessential'. After three-quarters of a bottle of Minervois everything became quintessential. He was actually wittering on about the model of car he wants – 'The quintessential thing about that particular marque . . .' It's just a Jap fleet car he gets with his job, for goodness' sake! I risk a sideways glance at Rachael when he's like this, when he's had a few and he's dribbling on like this, but she never lets him down, betrays him, though I'm sure she feels embarrassed by her husband these days. She must be embarrassed when he drinks, because she's smarter than him. Not by much, but it's there, the gap, and as they get older it's becoming more obvious, more of a social nuisance. And glaringly so at lunch – In vino veritas, Alex! How about that? Am I keeping up? She used to do some laughing for him. When he started one of his funny stories or exaggerations she would laugh at the right places to cue me in. I never joined her. Face of stone throughout. Lately she's given up her canned laughter, and the bogus chuckling from Alex is louder and lonelier than ever. They're drifting apart but he can't see it and she won't admit it; well, either that or she's slyly biding her time. I wouldn't put that past her. Some secret plan. She has a heart-shaped face: I've always connected that shape with slyness, infidelity, treachery.

Last Christmas we had to sit through half an hour on the Napoleonic wars, of all things. Alex had got a free book on it from his book club. I know that because he tried to sign me up to the same club for a case of wine – I saw the literature about it. "Look, Dad, there's a book about crosswords here somewhere, I saw it . . ." He'd have conned his own bloody father into yet another bloody book club for a case of Minervois.

The Napoleonic wars. Oh, really. Napoleon – just another preening booby of the military kind. Wars and warriors – such trite and trivial Boys' Own stuff. When I played bridge at the Conservative Club they were all like this. I called them iceborgs: one third of their education on show, two-thirds they hoped you'd think lay under the surface. The women were the worst, and the place was full of 'em, as they say. Widows who'd buried their donkey husbands, or divorcees staying on, mortgage-free, in the country houses their husbands had abandoned for other women, other climes. Women pontificating about politics, history, war, education and tradition, fiddling with their amber beads on their ample bosoms. Women who'd never held down a job in their lives lecturing on the evils of unemployment. Most pointedly to me, of course.

And they tell me to go out again. Go back to the bridge club. Put on your charcoal suit again, slip a carnation in your buttonhole and go to places like that for a round of whist or a rubber of bridge. Make new friends.

No bloody thanks.

I'd rather die here, in the freezing hallway, no-man's-land, between kitchen and study, standing crooked in my grubby tracksuit, than go through any of that petty human abrasion ever again: the ducking and weaving through the conversations, glancing over this or that about my background, clinging for dear life to the driftwood of my assurance through the drowning waves of silence, while the cards are dealt or the tea or sherry served. Alex, Rachael and

Joe, for all their faults, are enough humanity for me. Quite enough.

Sometimes I wonder about my own nuclear family, my brothers and so on, hidden away under so many accounts of the past. They stayed in the East Midlands. Geoffrey, my youngest brother, was something of an engineer and entrepreneur. With his clever sons he perfected a moulding process to produce plastic which looked exactly like wood, completely indistinguishable from seasoned oak, walnut or mahogany. This was more than twenty years ago, mid-seventies. They were all set to make their million, that prickly branch of the Roses. What happened? The process could be used for anything. Picture frames, architraves, shelves, ornamental animals, knick-knacks of all sorts. I saw brochures of flint pistols and wine kegs, freshly hewn rustic carvings of squirrels and donkeys, goats and monkeys. And there were walnut dashboards, I remember. "Nissan is interested," my elder sister told me. She wrote to me when business was taking off, enclosing photographs and local press cuttings and these brochures. As the eldest, she assumed some proprietary right over the whole success story. She was so full of exclamation marks because Geoffrey's boys had been so clever, and there was talk now of industrial plants or of selling the process to the Jap. Hah! I should think Jap got there years before. But of course her real glee was that this brother of mine, and my younger brother too, had done better than I had, when all my life I'd been the one who'd got away. That was her real story, her real reason for writing, for sending all that stuff, that evidence of Geoffrey's success. She wanted to let me know that brother Geoff had got ahead through native wit and invention, not via the R.A.F., marriage and social climbing, and furthermore through family loyalty, no less, though quite how she worked that out I don't know; and finally, most singular of virtues, he'd stayed put in the East Midlands all his bloody life. Something, she believed – I'm sure of it – that would have made our parents proud. But she was wrong about that. Our father was a tradesman, a painter and decorator, and he loathed his work and his station in life. All his life. He hated it. He looked up to me for getting away so young. It took guts. Part of the reason he left mother in the end, when all the child-rearing was done, was that he couldn't stand her parochial horizons. He believed in getting on, breaking out, for better or worse. But he did it too late himself, poor sod, and the gamble never paid off for him at all. He died alone and derelict in a Worksop bedsit, at what for me is an unforgettable and irredeemable address: 11 Netherton Road. I never went there and never attended the funeral, but I can only too easily imagine that last address. And he was teetotal, like me. Never a drunkard, even at the end. So no anaesthetic either. A cold turkey died cold turkey.

Neither did I stir to attend big sister's funeral last year in Hinckley. Too much to ask of any human soul. Sorry, sis. They wrote several times. Are you still there? But people don't seem to know what they're asking of you when they send out black-bordered invitations.

Aaron stopped me entering the pool this morning.
"Take a shower. It's The Rules. Look."
He pointed to The Rules on the wall. No spitting, no

pushing, no petting, no jumping. I can spit, I can push, I can jump, but I cannot pet.

At the foot of the proscriptions:

*All patrons must shower before entering the pool.*

Each notice above, except the spitting one, has a picture with it, crossed out. The couple petting, crossed out; the boy jumping, crossed out.

I was standing on the very edge of the pool. Ignoring Aaron, I executed another graceful swallow-dive towards the middle. I heard his whistle as I hit the water.

Twice I landed at sea. The second time I simply ran out of fuel. Not uncommon, particularly for the other side. The Hurricane's range was only six hundred miles and I'd squandered the last of it in evasive action. Instructions were to bail out, but the sea, the North Sea this time, was very calm and I couldn't bear the idea of knocking loose the side panel again and falling off the wing, and besides I was too low for the parachute. I kept the nose up and belly-flopped, hoping to aquaplane to a gentle stop. Hah! The unretractable rear wheel ripped away the tailplane on the first wave – box-frame and canvas against the metal North Sea – and then the radiator, slung beneath the plane, hit the water and brought the nose down, and as soon as the propeller touched the plane tried to flip, but there wasn't the momentum to carry it over.

I thought there would be a few seconds grace, with the buoyancy of the empty tanks in the wings, but the nose started down immediately, and with a wild hiss and split of metal as the freezing sea swilled around the crankcase. I had the cockpit back and the harness off, but getting out that tiny space with the plane already listing was unmanageable. Again, I thought of knocking loose the side panel, then realized I'd caught my foot in the harness, and I remember thinking, to this day I remember thinking – That's easy, it's not tied or twisted, it's only looped, but my own weight was making the plane list and I had no balance to move my foot to free it.

Only then did I think of the weight of the flying jacket once it was wet.

Nothing can prepare the body for the shock of the North Sea: the iron grapple of cold that stuns all motion, the sudden sense of being so completely out of one's element, brought to book, as it were, by Mother Nature for an unforgivable trespass. The motion of the plane pulling me round beneath the cockpit undid the harness. I started working my way to the tail for no other reason than it was still above water, but by holding on like that I couldn't get rid of the jacket, and my grip in the freezing water wasn't strong enough. I lost hold. Sank. That jacket, just as I had realized seconds too late, became a thing of lead. Total immersion in the freezing brine with nothing whatever to hold on to, and the grey of it all around – and beneath you, beneath you, the sense of its infinite mass, its fathomlessness shading into total blackness below.

Not like Kittinger, because everything was taken up with the instinctive struggle to shed the weight of that flying jacket. Whereas for him the moment was pure and without struggle: it was contemplative, for fourteen minutes, with just the nag of some painless bleeding. He could think. The universal emptiness behind him, over his shoulder; not a fathomless menace below that crushed life from the body. The undertow of the plane as it went down tugged me deeper. I remember seeing the broken tailplane beneath me, to my right, still loosely hinged, in a stream of bubbles, a blurred outline becoming fainter, erased by the grey water like a sketch as the plane accelerated gently, silently, out of sight, on its way to the very bottom of the North Sea.

Much later I found out the North Sea is actually very shallow, only seven hundred metres at its deepest point, but just then it was infinite.

A second blast from Mark's whistle as soon as I surfaced. He shook his head and pointed at me, wagging his finger.

*No no no . . . Bad Old Man . . .*

I began my lazy breaststroke away from him, to the other side of the pool. Twenty widths I set myself, twice a week.

Keep fit. Stay strong. Stay sharp, as Rachael says. On guard.

Rachael's dress had its desired effect, but intensified suspicions. Altogether too summery for golden October. And it was so low cut that as the afternoon died delicious goose-pimples stiffened in the breeze. We were watching Joe and Alex collecting cooking apples. A perfect, familial, autumnal scene.

The tree where they were picking is Alex's own apple tree, nominated by Laura the very morning we packed him off for his first term at boarding school. He was still carrying a paper bag of small, sour apples when he got out the car at the other end. They were *his* apples, even though he couldn't eat them. Still so unsuspecting, the seven year old. Two guards, house prefects, one at either side, led him to his dormitory. Two more took his trunk. He nestled the bag of apples on the bed next to the trunk, then came back down with us, suddenly in a panic – Where were we going? What betrayal was this? He'd never properly understood the implications, though we'd been through it half a dozen times.

I wonder if Alex remembers all that now, as I do. If so, he never mentions it. He seems far more at ease with his upbringing than I am. About his or mine.

There was just one more diffident apology early on, to clear the air, about The Grosvenor business and Mr & Mrs Simmonds. From Alex, nothing from Rachael. I'll leave it that way because it suits me. Her dress conducted away any remaining static, cut off my aggressive questions and manoeuvres – and that was its purpose, I'm perfectly sure. There won't have been anything said or planned of course, but I'm convinced that the dress was for me, certainly not for Alex, poor chap. She remembers the whisky advertisement, my little cupboard, my staring down her cleavage from the miniature step-ladder, and she knows she has that power. Of course, I don't dismiss the possibility that she is also thinking of someone else entirely, neither me nor Alex, when she puts on a dress like that. Some new colleague at work, for whom she wears that dress to enjoy the effect it has on him, and the pleasure of thinking about him slowly unzipping it from behind, slipping it away from her, letting it fall to her feet and ruffle there, and the pleasure of feeling his cool fingertips slide beneath the undefended borders of her underwear . . . I know the kind of creature she is. In his Christian smugness Alex would never suspect, just as he never suspected when he was seven years old that he was being betrayed.

Back indoors there was more for me when she helped me with the computer, bending down to operate the mouse when I got confused. She's definitely better than Alex now. Much quicker, more intuitive, as they say. I can't download a game I want, a bridge game. With *planetbridge.org* you can play with people all over the world without having to meet a single one of them. Perfect!

She admonished me: "You double-click on everything."

"Oh?"

"You don't have to. You're a compulsive double-clicker. That's why there's this mess, these duplicates, and it crashes. You keep fetching things up twice, look . . ."

"If that's all, even I can fix it."

Then Joe came in. The door whined. He whined.

He should have some purchase on my feelings, my grandson, standing there in his dungarees and looking at me with his mother's grey eyes. He has his father's, and his grandmother's, droopy mouth, that lends him a pitiful, lost puppy look. I wonder if that will work for him, help him make his way in the world, as it did for Laura. Somehow I think not. The world now, the competition, is much harder, brasher, less merciful. There was some colour in his cheeks from the October sun. Their sunny apple-picker.

Yes. I feel nothing. I look down at him as I'd look at a photograph someone has handed me of their pet dog or cat or hamster. How is it possible that I feel so little for a grandchild? How is it *possible*? Alex nearly lost his precious temper with my joke last Christmas (I'd already forgotten Joe's birthday) when I gave him a two litre bottle of Ribena from the Co-op. Well, I know he loves it, and I'm not dragging myself into town to wander around *Toys-R-Us,* filling some monstrous trolley with Chinese trash and shoving it to the check-out. Not at nearly eighty years old. Come on! Besides, he's already got more toys than he can possibly play with. He doesn't need me to spoil him too. But it is strange, even to me, this absence of sentiment for a grandchild, this atrophy of feeling, like the atrophy of muscle that happens over the years. It must be his father. That's where it backs up, the feeling, like effluent.

He headed towards my computer, as he always does. Rachael put her arms around him.

"Do you want a go on Grandpa's computer?"

He nodded. She shouldn't let him get away with that. She should make him speak. Say, Yes, please, or No, thank you. Make him humble himself, as manners demand.

I looked back to the screen, idly moved the mouse.

"Best not, Rachael."

"Oh nonsense, you old misery. He won't do any harm. No more than you've done, anyway."

I was about to leave the chair when she stopped me with her hand.

"No, Antony." She was firm. "Joe will sit on your lap."

He made a fuss, but she lifted him onto my lap.

"Put your arms around him, then!" she scolded.

I raised my arms half-heartedly and set my ancient speckled hands on the melamine trolley, so my arms were crash bars at each side, as if to protect him.

"Good God!" she cried, whipping him out again, a flash of anger in her grey eyes, her ringlets in disarray. "You're a cold old bugger!" She rushed from the study dragging Joe behind her.

Hmmn . . .

After shutting down the IBM I rolled it back into its cupboard by the fireplace, symmetrical to the cupboard with the gramophone, the whisky advert and other relics. I won't have the trolley out all the time – too ugly, all that grey and melamine. One has feelings about the colour of the computer trolley and the IBM, but not about the grandchild. Oh, I've had my own way too long, I know. The feelings and needs of others just don't get through. If they do it means more work, more time given over to please and appease, attend and pretend, refrain and entertain – AND NO! I won't do it. Fool around making birthday cakes and all the rest of it. If I need a cake, I'll buy it.

Alex's patronizing sanctimony, "Doing things for other people, you know, Dad?"

Having reduced the world to what it is now, the only human contact a pair of loathsome lifeguards, the tiniest infraction ignites, blinds, deafens. The tolerance that comes with daily human abrasion has completely disappeared. The old do not feel as the young feel, and that is that.

After putting the computer trolley away, I sat back in the recliner and shut my eyes for forty-winks before the Madeira.

But they had gone when I woke up. This is a first, and it was awful. Waking up, drifting through October no-man's-land towards the kitchen, noting, with some dread, the quiet in there, then pushing the door wide, against its spring, onto a vacuum, onto the cold, just the transistor faintly trickling Frank and Nancy Sinatra, the incest song, of all things –

*"Then I go and spoil it all by saying something stupid like I love you!"*

What's that doing on Radio 3? What's the world coming to?

The tradition is they do the lunch and I provide tea and the Madeira cake. Their tea things were all washed up and neatly set out on the draining rack and the table had been wiped clean. There was a note at my place.

*We didn't want to disturb you. Madeira's in the fridge – what's left of it! Delicious as always, thanks.*
*See you in a month or so.*
*Rachael.*

I switched off the transistor, glanced down the empty drive.

The pigeons swooped. Crows cawed.

It was as if Alex, Rachael, and little Joe had been wiped out in a car crash. As if everyone had died, the aloneness at that moment was so acute. They had never done anything like that before. It must have been her – the incident with Joe and the computer had upset her more than I'd thought – and she'd told Alex she'd had enough, quite enough, and wanted to get away early. Couldn't stand another moment of it here, with the cold old bugger in his freezing rural slum. Let's get out of here! Get back to Peterborough and some humanity and modernity, the real world, some living souls.

My speckled hand settled on her note. The age-spots are so distinct you'd think they were spits of oil you could wipe away. In fact, I tried to clean them off when they first appeared with a scrubbing brush. I spread my hand on her note as if I were spreading it on her shoulder, or her head of slippery ringlets, or one of her lovely breasts, and squeezed hard.

Damn them. Oh, damn them.

I crumpled it into a tight ball and threw it at the sink. Never, ever do that again, Alex. Never accede to her demands like that. Coward. Gutless son.

Where was the teapot? I wanted to feel it, to know how long since they'd left, but it was washed up too, and stacked in the draining rack. In the fridge there was plenty of cake. They rushed it, or even faked the whole tea, took a slab of cake away in the car for Joe and stacked some cups and side plates in the rack. I closed the fridge and stood there looking down the drive again, my hand on the fridge door. The pines, the mossy white marker stones, and way up in the tops of the trees, the nests of crows, whose incessant caws crack the air all day, and I thought – I'll go out and gather fir cones for a fire and smell the pine smoke in it; gather them in a basket for that pleasure. One pretends that the reason one doesn't actually do things like that is because there is no one around to share those pleasures, encouraging the delusion that one did such things when there was. But we never stood contented with our lot and each other, leaning on grass rakes, before an autumnal bonfire, staring into the flames, cheeks reddening with the blaze as if we'd shared a hot toddy too. Rather, whenever there was a fire, indoors or outdoors, when I stared into the flames, I dreamt of being elsewhere, away from her spying and her insidious taunts and complaints, her dissatisfaction and disappointment with me; and doubtless she did exactly the same.

The drive divides just before my gate and the second drive goes on to the church. I assumed straight away that the new silver car, a Lexus, mid-range, driven by a woman, would turn off to the church. Some widow tending a grave, doing the flowers for the evening service, or cleaning the heavenly brasses. It's an instinctive defence against disappointment to assume cars are going the other way. But she didn't turn off. The silver car came through my gate, and boldly swept across my gravel at a steady, confident speed.

It disappeared from view round the back porch and turned all the way about but did not reappear. Only a mid-range Jap saloon, but it crunched the gravel much deeper than Alex's Micra. Did it justice, as it were. My next defence against disappointment, rather paranoid, I must admit, was to connect this car with the Simmonds, so I stayed where I was with my hand still on the fridge door, in hiding, the truth be told. Rachael's note had left me raw and vulnerable.

I heard her steps across the gravel. She did not press the bell or knock. The letter box clattered, then the steps returned to the car. She'd had no intention of knocking. There was no restarting of the car so she must have left it running, but the engine was silent. Bloody Japs.

And she didn't drive on to the church. This had been a dedicated visit to the residence of Sqn Ldr Antony Rose, no question. I hadn't seen much of the woman but she looked rather attractive, somewhere between forty and sixty. That was the fleeting impression I had of her face inside her car. Whether she was fat, tall, wore wellington boots or high heels, I had no idea.

On the dirty black tiles in the porch, amid the leaves and cobwebs, was a pale, thick, yellow envelope of the kind used for greeting cards. So far so good. I picked it up and found myself rather faint, and not just from the exertion of stooping and rising. Ridiculous to be so excitable, so suggestible! Plenty of feeling now in the old pipes and wires! I took the card away to the study to open it. Such games! I didn't even turn it over to see the handwriting until I'd settled comfortably in the recliner in the warmth of my study. There was my rank, correctly abbreviated, without clumsy stops, and name, *Sqn Ldr Antony Rose*, in fountain pen. A slow, jet black, italic script. What could we tell from this? Educated, certainly, but to what extent? Not too much,

I hoped. The thick yellow envelope contained a weight of expectations the sender could not possibly have understood. There was indeed a card inside, not a circular or a village 'Newsletter' or any such nonsense.

At last I removed it.

On the front was a photo of a house, named in a white caption slot, 'Long Cottage'. The house avoided chocolate box perfection because the photograph showed, perhaps celebrated, the completion of a restoration project, and the place seemed rather naked. The windows were brilliant gloss white, the gravel immaculately raked, still wet from the quarry or a shower, not a weed in sight. A brand new pergola led to the front door, the woodstain unweathered and the timbers unencumbered as yet with any foliage, though two handsome pots with something green were set at the foot of each of the posts to start things off. A brand new brass knocker adorned the door, and the handles and plated key holes were similarly shiny and unused. I know this cottage, of course. In fact, it is not much more than a mile away, up past the ford, just beyond what used to be the village school, now defunct. (That too has been restored and converted. A young dentist has done it up. There's a rumour he is homosexual.) But Long Cottage was being renovated piecemeal by newly-weds in the village – DIY enthusiasts – until quite recently. Then Carter's, a big Norwich firm, were contracted, and they'd been working on it continuously, rain or shine, ever since. The DIY couple had given up, sold on. And for a pretty penny, no doubt.

This new owner was someone who cared for details. The picture might have been touched up, perhaps, on her – oh, let it not be *their*! – computer. I opened the card before my expectations could capsize under their own weight.

Inside, on the left, was another picture, this time

of the interior. A long, low-ceilinged room, with beams exposed and stained, and an open fire at the end. But not actually an open fire – a living fire in a modern, expensive log burner, with the glass doors wide open. Chairs and sofas, in a warm red, were aligned for the photograph in a welcoming configuration.

On the other side my name appeared again, in the slow italic script, within the following:

*Natalie Stein*
*Requests the pleasure of the company of*
*Sqn Ldr Antony Rose*
*At The Warming of Long Cottage*
*On Saturday 10th October, 1999, 8.00 pm.*
*R.S.V.P. 0986 686 665*

Saturday? Less than a week away! Immediately I thought – Thank god they all went! Alex, Rachael and Joe. God bless them all! And particularly little Joe for causing the rumpus! If they'd stayed and actually been in the kitchen, or anywhere around the house, under the apple trees or wherever, and she'd arrived a few minutes earlier, they would have spoiled everything. Good timing, Natalie! They would have chatted with her and made her tea and given her my Madeira cake and smiled and amused her, and I, the old man whose name was actually on the invitation, would have been completely forgotten, left dozing in his study. Oh, don't disturb *him*! He's a grumpy old bugger at the best of times, particularly if you stir him from his forty winks! Even if I'd awoken by chance and come through when she was still here, I would quickly have bowed out and retired again, unable to compete. Thank God, then, they had not been around. And thank God I was so cold to Joe, in that case. Doesn't matter to him anyway. Just his mother.

Réspondez? My dear Natalie, of course I will! Wouldn't miss it for worlds, my dear!

The coin has flipped tails continuously for twelve years but now, on this gloomy Sunday, it flips heads. Natalie Stein! Not Mrs, either.

Laura was one of those who could not live without routines. If you haven't got routines you haven't grown up, she liked to say. Her job wasn't much but it regulated her life, gave it shape. She thought her working days left prints that were leading somewhere. Then, as retirement loomed, the fear came in. I heard it in her relentless, mindless, cheerful chattering, her twittering – How wonderful it was all going to be! How she was going to take that corner of the garden in hand and grow a few vegetables. How she was going to learn to cook all over again. How she might even buy some overalls and try to learn a little car maintenance to save on garage bills. Where were the old cookbooks? Where was Mrs Beeton's? Wasn't that a first edition? She was going to learn to play Alex's piano. After lunch every day she'd sit down and practise scales.

La La La.

Once the structures of routine and habit were taken away, time squeezed a shrill and implacable shriek from her, at a pitch inaudible as a dog whistle, but ever-present to me, whether she was there or not.

She took solace for all that had gone wrong in her life, starting with me, of course, by creating the idea that she was an endlessly suffering, giving and patient soul. Giving, grieving and aggrieved – that was always her way. She cut out two cardboard Christian dolls: I was some kind of invalid, and she a long-suffering nurse. If anyone asked after me I'm quite sure that's how she carried on: I was 'fine' or 'much the same' or 'much as always'. With the world at large she had always been successful at exciting pity for herself: that's how she got her way, and we are what we are successful at, are we not? And that's why we complemented each other so well, because I ran out of pity a long, long time ago.

An uncertain movement of her heavy mouth showed when she was wounded. Her mouth sagged as she aged and the lower lip crooked into a fleshy V. When offended she sucked it in to one side and her whole face fell at the corner. She wore glasses – cheap and wiry, from the national health, that were tilted on her nose, adding to the lopsided and pitiful effect. There would be a turning away, with a slight dropping of the shoulders, as she retreated. Maybe even a shake of the head. Her habitual posture made her seem small and shapeless and helpless, particularly in retreat, and as she aged she dressed more and more in dumpy cardigans and mid-length skirts. Horrible clothes that she knew I loathed, and that she hoped would throw me off the animal scent.

But sex is always there, somewhere, no matter how many the layers. She worked in the bursar's office of a dying convent school outside of town. The place was an anachronism even then, full of benign amateurs. She also helped out with 'extras' as required: netball (for which she had to swot up the rules) when she was younger, then classes in home accounts, typing, general matters of housewifery, which survived in her cosseted Christian world right into the mid-eighties. A new broom came in and swept away all that when she retired. Of course she had a secret life there, at work, or at least a secret fantasy life, surrounded by nuns and pubescent and prepubescent innocents, deep in the grey English countryside.

On turning fifty, sure enough, her hormones had a last flush through.

"You're doing *what*?"

"I'm going to be in the play!"

Am-dram? Laura? But after a moment I thought I understood it. Her whole life was a quiet, aggrieved performance – nothing unusual in that, of course – so am-dram was exactly what she needed to show the repressed side of her nature. Ayckbourn was still in fashion and the parents and staff association were putting on *Round and Round the Garden*, the last of *The Norman Conquests* trilogy. Laura's role was Annie, the lonely, martyred daughter, who looks after mother but wants to spend a dirty weekend with her brother-in-law. Perfect. Typecast. And that year the Tom Conti tv adaptation had come out, so she had plenty to feed on.

I took no notice until the dress rehearsal.

Then I told her I'd come along.

"Oh," she said. "Are you sure?"

"Yes."

I pulled up my recliner straight away and snapped off the television. She was taken aback. She hadn't expected this at all.

"Are you sure?" she said again, flustered.

"Quite sure!" I replied, with theatrical certainty, putting on slippers, getting out of chair – I was nearly in the play myself now, following my own stage directions. "I'll come to your play. I want to. I'm coming."

Tell-tale signs – more attention to her shabby hair,

less dowdy clothes, more expensive perfume – had indicated she was up to something. I was curious to see what kind of creature had taken an interest.

The cast were mainly parents, all supposedly doing their bit for the school – the play was an examination text – but as any actor will tell you, performance is for the performer, not the audience, otherwise there would be no am-dram. The star role was played by a youngish solicitor: a smiling, bald, ironic man, very detached, right for the part, though not really good-looking or suave enough. He wore steely glasses that he kept lifting and resting on his forehead to rub his eyes; a professional tic from the day job, his way of buying time to take stock of what had been said by clients, perhaps. But here, with Laura and the cast, it was a way to hide his boredom. Difficult to sustain the energy for am-dram after a busy legal day.

Before things started Laura sidled up to him two or three times with her text to ask his advice on a line, stage direction or whatever.

The dress rehearsal was slow, wooden, quite unfunny, really awful. They dated the play before its time. For some reason the director had to be one of the nuns: the appointee was a quiet woman with no lips who was extremely slow in speech and movement, as if each word or gesture cost her grace. As the director of a play, and a comedy to boot, she had absolutely no idea what she was doing. She sat in the shadows of the set, the text in her white lap, and said nothing once the thing was underway. She was understudied the whole time by the teacher of the text – a bounding, curly haired graduate who played Annie's brother, Reg, and who stole the show whenever he came on.

Act 1 limped by, and when it finished Laura went up to the solicitor again. I had to blink when I saw her nudge her breast against his elbow as she leant over to look at his text. He found an excuse to turn away to point at something upstage. All very, very painful. Worse than the play itself. I don't know if I was meant to see, but I really didn't care.

This am-dram lark is something of a family weakness because both Alex and Rachael, particularly Rachael, love it too, and before Joe was born they were in endless performances together, all of which Laura dutifully attended – "You were marvellous, darlings!" – until Rachael started her solo career, as it were, and entered what Laura called her Scandinavian period: huge female leads in plays I'd never heard of and had to look up – *Hedda Gabler, The Wild Duck, A Doll's House,* which I kept calling, by genuine mistake, *It's a Doll's House* – after the TV show, *It's a Knock-Out!* – something I found rather funny but no one else did. Alex, ever the innocent, decorated the house at weekends while she rehearsed her epic roles.

"I can't watch any more of those," Laura told me, coming home early, after just a couple of acts of some wintry triumph. "Why not?" I asked. She seemed upset. "Was she no good?" Laura shook her head, tongue-tied. She was upset. The evening had aroused conflicting feelings quite beyond the playwright's imaginings. "Well?" She busied herself with Ovaltine or Horlicks for the two of us. "Rachael was excellent, as always," she said, when the milk watcher started knocking. "Could have been a professional." She poured and stirred. "I just feel so sorry for my son, that's all."

She would explain no more about it. Ah, the sorority.

It makes perfect sense to me these days that her wounded look, which so irritated me in our later years, attracted me as a younger man. That and the straitlaced, innocent clothes she wore when we courted, and her aloof, class-bound posturing even then. Such things signalled naivety and vulnerability to me, bait to the predator within. And there was a stretch of our lives, when Alex was first away at school, when that worked well for both of us, and we encroached on the nasty delights I see brazenly advertised on the internet now, but which I never go near. Best not excite the predator these days, if it can be helped.

Rachael opens up the old shop, of course, but everyone else I know is either the wrong sex or otherwise accounted for. The grocer is a man, the butcher is a man, the bakers are a middle-aged husband and wife team, the pharmacist is a man, quite doddery now, and the librarian is a widower well past retirement age. His name is Eric. He keeps long hours he shouldn't keep in our tiny pre-fab library, hiding away in there, in the warm, saving on his fuel bills. He spends all morning stooped over the papers that he reads for nothing, a drip of mucus suspended from his nose. He completes all the crosswords too, every bloody one of them, every day. He does the Sundays early Monday morning, before the library even opens.

The young women are all in the supermarket, shopping or serving. I cannot venture there. Supermarkets are no-go zones. The strip lights, the muzak – often the local radio with its relentless cheer – the duff-wheeled trolleys shooting bolts of static through me at the end of every aisle, and the chill from the freezer cabinets – far too much alienation. I become so self-conscious. My speckled hands on the cold trolley bar. I am an alien in their world. Their friendly smiles and gossip only make me feel I'm trespassing. I'm beyond the pale. Everything is for the young, or would-be young.

The pretence of his parents' marriage was laid bare to Alex once only. He was ten years old. It was late spring. Another of those dreadful, ritualistic, Sunday lunches before his return to school. Laura had set up the dining room, moved the heaters in there, done everything as usual, but when I came in – Alex had called me excitedly from my study – I saw she'd put the heaters on too late, so the room was chilly and the windows were long, pale blanks of condensation. You could see nothing outside. The rose beds, just coming into their first bloom, all edges neatly trimmed with creosote, and the lawn I had mown every week since March, so that the gardens of the rectory looked like something on the cover of Country Life – all of that was invisible, just a green blur behind the rotting sash windows. You couldn't see a single Harry Wheatcroft.

Worse, she'd set out a mix of crockery that made the dining table look like something in a Bed & Breakfast parlour. She'd taken me back more than thirty years, to my digs in London, while I was studying for my wireless operator's licence, skivvying all hours in hotels in Paddington and moving from one Jewess's house in Canonbury, Stamford Hill or Golders' Green to another for the cheapest rent. The dining room, that I had so lovingly decorated with plush red and gold embossed wallpaper, and an eggshell blue handrail, had been degraded to a front room in a north London terrace. Bizarre how I'd become such a stickler for the class details, the matching tableware, correct cutlery arrangements, when it mattered little to Laura, the one who actually had the upper-middle-class background. "It doesn't matter!" she protested lightly, misunderstanding, setting down an open margarine tub, Marmite-soiled from breakfast, for the boiled potatoes. I stared fixedly at the steam billowing off the potatoes in their lidless Pyrex dish. More condensation. *It did matter!* She'd blanked my garden, my labours. Ignored it all. She'd put me back in my digs. The work that had gone into this room, all the tricks of my father's trade I'd brought to bear, to achieve this look-alike of bourgeois luxury in an upper-middle-class country home, all that I'd kept as a love-secret until it was finished, and that she'd complimented me about when she first saw it, all of this she'd turned into a front parlour in Golders Green!

We cut through the undercooked chicken in silence, ignoring the stringier, bloodier bits. Alex got on with the meal, polite boarding school boy, saying nothing. I grunted at some further shortcoming – the salt had stuck in its salt-cellar with the damp. Then I stopped eating and stared forlornly at the windows. Long, algaed slabs of aquarium murkiness, through which I couldn't see a single rose.

I sighed.

"Oh for goodness' sake," she started, but she sounded more hurt than irritated. "He's only here a day . . . " On saying that, she couldn't continue. Her heavy lower lip began to tremble. She was so upset by my behaviour, for creating such an atmosphere in complete ignorance of my own son.

Alex looked uncomfortable, didn't know what to do. The manners his school had given him didn't extend to this ugly scene. He was already in his uniform for the journey back because I'd told him to change before lunch. No delays.

"You're impossible!" Laura burst out. "Impossible!" Through tears now. "He's only here a day – I mean, why can't you – "

"Now I want you to listen to this, Alex," I told him, the ten year old son. He was looking down at his chicken and potatoes, not eating any more. I was pointing my knife at him and the blade was trembling with anger. "I want you to listen to this!"

"You're pointing your knife, Antony!"

I turned to her.

"You're pointing your knife!" she repeated. "Like a peasant!"

Still I pointed my knife at Alex and turned back to speak directly to him. "Listen to this, Alex." Then to Laura, "Why did you marry me, then? Hmm? Impossible peasant that I am. Hmm? Why? Why did you marry me?"

She put her head in her hands, sobbing freely. She didn't care.

"Because I was desperate."

I nodded at her, and at Alex.

"There you are, you see."

I put in one more mouthful but couldn't chew it. I stood and left the table, still with my mouth full, and retreated to my study, to the papers I pretended to read until it was time to take him back.

*The average age of a pilot in the Battle of Britain was twenty years old. Your chances of survival were one in three. Some may say such odds would deter only the –*

Ah, the great testament. She would not stop looking at what she called, "his work in progress". I told her not to.

I warned her. But she ignored me. She behaved as if it were her right to inspect, correct, emend. Part of it was revenge, pure and simple, for a certain letter I took of hers, once upon a time, but the rest of it was spite, also pure and simple, I'm quite sure. I locked everything up, but too late. The damage was done. The sense of her vigilance was irreducible. And time did not wear it out, didn't even thin it out. I left my typewriter, my papers, my log, my maps, photographs, all of it, locked up for a whole six months, but when I came back it was as if she were actually looking over my shoulder, all the time, smiling her fleshy, condescending smile. I had promised her she would see it when it was done, when I thought it was finished or as good as I could make it. She would be the first to see it and she could help me with it then. I solemnly promised her that, and admitted I would need her advice, when the time came. But she only smiled in that heavy-lipped, blunt, stupid, teasing, superior way. Even though I could not have been more in earnest, she would not give up treating it as a bloody joke.

"Antony. You're not being serialized in the Sundays just yet. Don't take yourself so seriously."

"Once it is all done as well as I can do it, I will show it to you. I want to show it to you and I want your help. Your education. But until then – Please Stay Away!"

But she refused. She behaved as if she owned the copyright.

"Why?" I asked. "Why this insatiable curiosity?"

"Pah! Don't flatter yourself!"

She must have known she ran the risk of destroying everything but it was a risk she did not seem to care about. In fact, it was her subconscious intent, or even conscious intent, I now believe. Because, what would have been the consequences for her if I had discovered something in myself, some means of telling my story, from uneducated working-class youth to Battle of Britain pilot, one of the very fewest of The Few? Something that said so much about England, and about the war. What would have been the consequences for her, if I had achieved, god only knows, success? What if I had turned out to be more than a gardener and odd-job man, living on a commuted pension and his wife's pin money?

Now that I have broached this, I am sure her intention was destructive. When I first discovered she had been in there, into the drawers where I kept everything – my pilot's log, my notes, my desperate attempts to begin the epic – she told some half-hearted lie, some excuse about looking for Sellotape or scissors. I was outraged, and naively thought that would be enough. To be *outraged*. A little human privacy, if you please! A little human decency, for goodness' sake! But no. She did it again. As if my outrage had provoked her or amused her. The second time she was quite brazen. I came into the living room and she was sitting there reading, in the cold. The central heating had packed up for good by then. The image of that is so vivid, even now. Her dumpy figure hunched at my desk. (In fact, it was her desk, something from her father, a beautiful Edwardian thing of some value, which I now have in my study.) Back then I'd set the desk in front of the bay windows, where Alex's piano now stands, overlooking the lawn and the rose beds, my garden. The chapters were all out, pulled about, tossed about, on her desk – not just a few sheets but the whole thing! – and she was sitting there reading, invading, stealing what I had done. She didn't even turn when I came in. The sense of downright treachery was ungovernable. Then she did turn, and looked over her glasses at me. She was smiling but there was no kindness or sympathy or respect there. The same fleshy, complacent smile as before. Superior, patronizing. I must have looked more distraught than angry.

"*Some may say . . .*"

"How dare you!" I thundered.

"*Some may say* you're taking yourself a mite too seriously, Antony . . ."

She got up, straightened her dowdy, loathsome skirts, and as she went past me she shook her head.

"Must get on with lunch. Peel some potatoes."

The real world. Lunch. Potatoes. Get away from this nonsense.

Of course, when I leant on the desk and looked down at the words, they were all, each and every one, filled, sodden, bloated, rotten with her tone, her scorn.

Ruined, blasted, blighted . . .

But I am a military man. I steeled myself and put the papers back in their drawer without hysteria, without tearing everything to pieces or making some romantic funeral pyre, and I collected my thoughts. I sat down in an armchair and shut my eyes for twenty minutes.

I stood and went to the kitchen. With the door half open on its closer, I asked her:

"I should not have said, How dare you? I should have said, How could you, Laura?"

"Oh, Antony. Such subtleties!" She was draining the potatoes at the sink, shaking off the drips. She took them steaming to the table. "Does it really matter, dear?"

Dear!

"It does to me. A great deal. I told you that."

"You need help with your grammar. You said so yourself. And you do. Indeed you do!"

She sighed and tipped the potatoes onto a small ashet. One of her grandmother's ashets, from the Scottish side. Worth something. Everything she had was worth something. Not like my bits of paper.

She looked at me a moment, the empty colander in her hand. "Come on. Have some lunch. You're not going to make our fortune just yet, are you? May as well have something to eat meanwhile."

I couldn't eat lunch with her. I turned and left the kitchen. But neither could I go back to my study, which would have looked too much like sulking, and I wasn't sulking. I felt betrayed and alone, and as if everything in that drawer was useless and worthless and the shame of it was all mine. I had to get out, into the air, even though it was raining, and walk and walk and walk around the three acres until some equanimity returned.

What I didn't understand then was that if things had started to get underway, and this was her secret fear, I'm now convinced, if things had started to get underway, and my confidence in what I was doing had begun to burgeon, which would itself have led to a greater command, a greater skill, a virtuous circle, then she would have been less necessary. Her help might have become only secretarial, rather than critical. Given time and a lucky break, her family money, even, might have lost its leverage. All of that was her secret fear. If I had just managed to get my blundering, ungainly thing airborne, I might have been out of reach and she would have been left behind, and that must not happen, not at any cost. Female vanity, jealousy. Better the sorrow and conflict, the endless bourgeois mediocrity, the endless boiled potatoes, the broken, unaffordable central heating, than the actual prospect of my success. It was sabotage. That's what it was. Only now can I get this done, just slap it all down, when I'm too old for it to matter a jot one way or the other any more – *Not a bloody jot!* – when I'm done for, when the game's up, off, over – Oh, I can end every clause with a preposition now, right enough. I can do as I damn well please.

She never used that phrase in innocence again. She taunted me with it. *Some may say* . . . She used it in company, if she thought I was getting above myself. During her sister's visits it was always there. I just had to wait for it. I don't know if she ever told her sister about my pitiful sheaves of false starts, or if they giggled about them together, but when we were eating lunch, if I'd ventured a stupid opinion of some sort, some bigotry no doubt, she'd remark, pouring her sister more white wine, or exchanging smiles – "Antony, *some may say* that's a little extreme, you know . . ."

No. It *was* a shared joke between them. I never thought till now she'd actually shown her sister my efforts because to do so would have been to invite her mockery of me too, which would have been to Laura's own shame – Oh, her embarrassingly uneducated husband! What pretensions! But now I think about it, and set it down here, I'm sure she showed my epic to Sylvia, and that it was a shared joke between them. The ugly sisters. I know Sylvia laughed at how I'd done the house. I could sense that in the way she spoke about it. She said all the right things, but always with some peccadillo lightly mentioned, to let me know, if I had the sensitivity, that she was only being polite. And even that was not what it seemed. It was also a way to get back at

Laura, because Laura had a big house in the country, and a husband, and a son at boarding school. Sylvia had her flat in Broadstairs, with the beautiful sea views, that she'd bought outright with her inheritance, but that was it. She had her charitable work for the soroptimists, for goodness' sake – 'doing her bit', she called it – but she'd achieved nothing in life. She was just another of those gentle, useless, vicious English dames that crowd the Conservative Club on bridge nights. She was the spinster Laura would have been if she hadn't married beneath her. In fact, they would have lived together, I'm sure. Grown old together, in Broadstairs, Kent, staring at the sea, where I'd once bailed out.

Sylvia told us Alex had flat feet when he started to walk. "Hadn't you better see a doctor about Alex's feet?" She never stopped sniping at him one way or another, every visit. And the vicious cunning of making him look stupid, of course, every adult's prerogative. "What are they teaching you at that strange school, Alex? Now, remember: desiccate, moccasin, inoculate and sacrilegious – just those four – and I'll test you again after lunch."

She counted on my ignorance to keep me out of it, but I wouldn't have it.

"Never mind, Alex." I told him. "Those are horrible words. No more tests, thanks, Sylvia, or Alex won't be able to enjoy his food."

She considered this while taking her napkin from its ring. "Well, you know, Antony," she said, her eyes hooded – that was a habit of hers, when speaking to me, to half close her eyes, as if it made her sleepy or bored to explain things to me – a conversational tic, I've noticed, that belongs exclusively to her class. "They just don't teach spelling in schools properly any more, do they? It's a terrible shame, don't you think? Not like when we were at school."

So she sniped at me too, once I came within range.

After Laura's funeral she was the last to go. She seemed to expect to spend the night under my roof! What on earth was afoot there? Such sisterly loyalty! I told her plainly, without context or provocation, when I came back into the kitchen after seeing off the last of the drunken mourners, that I never wanted to see her, or hear from her, not even in a Christmas card, ever again.

"Do you hear? And what on earth are you lingering around for? Do you hear me? I never want to see you or hear from you again, dear Sylvia! *Goodbye*!"

She actually burst into tears with the shock of it, but the taxi I'd ordered without telling her was already coming up the drive. "Take her to the station," I told the driver, giving him his money. "And good riddance!" I added, slamming the door behind her. Take her and every splinter of her English spite away forever.

Hers was a whole life, every scrap and tittle of it, sacrificed to English one-upmanship. As was Laura's. As is mine.

I swam twenty-one widths today, one extra in order to leave Aaron safely the other side when I climbed the steps. But he called across and signalled for me to wait. I slung my towel around my shoulders and stood there like a fool getting colder and older.

He smiled as he lumbered round – nothing to worry about, sir . . . just a mo, sir . . .

When he reached me, he put a hand on my towelled shoulder and leant down to my height, fixing me with his stare. "The reason we want you to take a shower before bathing, sir – " he lowered his voice for the next bit – "is that we don't want your prehistoric pubes floating about in our Leisure Pool. Why don't you go and drown somewhere else, eh?"

He stood back again, still smiling. Mission accomplished. He clapped his hands as if he'd just offered a swimming tip.

"All right, sir?"

"You young turd."

"Yeah, I know. I know." He started to retreat backwards, rubbing his hands, smiling, so pleased with himself.

I nearly said it. The war, you young turd. For the likes of you.

Then I did say it. "The war. You turd. The war."

He didn't stop retreating.

"What war? Falklands? Nice one."

Ignorant peasant. Life is not serious to this young man. To make it so he needs to hear Mark scream at the top of his lungs, scream as he burns, or as he stares at the ground or the sea spinning up at six hundred miles an hour. Scream like a young warlock burning at the stake, with his legs about to flip out and his belly blow apart. Or hear his shock and agony when a 20mm cannon bullet bursts through his elbow, his wrist, or through his guts, or blows out his groin and splits his hips – and you heard him all the way down, down, down to the earth or the sea. It was wrapped to your ears, his young tearaway goodbye.

This incident tarnished a pleasant start to the day. There had even been some sun at seven but by the time I left the baths it had gone. I ignored Miss Doe-eyes in her booth this morning. In no mood for that game, not after Aaron's quip. Felt too old and alone after that.

Above was a car park sky, wide and flat and grey, one and the same thing above as below, just no white lines up there. Why did they build this place on the outskirts, in the cabbage and beet fields? It is so very desolate.

At home, instead of the customary boiled egg, I comforted myself with two, scrambled, and ate them with fresh brown bread and garlic salt, staring down the drive through the kitchen sashes as I ate. I made a small pot of tea for myself as well, rather than just the usual bag in a mug. When you stare through these kitchen sashes you have to stare through their ice-water draughts too, you have to take them on, resist their pressure to move aside, quit the kitchen. They become part of the view, through the drip-strewn glass. I could feel their ice-water across my knees, dampening my tracksuit.

A voice inside me, maybe Aaron's, maybe Mark's, maybe Frank Simmonds' or his wife's, or the greengrocer's – as he fetches me one more bruised apple to slip in with the other bruised apples – I heard that voice say, *This is nothing. This is not living.* The old refrain, the refrain of the old. I heard it as I chewed my toast, heard it with that slight squelch where my dentures have fallen loose, heard it rising on my pulse, sinking with the swallow of my tea. This is not living. "Well, it isn't," I answered myself aloud, matter-of-factly. "It is waiting for death. What did you expect?" I swallowed again and stopped eating. I stared down the drive, at the mossy stones along its curve, at the ragged border. I used to creosote that border down the drive to stop it growing so fast, just as I did the borders of the rose beds, once upon a time. A pigeon swooped down for something on the tarmac, pecked at it, gave it up, flew back into the pines. Cooed. Good. Jolly good.

Whenever I'm pushed against the limits of what I can do it wells up – not sorrow, not grief, not even dread – but Anger. I swept the half eaten scrambled egg, the fresh brown bread, and the plastic pot of garlic salt onto the floor, and I looked down at it there, my comforting treat – "Why don't you go and drown somewhere else, eh?" – on the ancient lino, a stinking, steaming, pale yellow mess. I looked back down the drive. I get nothing from living. After nigh on seventy-nine bloody years of it. Going to the baths twice a week. Twenty-one widths. The terms by which I must exist in this glum, cold, shabby heap of England are terms determined not by me but by my only begotten son – or rather, I'm damn sure now, not so much by him but by his artful, subtle, scheming wife. She's taken control. I am living out my final years here according to what she wants, not what I want, or even he wants. It suits her well enough to have me keeping the house aired, keeping an eye on things, stalling the inexorable decay, while she waits for the precious "window" to maximize capital gains. If she winkled me out, got me into a Grosvenor or a Claremont or Beaumont of some sort, she'd be in clover. She'd get Alex to take out a loan and tidy the place up, fix the sills and windows, give it a lick of paint, put the central heating right, then let it out until the market turned, paying off the loan with the rental. They wouldn't even have to put that towards my care because the home would take my pensions. I've done the sums. The research. I can use the internet. I know all this. Then she'll dump him, poor old Alex, as soon as the sale is made and she's secured her share, and more, somehow, by some cheat, and she'll start life over. Laura's premonition: 'I just feel so sorry for my son, that's all.' Life really will begin again at forty for her, which is not long before mine ended.

Lucky bitch.

But how lucky I am too that the proprietors of The Grosvenor – those bloody names again! – Grosvenors, Claremonts, Hamiltons, Carltons, Mayfairs, Castlemonts, Beaumonts! – were too keen and greedy; how lucky that Frank Simmonds and his good lady wife graced me with their visit, let me know the plan's afoot, the countdown has started, so I stand a chance at least of staying one step ahead.

One's charcoal suit with a carnation, one's black brogues with insteps polished (the mark of a gentleman, one learned in the mess) is the chosen outfit for the big occasion. One tried a white silk handkerchief in the top pocket but one decided that was going too far. Bored, at last, with preening oneself, handkerchief still in hand, one stepped from the mirror to the window of one's bedroom.

At twilight the view is beyond belief, and I am in such a benign and charitable mood to enjoy it! My airman's vision not blurred by anger and resentment for once. What a little hope can do! The ford, at the end of the strip of woodland by the lane; the glebe field to the left with a tethered horse, quite still and at peace, quite magnificent; and the giant elm down at the ford, which fills with bees every year. They nest in a hollow twenty feet up, out of reach. Then a shallow valley of fields into the distance. All so unspoilt and precious. And valuable, of course, and will redouble in value, no doubt, before very long, the way the property market is going. Laura was right to cut me out of it. I would have sold up long ago for a stupid price and moved on – a world cruise? Hong Kong? Barbados? A bungalow by the sea or the golf course? – and left Alex and family with none of this, with nothing at all, in fact. She knew I would behave in that way, and she was quite right.

Return to the mirror. It is full length and swings between two rosewood stanchions. Laura's, of course. I have it tilted back to make me look taller than I am, and the darkness of my charcoal adds loft as well. I have always hated being on the short side. It's not very noticeable, shod in a pair of solid brogues, but no one has ever called me tall, and of course with age there has been a compression of the cartilage, leaving me stumpier still. But I stand tall, shoulders pinned back. There is a shine on my forehead from some cream I've used to keep the eyebrows shapely, and it emphasises the slight protuberance there, a slight apishness, the primordial forebears coming through as I shrink towards extinction. The long sweep back of my thinning hair is youthfully softened and darkened by a modern emollient from the Americans, God bless them, invented for that purpose alone. The angle of the mirror makes me a touch severe, intimidating even, in my charcoal suit, which is rather what I want this evening.

She is not forties or fifties as I had thought, but early sixties, I now believe. Given that I look about ten years younger than I should, she's within reach, as it were. Her face is moonish, well made-up, with a melon-pip smile of well-kept teeth, and my impression is that behind the powdered face lies a simple, uncalculating mind. Her eyes are a distinctive grey, the same as Rachael's, in fact – that is, a genuine grey, not just a different shade of blue. I love grey eyes. But most interestingly of all, Natalie Stein is rich, rich, rich. She's possibly the richest person I've ever met, and certainly the richest ever to settle in these parts. There's a titled couple living further up the village in a manse (the church were great property developers here a couple of centuries ago) but these particular nobs have no money left. He runs a pig farm. How the mighty are fallen, and a good job too. But Mrs Stein really does have independent means. Her money humbled me immediately, undermined me, and I had to bluff superiority and indifference to it straightaway, and remained stuck with that posture all evening. However, I didn't outstay my welcome; I'm sure of that. I mean, how long can you spend standing around with a glass of sherry talking to neighbours you don't know, about things you don't understand? We spent a half hour or so exchanging views about a young towny who has set up a tool-hire firm at the top of the village, and whose customers sometimes block the road up there because he hasn't building permission for a proper car park. Some jealous carping about this young man's success, a general relief of spleen – but then what? To spend half an hour on just this alone? Far too stressful and demanding.

I think she is a lush, as they say. But I don't mind. Somehow with women it's more acceptable. Women don't brag and bray as men do once they're tanked up.

The other guests: some gentlemen farmers manqué, one of whom I know; the young bachelor dentist from the village school conversion (not a trace of effeminacy about him, now I've met him); a solicitor on his own because his wife was "Too under the weather to come along. Quite unchivviable!" (I'll keep that phrase for later; thanks, mister);

and a larger than life artist from Norwich called Logie, of all things. She'd obviously met everyone before, except me, from her familiarity with them all, and one or two seemed to be there because they'd offered her help or advice with the restoration, so the event was a kind of thankyou too. That's where the tool-hire conversation started. Steggles, the farmer I know, had brought his drinking partner instead of his wife. In fact, there were no other women present, but Natalie seemed quite at ease with that. After we'd buried the tool-hire entrepreneur, the artist tried several times to publicise an exhibition he is holding in Norwich in November, directing our attention to some handsomely printed flyers on a nest of tables, and hinting he'd give us a discount on his 'works' - as if any of us gave a damn. Recently he'd been helping Natalie become a miniaturist, he told us. "I'm a miniaturist, don't you know!" she laughed, when he announced this. We had to gather round and gawp at her efforts, which were set out on the far wall of her lovely new living room in a tight squadron. No less than ten postcard size pieces in oils, four along the base, each in a very costly looking matt black frame with gold beading. Subjects were all of a rural nature, taking us through the seasons. Such an expensive waste of time and money! Logie, in a baggy white suit, with some unfortunate stains below the belt, a rather large and unlikely looking artist, it has to be said – much more a hunter-gatherer, in my view – was one of those men who believes it lends irony and authority to speak out the side of one's mouth the whole time, so when he turned from his audience to address the paintings squarely I *lawst* much of what he said. But it was of no consequence because there really wasn't anything to say about Natalie's miniatures. A childish field of flaxen corn, trimmed like a haircut; a brave attempt at a horse, with hooves like door-stops; some snowy woods slipped off a

Christmas card; the ford in rampant flood but looking quite static and glacial: all in all, a general waste of oils, time and someone's hard-earned cash. Not *her* hard-earned cash, I'll be bound. However, to her credit, Natalie was dismissive of them too. Catching my critical eye, she told us all, before it was too late, she was only learning. "Painting by numbers sort of stuff!"

Following the art talk, and perhaps because we needed it after that, we moved on from sherry to wine, beer, gin and whisky, and half an hour or so later I decided it was time to get out while still ahead. Gamble no more. Remaining aloof from the bonhomie, I thanked my hostess and made my gentlemanly exit. I'm not sure if I left with my reserved impression altogether undented. However, I did leave with my fantasies heated up, if not inflamed, by The Warming of Long Cottage. Her behaviour towards me had both excited me and made me anxious, as shall be seen.

Midway through News at Ten, still in my suit and still feeling a modicum of elation, not least on account of the sherry, because I'm not used to any alcohol whatsoever, I was watching a report on house prices. This always interests me because I imagine Rachael and Alex watching the same thing and wonder what is going through their minds - or rather, through her mind. The rate of growth per quarter had slowed from 4.9% to 4.6%: which means the rectory, despite the decrease, must have gone up around £20,000 in the last six months. Talk about money for nothing! For some, fortunes will be made from this boom without anyone lifting a finger. Just a question of being of the right generation. Nothing clever about it at all. While all this was gently tugging at my attention, I received a rather ambiguous telephone call.

The central heating wasn't working. Could I come back and have a look? I seemed the sort of fellow who'd know what to do, and I was the closest of her guests this evening. Well, that wasn't true. The dentist was closer. I was careful not to read too much into that, but suspicions were aroused. I see all women through disillusioned and jaundiced eyes.

She welcomed me in stockinged feet, still wearing her tight black cocktail dress, and quickly drew me through to the living room where the wood burner was blazing, but apart from the six foot radius around the fire, the house was chilly and cheerless. For me, home from home, of course. Her other guests must have left pretty smartly after I did – ungracious curs. After I'd warmed my hands we returned to the kitchen to investigate. A rancid smell of booze hung in the air and plates and pots lay unwashed by the sink, and the residue of the party – prawns, crackers, trout vol-au-vent – was all heaped up on an ashet she'd used for cold meats.

"Dishwasher's conked too," she muttered.

She couldn't find the fuses.

Well, she hadn't looked very far because they were exactly where they were supposed to be. The stairs were steep and Carter's had set the cupboard door at the end so that it was virtually full height. Tall enough for me, anyway. And there was a battery light that worked in there too. Well done, Carter's! The cupboard was carpeted, and the smell of the new carpet and stained wood trapped in there was heavenly to me. So different to all my chilly making-do at the rectory; my accursed telephone cupboard, with its all-year-round condensation. There was the clutter of a modern Dyson vacuum cleaner, not put away properly, and various lamps and boxes, some of them still taped up. The fuse box panel was hidden behind the seat of a small step-ladder, but not difficult to spot with so many fresh white cables running up and down from it. The floor was blocked by some open boxes of books.

"Let me give you a hand," she said, bending down to help shift the books.

The black dress was low cut with some lace frill woven inside. Can't stop myself staring down women's cleavages, whenever opportunity arises. And I thought immediately of Rachael, young enough to be this woman's daughter – my daughter-in-law! – in the confines of my study cupboard, my captive there to look at the whisky advertisement; lured into my cupboard, in part, at least, under false pretences. Had I been lured here similarly?

"Best leave them to me," I said.

"Nonsense."

There were four boxes to remove, then the little ladder. In her drunkenness she let the ladder slip open and scuff the woodwork of the doorway, the new paint. She pretended it hadn't happened.

"Don't trap your fingers," I cautioned, as the ladder flapped away from her, out of control.

When I opened the panel, she leant in close to take a look too. We didn't actually touch, but I thought of Laura and her solicitor at their Ayckbourn rehearsals.

"I needs me glasses," she said, in that Professor Higgins way of imitating the lower orders. But she didn't go to get them. "What's it say?"

I studied the rows of fuses and the writing on the inside of the panel door, taking my time, sensing the closeness of her body, the weight of it so near me, inches from me. Twenty, or maybe just ten years ago, such positioning would have been overwhelmingly exciting, but bodies do not mean the same to me now and it is easier to control myself. These days bodies come suffused with other associations. They are heavy with excrement, shit and piss, between five and twenty-five pounds of it, and big meat-eaters like her – I'd seen her tucking into her cold meats – would have a column of rotting flesh half a metre long inside, and it might well have been there a day or two. Such understanding was the legacy of Laura's illness.

"Well, it doesn't really matter what it says," I said. Even my eyes couldn't decipher Carter's script on the door panel without a torch. "It's clear which ones are down, look."

There was a row of three chunky switches in the off position. A 13 amp circuit.

"Shall I try?"

"Go on, then," she urged, as if there were some mischief in all this, as if she were about to giggle.

The fuses went up and stayed up. Immediately there were electrical hums and lights flickering from outside the cupboard.

"Oh good! Well done, Antony!"

"But you have to find out why they went off," I advised, closing the panel.

"Let's take a look at the boiler."

For that, we had to go outside. She slipped on a pair of house shoes and took some keys from a row of brass hooks behind the door. Such an organized person, and yet she'd forgotten the whereabouts of the fuse box?

The utility room, which she'd converted from some store or animal pen adjoining the cottage, was purpose built inside and full of brand new, top brand gardening tools: Fiskars' rakes and shears, Sandvik forks and spades, as yet unused, hung neatly around the breeze block walls – painted green, of course – on galvanized brackets. A new Husqvarna sit-on mower was parked to one side and the place was filled with the smell of its belts and grass cuttings. Beneath that, a faint whiff of diesel oil came from the boiler. I felt I'd been led in here to stare deeper into her bottomless pockets.

There was a control panel on top of the boiler and a large red reset button. I stepped over and pressed it without asking. The boiler growled into life.

"Oh, you are wonderful!" she exclaimed. "Come and have a drink!"

She put out the light and locked the door carefully behind us, and we went back inside.

"You have to find out why the fuse tripped," I repeated behind her, but she didn't reply.

I have always been incapable of flirtatious behaviour. I loathe it in the same way I loathe drunkenness, and the two are much akin, of course. It's the vanity and effrontery of the flirt that I despise. So many flirts, of both sexes, that I came across in my youth, were only interested in the preening, not the sexual relief itself. At the party I'd noticed Natalie's flirtatiousness, and put it down to just this kind of behaviour, because what woman of her age has much hormonal stuff left in her, when all's said and done? After the first round of top-ups she'd picked up on some lewd innuendo from Steggles, the youngish gentleman farmer. I say youngish but he wears his hair slicked back and brilliantined in the style of my own generation. He was there without his wife, as I said, whom Natalie had expected. Steggles' drinking partner was short (that is, shorter than me) and seedy. Two rogue males in sports jackets, jangling change in their pockets, impatient to be off to Norwich or Yarmouth, because for them Natalie's house warming was just an excuse to get away from their families and 'go out on the town', 'enjoy some nightlife' – meaning, find a red light district and enjoy a prostitute. Steggles was full of libido and his drinking partner, whose name I never caught, was a truly vulgar fellow. I followed him to the kitchen to refill some bowls of snacks for Natalie, and once in there he stopped, thrust back his arse, and let out a long, sly fart. "Vol-au-*vent*," he quipped, for my benefit. "Let some out to get more in!" At the sink he refilled his beer glass from a tartan can, and farted again. "Oh dear oh dear! Vol-au-*vent*!" he repeated, very pleased with himself. I must have looked rather aloof and unamused because as he left the kitchen he farted yet again, on quite a high and rasping note this time, and called back over his shoulder, for the benefit of Natalie or anyone else approaching –

"Stoma-bag alert! Scramble! Chocks away, old boy!"

Horrible little man.

Back in the living room, Steggles set the innuendo rolling again with some ribald lines about the tool hire firm, something like a limerick that had spread round the village. *There was a young towny called Hunt* . . . Then Natalie came up with her very own double-entendres about her cocktail sausages, and Steggles asked if she'd pricked them properly and then – ye gods! – just before I left, she caused great merriment and disturbance by bobbing down on the young dentist's lap, because he sat looking rather bored and fed up in the corner. I couldn't stay after that, not once the open flirting and drinking had really got underway.

To be honest, it wasn't just that which drove me away early. Natalie had also started bragging, which rather goes against my theory about the difference between men and women drunks. Be that as it may, her bragging was about her education, and nothing shakes me more than that.

"Both my husbands were Oxbridge grads!" she declared, as some triumphant non-sequitur, when Steggles spoke proudly about his stepson doing well at university in Wales. "First Cambs, second Oxon, degrees commensurate!" These declarations were mainly for the solicitor's benefit, I think, as he seemed the most educated and intelligent person in the room, but she looked my way too. "And I married the first in a mini skirt! How about that, Antony? Good God, but I loved the sixties! Didn't you? Bet you were sex on legs back then, eh?" She threw her head back and laughed, showing too brazenly that she meant no harm. With some anxiety, I realized she might not be completely taken in by my haughtiness and reserve, my charcoal suit and carnation. That sounds presumptuous but most are taken in by it: my posturing, my fruity accent and diction, my bourgeois circumlocution and British understatement, cultivated during thirty years in the mess, make up a formidable disguise. But now it seemed she sought to test it, get underneath it, break it up, my dark carapace, as if she'd heard some rumour about me in the village and wanted to get to the bottom of it. Quite how she expected her boasts about previous husbands to go down with the local gentry I do not know, but when she'd glanced *my* way at that moment – "First Cambs, second Oxon, degrees commensurate!" – and it was a hooded, grey, sidelong glance, it was as if she had already found me out, as if she had prior knowledge about me and recognized me from the start as a parvenu at her feast. If my air of superiority had been genuine, I suppose I might have responded with a disdainful look, one that showed I felt equal to the social trump she'd played, and therefore held her beneath me for her lack of finesse. By not responding in any way, I hoped to leave my opinion of her unclear, but worried all the way home that I had not.

However, after fixing the fuse and the heating and getting her dishwasher going, I was very much her friend, and she poured me a large single malt whisky from Isla or Jura or some Hebridean nowhere. I only sipped at it, by the fire, and adopted, as far as possible, the pose I'd been given all those years ago by Whyte & Mackay. I don't trust myself to drink a glass of spirits, particularly as I don't eat a great deal. And how would her first class scotch settle on my all-day breakfasts, my sandwiches, porridge or scrambled eggs with garlic salt, and the three or four trout vol-au-vents I'd taken from her lovely Wedgwood china?

Some of the alcohol definitely did get through to the bloodstream, though, because I began to see the woman in front of me in a different way. She sat on the edge of her elegant, crimson, fireside chair, rolling her glass in both hands as she spoke, and her slightly forward posture exposed more of her lace-trimmed cleavage, and I thought – she's making a play, she's casting me in the old role, waiting for the shop to open. Well, I look at least ten years younger than I should, and in my charcoal suit I still cut a bit of a dash, I thought, grasping at the clichés of my youth. But I also remembered – as she babbled on contentedly by the fire, talking about the problems she'd had with the fireplace, ripping the old one out and searching all over Norwich for the right mantelpiece, don't you know – I also remembered that at the party we'd been given to understand she'd had no children, that she'd skipped that part of a woman's lot. Not even step-sons or step-daughters could be traced between the lines of her conversation. She'd made some remarks about her late husband's family and friends, whom she'd seen recently at a reunion on the Thames – "I love boats, me!" – Henley regatta, yacht parties and riverside parties at Cookham and Maidenhead were mentioned. "But good God, those poor, worn-out women!" she'd called out to everyone, and she'd laughed again, looking around the all-male guests, catching Steggles' eye. "Flogged out, misshapen by their awful childbearing, then cheated on by their husbands! My God, what a life!" These same women had evidently been

nice enough about her – "Natalie!" they'd called across the
decks and lawns, "You don't look a day older than you did
fourteen years ago! No! *Twenty* years ago!" It was another
way of drawing attention to her looks, and she'd glanced at
me, definitely at me, with mischief in her grey eyes, when
she came out with that line, as if to see how she was doing.
I blinked and smiled in my superior way, and that drew her
over. "Nice for the old ego, I'd say!" she said, picking up
a bottle of claret to start another round of top-ups – "Now,
how are we all doing?" – stopping at the solicitor, the dentist,
and then me –

"How I love your carnation, Antony!"

She asked me where I'd got it, and did I know
anyone that grew half-decent carnations in the whole of
Norfolk, because she quite emphatically did not. She started
talking haughtyculture, as if it were a science, a profession,
not gardening at all . . .

But now here she was in front of me, leaning forward
in that way, and with a few sips of whisky I'd clean forgotten
the half metre of shit inside each of us. The predator was
surfacing. Something in me wanted to squeeze and hurt
that soft, abundant, vulnerable flesh, all rolled up in its tight
black folds of cocktail dress, trussed and meaty. She is not
a tall woman and her fireside chair is too big for her. Man-
size. Meant for some shortish idler like me, not her at all.
Even at five foot eight I felt tall, powerful, sitting in the chair
opposite, and felt strong enough to take her in a cruel way.
And right then it seemed to me that is what she wanted too,
or that is what she wanted me to try, at least, and this was
why the chairs, and our bodies, were arranged in this way by
the fire. And when she glanced up at me from staring into the
fire there was that fleeting penetration that happens between
men and women – nothing to do with flirting, which is an

exercise of the ego, a performance – no, this is to do with the instinct itself laid bare. The naked fact of attraction passing from one ape to the other without guile or guise, and once known it cannot be unknown. Of course we can pretend it never happened, that the other was mistaken, and so on, as we do all the time, but both apes know what has taken place.

"I suppose I'd better go," I said, setting my glass aside on a nest of tables, there for that purpose.

"Excuse me! That's my twelve year old single malt!"

"Oh, I'm sorry. But you can have it. Don't waste it."

"I shan't drink from your glass," she replied, chuckling. "I hardly know you, Antony!"

"I don't trust myself to drink it, I'm afraid. I hardly ever drink, you see."

"Don't trust yourself to do what?"

She laughed again. We were moving much too fast here, and it crossed my mind again, with squiffy certainty now, that the whole business with the fuse box had been a ploy. She'd put them down herself to lead me up her garden path in the dark. Second time around the thought rather shook me, rather vanquished the powerful, predatory notions of a few moments before. The thought of being outsmarted in that way suggested she was not at all simple-minded and uncalculating, as I'd so pompously judged on first impression.

She was on her feet before me and took my glass away. I followed her short figure, that suddenly seemed heavy and dumpy, through to the kitchen.

"It was really so kind of you to come out, Antony," she said, formality returning. "Saved my bacon. I do appreciate it."

Just then it seemed absurd to leave. Why on earth was I in such a hurry? What was there to get back to? Didn't

I need company too? But this was too complicated, and I needed time to think.

"Anytime, Natalie." I risked her name. "We're virtually neighbours, after all."

"We are indeed," she said tonelessly, giving and taking nothing any more.

She let me out into the chilly night and I walked unsteadily across her deep and weedless gravel to the freezing Allegro.

A couple of weeks passed. Well, I couldn't ask her to the rectory. The place is so shameful, and so cold already. To imagine her hurrying through no-man's-land! When she phoned again, Alex, Rachael and Joe were here, a fortnight early, on a patently compensatory visit. Guilt on Alex's part for leaving without saying goodbye last time.

"Who was that?" Rachael asked, when I returned to the study.

Funny to see her immediate suspicion. I glanced at Alex, who was looking up too, from putting new batteries into Joe's digger. Joe has too many toys. I keep telling them that.

Now, despite his unwarranted assurance, Alex finds it difficult to hide his uglier feelings. He hasn't the am-dram talents of his lovely wife. I wondered how had he, or she, come to think there could be anything suspicious or of interest about the call. It struck me that they might have gone to the study door and opened it, then held it ajar so they could hear my end of the conversation from the broom cupboard. And I suppose what I said would have been rather suspicious, because I'd told Natalie that I had guests, from which they would deduce that I was telling someone not to come round.

But how petty and underhand of them to do that! To listen in to the old man, check up on him like that. Joe had been on my computer when I left the room – he's addicted to *Donkey Kong;* he and Rachael take it in turns and have their own scores online – but now he was on the floor with his re-charged digger, and with the new batteries it made a horrible revving noise every time it raised its bucket. I looked at him irritably, as if distracted by it.

I answered Rachael.

"Neighbour," I said. "Promised me some logs. I made an excuse."

Rachael cut more slices of Madeira. It was Madeira hour. They would soon be gone.

I walked round Joe to my chair and added, with a groan, as I sat down, "I don't have much luck with logs."

"You've nowhere to put them," Alex said. "You need to put up a lean-to."

"Of course," I replied. "A lean-to. A shed. Get planning permission. Sharpen my saws. Why not."

"Put them in the garage, then. Leave the car out. Or half out," Rachael suggested.

"Logs have to be chopped," I said. "I'm past chopping logs."

Rachael laughed, ate her cake, swallowed too quickly and continued. "Rubbish. You're fit and strong enough. No one would believe your age! And it would be good exercise."

It was all I could do to stop myself asking her: *'Do you want me to last forever, then? Till you're fifty? More than halfway through?'*

Why this phoney concern, suddenly, after that call? They must have had the door ajar.

"Which neighbour was it?" Alex asked, sipping his tea, as if he were only interested in continuing the conversation.

None of your bloody business.

"Steggles," I said. "Farmer at the top of the village."

"Oh god! Not *him*!" Alex laughed.

"You know him?"

"I know of him."

"And?" I felt piqued that he should know more about the locals than I did. How had that happened? Perhaps he made it his business, dropped by the pub on the way back for a hair of the dog. But no. Sundays it doesn't open till seven.

"He's a bit sharp." Alex tightened his lips and put down his tea cup delicately, savouring his understatement. "Don't buy logs from Steggles, or anything else, Dad."

I very much wanted to know how he knew anything about Steggles at all, but to ask would have opened up a vein of conversation I didn't want them to mine. What he said seemed right, though, from what I'd seen of Steggles. And his drinking partner, young 'Vol-au-*vent*!' They'd have built up some notoriety between them, no doubt about that.

Talk of logs brought me back to my favourite subject, electricity bills, which was too much for Rachael, who couldn't bear to hear us bickering about that, so after the Madeira and tea they soon packed up and left.

Interesting, though, that they are quietly observing me like this, and wanting to know of any change in circumstances, anything which might affect the status quo. Rachael has the measure of it. She can see that I'm in for the long haul. "You're fit and strong enough. No one would believe your age!" I really could still be knocking around when she's fifty, into her own health problems and looming pension worries, and she doesn't want that. She wants change *now*. She wants the short-term prospect, at least, of a better life – more money, more freedom, more for Joe and for her – not another decade, maybe, of weekend visits and sacrifice and pretence, waiting for me to conk out, kick the bucket, pass away.

Die.

How I have come to hate the bloody telephone. I can't use it properly, never have been able to. On the phone I become much deafer than I really am, and I get into a panic and cannot understand the simplest things, so I sound rude and abrupt. Given I was a first class wireless operator, I don't know why deciphering on the phone should be such a challenge, but there it is. A side-effect of all this withdrawal and anti-sociability, perhaps.

So I didn't call Natalie back. Instead, I changed out of my tracksuit into some second best tweeds and popped round to Long Cottage. I had a pretext.

After my apologies for calling unexpectedly, redoubled with my apologies for being abrupt on the phone, which I wanted to offer face to face, we settled in very easily for some tea by her fire, in the same chairs as before. With the Madeira ritual not an hour past, I didn't want tea, but accepted it because I certainly didn't want whisky this time, and that was also on offer; I sensed that part of her hearty welcome was the excuse to bring forward her evening session. She is a lush. I'm certain of it.

She was in her gardening clothes: a rough polo neck sweater and a pair of thick corduroy trousers. Her hair was wild. All very becoming, in a just-got-off-the-lawn-tractor sort of way.

"The other thing I need to say sorry about, Natalie, if you can bear any more apologies from me, is for not inviting you over to the rectory."

"Oh, don't mind that," she said graciously, and for a moment I was shamed by her friendliness, her innocence. She seemed, this afternoon, in broad daylight, in her gardening clothes, with her pretty moon face and big smile, far too good a person to deceive, and my suspicions of her from the party night seemed just more of my paranoid nonsense.

"I haven't done so because I'm ashamed of it," I confessed.

"But it's a marvellous place! Very grand. Quite the nicest house around here – including the Laiths." These are the titled people in the manse, fallen on hard times. Pig farmers.

"Since Laura died I've let it go," I began. "You know all about grieving, so I won't bore you with that."

She looked down and frowned, put her hands together, but not in any kind of prayer. She spoke softly.

"When my second husband died, I thought I'd be able to deal with it because I'd dealt with it all before, and I was much closer to my first. But actually, it was just the same. Don't know why."

"I'm sorry," I said to her, but sorrier still for the change of mood I'd provoked. "Don't go into any of that. I shouldn't have brought it up." I offered the last almost in a mumble. I was rather better at this than I'd thought I'd be. Little Lord Am-Dram!

"No," she said, still frowning at the hearth rug, and rubbing the calf of her leg through her trousers. Mosquitoes, I thought, and immediately – my god! – leapt up the fantasy of applying soothing oils to her bites. "I just meant I know what you're talking about." She looked up at me again and smiled, still rubbing her leg. "And you and Laura had been together a long time, yes?"

"Twenty-nine years."

"Well, that is a very long time." Her tone was sympathetic, and now sympathy and sentiment were everywhere, suffusing the atmosphere to flammable limits by the glow of the log fire. But that made the next part easier. I sighed.

"You want to turn the place into a shrine. I've read about this. Nothing unusual. I wanted to leave everything just as it was. It felt like a kind of reverence. Or rather, it felt irreverent to change anything. To redecorate or clear anything out."

She looked at me narrowly, knowingly, as if my distinction had a deeper meaning, which it did not, or – alarums severally! - as if she saw right through me, as before, at the house warming, and knew this was complete nonsense! Knew me for the lazy old dog I am! Without a bone to my name! My confidence wilted but I carried on.

"Then I lost the habit of keeping up the garden and so on. For a long time it all seemed so pointless. No one to share it with. You know what I mean, I'm sure."

"I do know," she said, coming to my rescue, and she nodded her big head wisely. "With Rafe, I thought – Come on, you've been through all this before. And as I say, I was closer to my first husband, but somehow it didn't work like that. I was devastated. Even though that had always been there, in front of us, because we were different generations, you see."

This was looking better than I could have hoped. But I didn't know of how to invite her to continue. Then I didn't need to.

"It was just the same, though. Devastating. One's

world is so fragile, you see? You think it's all so solid, and then there you are. Alone again. Devastating."

But not so very devastating, I thought, if you can rebuild Long Cottage with the proceeds and start flirting with the locals . . .

"Well, I know all about that," I offered, after a measured pause.

"I'm sure you do, Antony. I'm sure you do."

I knew what she would ask now.

"How long have you been on your own?"

"Twelve years." I sighed again and stared into the fire. I nearly said something more, something like, 'twelve dark and lonely years without her', but pulled back, couldn't carry it off.

"Freddie and I were different," she carried on, wistfully now. I could see out the corner of my eye that she was looking at me, not the fire. I was glad I had timed this in the way I had. No whisky. Sobriety, clarity. "Can't say it was the same with Rafe, but as I say, it was still awful."

"Well," I said, standing to take my leave of her repetitions, because I really couldn't sit through Freddie – we'd hit the buffers of my sympathies for the moment, I'm afraid – "I have to make yet another apology, Natalie, for dragging up mournful thoughts. I'm sorry. But I felt I should explain my rudeness in not reciprocating your generosity." Such wordiness stood in my favour, made me come across as awkward and upset. "Don't get up," I told her, raising a hand. She obeyed, looked up at me. I stood there a moment, staring around her wall-to-wall carpet, her fire, her expensive fireside rug. "I need to break out of these habits I've dug myself into. These ruts," I said. "I'll get something done about the house. Renovate, refurbish. Start again. It's about time!" I couldn't help but exclaim the last, then offered an awkward smile, as if embarrassed by my own frankness, as if remembering suddenly that I didn't know her very well, and I stared around a second time at her freshly rebuilt, tastefully and very expensively decorated living room – Good grief! I had never in my life had the money to pay someone to do what she had done to this living room, let alone the rest! "You must give me the name of your decorator," I added. "You've inspired me!" She moved to get up from her low chair and I repeated my injunction, with a flattened hand this time: "Don't get up." I started towards the kitchen. "I've disturbed you enough for one afternoon."

That, "You've inspired me!" was a bold plant. I felt very pleased with that, once safely outside on the coconut mat, closing the door gently behind me.

Then all this happened in one fell swoop. Why shouldn't good luck come in threes, same as bad?

Outshining Natalie's chocolate-box card (even though that has opened so many diverting possibilities) a far more wonderful invitation arrived this Monday morning. I didn't discover it until I'd returned from The Leisure Pool. It has nothing to do with Natalie. In fact, it bears me aloft not only of the strains and joys of that particular soap, but also of all the woes of my filial relations, and my sweet, delicious memories of married life, my conflicts with Aaron and Mark, my pointless drives into Norwich, the Last-of-the-Few boobies, the ghastly Simmondses, the swindling grocer, miserable butcher, lying baker, crossword-hog librarian – the whole bloody cast of my rotten lot. They can all just carry on very well without me. For a while, anyway.

The card is 3/16ths of an inch. I actually went out and measured it with the rusty micrometer from the greenhouse. It arrived in its own magnolia, tailored envelope, of a distinctive and irregular size, with an official letter. The card too is magnolia, around A6 but with the corners rounded, rather like a wedding invitation. The border is gold, a beautiful, smooth, rolled gold, and the writing is in a fine, black, stately script. (I idled away a half hour trying to find the font on my computer, but failed.)

Everything about this invitation denotes what the late Dan Maskell, the voice of Wimbledon, tennis coach of princes and princesses, used to call, "A Royal Occasion":

*At the annual commemorations of The Battle of Britain,*
*25*th *November 1999, by kind permission of*
*His Excellency Crown Prince*
*Sheikh Abdullah bin Abdulaziz*
*and Mr Richard Evans, CEO British Aerospace,*
*Group Captain Christopher Rogers DFC DFM OBE*
*requests the pleasure of the company of*
<u>*Sqn Ldr Antony Rose*</u>
*during the Roll of Honour and Flypast at*
*Dammam Air Base, Kingdom of Saudi Arabia.*

I am not filled in: my name is actually part of the script! My own, individual card no less. Of course, there can't be many of us left – 50? 70? – so such personal attention is perfectly feasible. Nevertheless, the trouble someone has taken to do this properly makes you think. Quite humbling, in fact. That is all it says on my personalized, gilded card. The accompanying letter from Dammam Air Base goes through protocols, advice on flights, preferred group flights, visa business, websites, R.S.V.P. etc.

The first problem is my passport. I haven't used it since I retired, more than thirty years ago.

But rolled gold on magnolia! With rounded corners! British Aerospace, no less! His Excellency! Petrodollars! All expenses! . . .

I shall go. I will move heaven and earth to go! The pearl of great price never shone with such lustre! Of course, I cannot help but suspect my excitement is disproportionate and there will be some calamitous disappointments along the way – can't completely escape my ingrained, protective pessimism – but no matter: I will overcome. I will prevail! There are aspects to this that are no less than thrilling to me. Travelling on a modern aircraft, not least. I haven't been on one since the annual ski-trips with R.A.F. Coltishall. But it isn't just the trip, nor really the occasion itself. It's this out of the blue, stately, dignified, gold on magnolia *recognition* that is so marvellous to me. Rather than ducking and weaving through interviews with Natalie, or bearing up against the hateful scorn of Aaron and Mark, or suffering the quips and jibes and petty sparring of my own bloody son – because in all these ghastly relationships, I am in some way or measure the aged underdog, the supplicant – rather than any of that, here is bold and public recognition that what I once did was ungainsayably, uniquely heroic, and none of these other lives, which now have such leverage and advantage over me, can hold a candle to it. Such recognition isn't part of the psyche of these people and never will be. Their imaginations can't span or comprehend it. Whereas, that's what this whole event is about. That acknowledgement. Respect. Well, I'm up for a bit of that! If only this had been lying on the refectory table when Mr Simmonds and wife dropped by from The Grosvenor!

Sooner than I really wanted there was an opportunity to break the news. In fact, my hand was rather forced. After a somewhat restless forty winks I had a call from Natalie inviting me to afternoon tea. There was something "of a social nature" she wanted to discuss. She'd say no more on the telephone.

With beaming smile and warm welcome, she barred any return to the mournful conversations we'd so much enjoyed on my last visit, and steered us on to the here and now, and the gay future that lay before us both in village life. My one dampener, early on, as I settled again in my seat by the fire, was to inform her that I might not be the best person to discuss prospects "of a social nature", because I knew no one in or of, and nothing whatever about, the village; not out of snobbery, I insisted, but simply on account of anti-social instincts and bad widower habits, you know. I smiled modestly when I finished, lending myself a righteous air.

Oh, she had a field day with all of that.

"Stuff and nonsense, Antony!" she declared, throwing her head back and laughing at me goodnaturedly. "What flummery you talk! You're only anti-social because you're hiding something, you know, and you're worried about being found out. That's the only reason any of us is anti-social. We all need each other to some degree. Live alone too long and you go mad. Believe me, I know!" This was rather too close to the bone, horribly reminiscent of Alex's platitudes. Oh dear oh dear. What was coming next?

Was I to run the tombola at the village fete?

"So, what are you hiding, Antony? You poor old thing!" she asked, leaning forward. Her own elderly moon face was full of shadows and mischief and secrets this Monday afternoon. We were only drinking tea. There was no whiff of booze about her either. I sensed she was very sober and alert, and on the lookout for something again, a chink in my reserve.

Nothing I care to share with you, I thought primly. But it struck me then, with some misgiving, that it would have been difficult to say anything honest to her now, having already laid down two or three layers of deceit, thick as cake-mix.

I laughed at her in turn.

"Natalie," I reprimanded, shifting in my chair, wagging a finger. "Don't be nosy. We hardly know each other well enough to share such dark things." It was the nearest I'd come to flirting with her, and having gybed the conversation in that direction, I trusted she wouldn't sail quite so close to the wind again; not unless she started drinking.

"Aha! Touché. Well, we'll find you out yet, Antony Rose!" she promised, and she moved gaily on. "Now. To the real business of our tête-à-tête . . ."

The French was taking hold, a sure sign of something. Nerves, I suspected, despite her bluff manner this afternoon. But nerves about what, exactly? Her 'real business' turned out to be nothing more *risqué* than a bridge four. Oh lord. She said she had sounded out some authorities in the village, and discovered that "in times of yore" – no going back to specifics – I'd been a regular at the Conservative Club bridge evenings. In the picture she painted I was coming across as a bit of a Tory grandee. What larks! But I was happy enough to be thought of in this way for the moment, and nodded on through her explanations with tea cup politely poised. She proposed that the first "soirée" would be there, at Long Cottage, and, looking down to the carpet a moment before facing me directly, she asked me, gently, "Would you care to be my partner?"

Aha!

"I'd be delighted," I said, stepping up to the plate without hesitation.

"Oh good. Thank you, Antony."

That seemed from the heart, and really quite humble.

Our adversaries would be Mr & Mrs Steggles.

Steggles? *Steggles*? The man whose drinking partner, arse bucked, had farted in her kitchen? Thrice? Young "Vol-au-*vent*!"?

"Steggles is a churl, Natalie. A man of some notoriety. Have you invited him already?"

"No. I wanted to speak to you first because we're partners. I know they play, that's all."

"Well," I said, putting down my teacup for some gossip. "I know nothing of Mrs Steggles, but her husband's an infamous layabout. Pub-crawler. An altogether uneducated and rather vulgar chap." With language like that, who could possibly suspect I was just such a peasant myself, except teetotal? The teetotaller who despises drunkenness in the way I do, has licence to scorn and condemn to his advantage, so long as he doesn't for a moment sound a prig, of course.

It was when she told me the date she had in mind, Sunday 28th November, for the first of these delightful evenings, that I played my magnificent, magnolia, Arabian ace, to scotch her plans, which were utterly abhorrent to me, and I played it with some finesse, I'm bound to say.

"I am very sorry, Natalie, but I cannot attend that evening."

"How do you know," she teased, "you old pretender, without consulting your five-year, leather-bound, social diary?" She laughed at me again.

"I'm away."

"Oh? Where?"

"A flypast."

"Flypast? Fly past what? What are you talking about? Fly-sticky? Could do with some in the kitchen."

"Battle of Britain."

"*What*? . . . . Good Lord." She frowned in disbelief. "*What*? You were in that?"

"To the hilt."

"Gracious me! One of The Few?"

I nodded.

"How glorious, Antony! My oh my, but you are a dark horse!"

"Well," I said, "that was one life." I don't know where it came from but I felt, once I'd said it, that the line was truly masterful. It certainly had an effect.

"I'd love to hear about that - if you can bear to go through it, of course. One of The Few! Well well well. What a privilege to know you, and to have you in the village. Indeed! Really, I mean it." She opened her eyes wide and shrugged her shoulders, as if dumbfounded. "But look here, can't you come along after the celebrations? It won't take all day, will it? They only buzz about for a few minutes, don't they? Then you can tell us all about it. And that would be absolutely marvellous! A tremendous start to our evening, and to all subsequent – unless there's a dinner or something?"

"I'm afraid there is. But that's only part of the problem."

"Oh?"

"The flypast isn't here, you see."

"Not here?"

"No. It's in the Gulf. Saudi Arabia."

She clapped her hands in delight and laughed again at this, and I saw she was close to tears of pleasure for me. In this there was something very touching, and I at once felt awful for so misleading her in our previous conversations. Here was someone who might be persuaded to give a damn about me, who wanted to involve me in her own pursuit of diversion, happiness, call it what you will, and I was set to wreck any prospect of it by deceiving her and pretending as usual that I was someone I wasn't, as I'd deceived and pretended all my life. After that thought, I couldn't stay long.

"Here," she said, when I was leaving. "Have some eggs, Squadron Leader."

Taken by surprise, I must have looked askance. Typical. She had them ready for me in a polythene bag. I opened the bag and peered in at nine large, very healthy looking brown eggs, lightly dusted with fragments of feather, chicken shit and dirt. Free range, all right.

"Now, don't look a gift horse in the mouth," she reprimanded. "Steggles keeps some hens for me and they've been a bit over-productive." She lapsed into the accents of the lower orders again, Professor Higgins style: "Can't 'ave 'em 'ere coz of rats. 'Ens brings rats." She pointed at the bag. "And don't eat 'em two by two or you'll get egg-bound!"

She chuckled and I was transported, for some reason, just for a second, to that morning on the jetty, in blustery July, twenty years ago, with Alex explaining the Elsan to Rachael, and Rachael laughing in that way, knowing already, understanding everything, something of that youthful shamelessness about bodily functions. A most promising association, yet it brought no joy to me, just a vague unease. To do with being old, I suppose. Why are my feelings always alloyed, adulterated with guilt or fear?

"How kind, Natalie," I said, tying the bag.

She chuckled again as she opened the door for me. Lots of smiles, chuckles, laughter and bonhomie this afternoon.

"Not at all. Least I can do for one of The Few!" She was beginning to close the door while I was still on the coconut. "Won't come out. Too damn cold."

There was something about her closing the door so quickly after me that I didn't like, too close to my own parsimony about keeping the heat in, but I dismissed it and gingerly took her bag of eggs to the car.

"You know, there really ought to be two of you when someone's in the pool."

"No one's in the pool."

"I know. But when - "

"You're in here."

It was Aaron. The one who didn't save my life. Usually he lies on his side in the pose of a 60's centrefold. Usually we don't even exchange 'Goodmorning'. Not all of him was visible in every detail, and of course I made a point of ignoring his nakedness as far as possible, but today he was sitting upright, and because I spoke to him I also looked at him: I noticed that despite his narcissistic workouts, there were the folds of an incipient beer-gut where the six-pack should have been. He sat with hands under hams, slightly hunched. Even in the dim red light his aggression was obvious. His cropped hair bristled with it, and his eyes were hooded and his face heavy and sullen. His scalp shone faintly with beads of sweat that wouldn't run because he'd covered himself from top to toe with aromatic oil. A strong scent of sandalwood, not the sauna's natural pine smell, hung in the burning air. But there was another scent coming off him, more powerful than that: the animal scent of him being on heat, as it were, if he'd been female.

I didn't pursue our conversation, even though I had started it with the clear intent of ruffling him. These days I want the sauna to myself, I have decided. So I was going to put out the veiled threat that I might report him to Our Lady of the Leisure Pool, the new Facility Manager, a short Welsh termagant, with a cockerel comb, who styles herself on some tv toughie - desk sergeant, prison officer, ward sister or similar. A real man-hater, though I can hardly blame her for that, of course. She struts about in a light blue shell suit with a large ring of keys. She'd love to throw the book at Aaron, or her keys, or anything else to hand.

But a thought had taken hold. A thought which, in the new mood brought about by my magnificent invitation to the Middle East, might almost be seen as merciful.

For a moment, fleeting though it surely was, I actually empathised with Aaron. With the frustration of his life. I remembered what it was myself to be so full of heat, yet to have no outlet for those ungovernable urges. The sense of waste you had to live with. I was a rather dapper and attractive fellow myself at his age – much more so than him! – and I remember how senseless it seemed to spend one's days wandering around with all this pent up drive and longing, with this young body to enjoy, and yet never able to put it to any use, even though the unguarded glances from womankind told you plainly enough they felt exactly the same. All those rituals to be gone through first. Wait until you're married, was the answer back then. That's all gone and the young have a much freer time of it but nonetheless, if you simply haven't got a partner – and from their behaviour with doe-eyes at Reception, it is clear that neither Aaron nor Mark has a partner – the sense of waste for both of them, the sense of time passing, of months, or maybe even years, without 'making love', without 'getting your leg over', without 'a fuck', despite all the braggadocio of Aaron being a "virgin-buster", must still be there for these young provincial folk, and that unspoken repression goes on, for these two at least, just as it did in my day. So it was a strange moment of clemency in the sauna this morning. A moment almost of pity for this young man, who preens himself daily for an event which remains just a perpetual and improbable prospect, as likely as picking up a beautiful, bra-less hitch-hiker, and bringing her back here for a swim and a sauna, when he doesn't even earn enough to run a car. Little wonder he hangs his head in here. True, he may meet someone, somehow, and have sex, somewhere next week – but where? In a bus stop? In a shed on the municipal park? – but it is much more likely, stuck out here in the beet fields, still shacked up with his parents, that he will not. And he may not for another – what? – twelve months or more? If some genie appeared, in a puff of broken wind from the virgin's booth, and said to him, with an absolute certainty – "Aaron, listen a minute. You will not have sex this year at all. Not with doe-eyes, nor with anyone else. Not for another twelve months from today, and perhaps, after that, not for a further twelve months." – such news would fall on him like a prison sentence, reduce him to despair. The endless, marathon reaches of masturbation ahead. And at the same time trying to stay in shape, prepared to mate, even while the frumpy, flirtatious mum cooks you her irresistible fry-ups on Mondays and Wednesdays, which must we worked off with more circuits, weights and meaningless, panting, grunting exertion. The irony is that in my own youth, while even younger than him, once the war came, I enjoyed more sex two generations ago! More than he's ever had, I'll be bound, and so much more exotic too. Not in England, of course, for reasons already discussed, but once we were posted abroad our squadron had weeks of idleness en route to Singapore: the brothels of La Linea in Gibraltar, where I bust my duck, as they say, like most of the other young men in my squadron (if they'd had the guts to admit they were virgins); and onward to hedonistic bliss in licentious Khartoum, with hostesses in long clinging dresses on the rooftops of a hundred nightclubs, and best of all the Capitool Restaurant and the Black Cat nightclub in Batavia, Java, which were legendary before I was there in '42, and continued to be so throughout the war. In Java I enjoyed women for the first time without paying for them. Some of them wives and mothers. Marvellous, secretive liaisons and affairs with bored and lazy, plump Dutch wives, whose husbands were away planning how best to evacuate with as much loot as they could before Jap came. Hah! A rather more exotic introduction to women and sex than Aaron's body-building narcissism in liberated, promiscuous, Cool Britannia!

I glanced at him again, about to speak, but did not. His face, with its blunt nose and nondescript eyes, is common, and he makes it more so with his aggressive look, his cropped hair and angry expression, that he supposes is attractive in its hardness and indifference, an understanding he's picked up from hours and hours of endless cop shows and American movies, no doubt. A plain face, as run-of-the-mill as urban England itself, whose owner could well think at times, I imagine, as the sexless months stack up behind him, and birthdays come and go, that he has a face simply *too* common and unappealing to win any mate long term. Womankind could demand of him, he might think, in his weaker moments, why anyone would want to reproduce someone in his likeness. Poor Aaron. And so confidence sinks behind the aggressive facade, leaving him still less attractive, his eyes lacklustre, filled with self-doubt and self-abusive anger, and such circular thoughts wrap around his libido, squeezing out the very will to carry on. And again I feel so lucky to have had the war, that threw me headlong into such a rush of action, heroism, excitement and adventure. In comparison to his life as it is now, sweating away in the sauna twice a week, trying to feign contentment with his frustrated, meaningless, onanistic existence, my youth was idyllic, and his seems contemptible, really quite laughable.

"You know something, Aaron?" I asked him.

He hunched: the recalcitrant movement of a reptile disturbed in the heat it cannot leave. He shut his eyes and said nothing. When he opened them again, very torpidly, he stared directly ahead at the egg-timer.

I carried on.

"This may surprise you," I told him, "but in a very real sense, you're just as old as me."

He grunted.

"You are, though."

At last he spoke. "If I thought that, I'd top myself."

I hadn't thought of it either in this way before, from his point of view, but I suddenly realized how my remark had a horrible, physical reality for him, with my decrepit frame – the curtain wrinkles, greying tufts, foul hollows, unsightly folds - just a few feet away from his lustful heat.

"Well, you might just do that some day. Mark my words."

"I don't want to mark your fucking words, you nasty old bugger. Now fuck off!"

"I meant – "

"I don't want to hear it. Shut it. You're ruining my fucking sauna. *Again*."

"Aaron – "

"*Fuck off!*"

Beneath that last *Fuck off,* which was not loud but came out with such plosive force some beads of saliva escaped him, was a swell of loathing and anger, not to do with what I'd just said or my hateful body, but hatred and anger that is always there for him, bubbling up continuously from his sexual frustration and his discontent with life.

Well, that brought our cosy chat to a close for today. And then, not an hour later, in town, as if to bring into sharper focus all that is worth leaving behind for a while, I had a second altercation when I went to the greengrocer's shop in the high street.

More Events!

Mr Benson bustles about between his trestles, reaching from box to box for fruit & veg with his stubby, tattooed arms, making noisy puffs, snorts and whistles. He's always short of breath because he still smokes – surely a death wish in this day and age. People have to bring their own shopping bags to Benson's, but I never do, and so for me there is only an old-fashioned brown paper bag for my apples, or for the occasional pound of carrots, which I eat raw. Every week in autumn, sometimes twice a week, with well-practised sleight of hand, Benson includes at least two bruised apples in my bag of Cox's Orange Pippins. He has been swindling me like this for twelve years, ever since

Laura died and I started shopping here. But last week he excelled himself. When I got home and put the apples into my fruit bowl on the card table, I found that four of the eight were bruised. Fifty per cent.

"Mr Benson."

He stopped bustling, put out his cigarette and set his short yellow fingers on the middle trestle. My tone put him on the defensive. His pudgy, squashed, boxer's face – Could he be related to Aaron? His father, even? – was wary. Then he burst out –

"Good morrow to you, sir! And how are you today?"

Ever the cheerful, roly-poly grocer, waiting for his lung cancer or pleurisy, as if it were a bus with his number on it, to take him away from this loathsome working life where he must be so nice to everyone all day.

"Mr Benson," I repeated. "The apples that I bought from you last week, the Cox's Orange Pippins – "

"Finished, I'm afraid, sir. I can do you some Golden Delicious if you like. Lovely apple. French. Cheaper too. My wife prefers them to Cox's."

Benson's wife is often mentioned to close a sale, but I've been in here when she's actually passed through the shop: a lean, tart, deeply parochial woman, who wears a transparent plastic raincoat in all weathers and exchanges vicious, whispery gossip with her husband's customers. I can no more see her eating a French apple than noodles or caviar.

"Of the eight apples I bought from you last week, four – four, Mr Benson – were bruised."

Benson raises his eyebrows.

"Are you sure, sir?"

"I have never been more certain of anything in my life."

He was clearly embarrassed and confused by my complaint, and my forthright manner. It wasn't British. Pecking order all wrong. To a British shopkeeper the customer is either beneath him or putting on airs. The British can't serve.

"I can accept one apple might be bruised," I continued. "Maybe even two, if I'm unlucky that day, but last week you selected four out of eight that were bruised."

"No sir!"

He shook his head. He wasn't having it. "If that happened it was definitely an accident. I can assure you of that. *If* it ever happened. I would never have selected a bruised apple for you on purpose, sir. Makes no sense."

Huffing and puffing he turned about and fetched, from under the trestles behind him, a box with bruised and rotten fruit rolling around in the bottom. "The bad ones go in here, see." Well, there were only three or four apples in there, and cookers all. "I would never have done that to a customer, sir. Deliberately sold him four bruised apples. I promise you that. Doesn't make any sense, sir. Bad for business."

But he was red in the face. His discomfort was palpable. For a moment I couldn't help doubting myself. Could I have bruised them on the way home? They were on the passenger seat next to me, still in their brown paper bag. The bag had not fallen on the floor. None had rolled out, come to harm.

"Let me get you some Golden Delicious, sir. On the house. No charge."

He whipped a paper bag from his rusty hook and took up a yellow Golden Delicious. He inspected it closely before placing it in the bag. When the bag was full of these cheap, soft, yellow apologies, he offered them to me with both hands outstretched across his boxes.

"I am very sorry for your trouble, sir."

I took the bag and left without another word.

These two altercations and their contrary endings, the *Fuck off* from Aaron and the abject apology from Benson, had an effect on confidence I was quite unaware of until back home in my study. I sat in the recliner without taking off my Crombie, selected a Golden Delicious from the bag in my lap, took a noisy bite and listened to the interlocking rhythm of my dentures, and the pulse behind my ear, which seemed mildly urgent this Wednesday morning. I had not put on the radio yet. The apple was just as I had thought it would be: far too soft, yellow and sweet.

And then it happened.

Quite slowly, involuntarily, like some kind of seizure.

My left arm slid down, collapsed. The apples spilled from the bag, rolled down my Crombie onto the floor, merrily bouncing, tumbling and bruising each other, as they went. One rolled all the way under the television, out of reach, as if at Benson's behest, only coming to a stop against the dusty cable at the skirting.

I felt perfectly all right.

*What* on earth had happened?

The pulse continued its old, square-bashing tattoo with the same mild urgency as before.

Tee-tum, tee-tum, tee-tum, tee-tum . . .

It seemed that the sudden, ungovernable Anger that had led me to scrape my scrambled egg off the table, making that dreadful steaming mess on the lino, and leaving a trace of garlic in the air for several days, had overcome me once more. Anger, then, was at the root, I rationalised. But there was no anger, or, at least, of nothing like the same intensity. This time there was just that collapse of the left arm, an absolute refusal to support the weight of Benson's Golden Delicious for a moment longer.

What new indignity was this? How would I manage in the toilet?

But physically there didn't seem to be anything the matter. I felt fine. I could clench my fingers, move my arm, lift my arm. No numbness either. All movement operative. Nothing untoward at all.

A minute passed. The pulse behind my right ear gently counted its seconds away.

A bird settled on the windowsill and I winched my neck to look at it. A common starling, but big as a blackbird. Overfed. Life too easy. It hopped about, turned its tail on me to face the unkempt garden, and shat on the windowsill, behaving as if the building were derelict, abandoned, as if there had been a death in the house.

'*What* had happened' was actually very simple: I had hit an air-pocket of the will. The Hurricane had dropped twenty feet or so. That was all, it seemed. But my thoughts ran off in dashes from that conclusion – just when everything was suddenly looking up – the burgeoning relationship with Natalie, and all the possibilities that set in train – the trip to the Middle East, all expenses paid – I might even meet an old airman from my squadron; there was still one left I knew about – just when there was all this expectation ahead, or perhaps because there was suddenly so much of it, too much of it, my will to believe in it all, indeed to believe in any of it, to suspend my disbelief as it were, had plummeted.

The reason I'd broached a conversation with Aaron this morning had been on account of my new-found optimism and confidence. I'd felt able to take him on, try to get rid of him, on his home ground, in the sauna. Now all such optimism and confidence had dissipated into the freezing weather that greyed the bay window, leaving me chilly despite the blow-heater on max, and the Crombie buttoned to the lapel. I winched to the window again. The starling had gone. Out there all was still. That wasn't it, not out there, the only-too-familiar still-life of moribund, English melancholy. Beneath me, then, into the cold and dark, into that pulling, sucking, freezing, North Sea dark beneath my chair. No. Not there either. But why, then? Why this collapse? Surely not just more intimations of mortality, because I am too used to those and inured to the feelings that accompany them. They could not, out of the blue, cause an air-pocket of the will in this way. This was different.

Yellow apples all over the floor. One under the television, stopped by the dusty mains cable.

My hand closed on Benson's brown paper bag, crumpled it slowly, without pressure.

I heard a dusty, crackling song drift down the corridors of thirty years or more. *My Fair Lady.* Marni Nixon dubbing Audrey Hepburn:

> *What a fool I was, what a dominated fool,*
> *To think you were the earth and sky!*
> *What a fool I was, what an addlepated fool,*
> *What a mutton-headed dolt, was I!*

Disillusionment, pure and simple.

I suddenly knew, and with an incontrovertible certainty, that the invitation to the Middle East was fake. It was bogus. A joke. A hoot. An out of season April fool. Of course it was. A laugh. A prank. Which was why Natalie had laughed so much and clapped her hands. But was she in on it, part of it? Such a good joke! Hurrah! My excitement and satisfaction – such recognition, indeed! – came back to me now in wave after wave of embarrassment and folly. What a gull, what a fool, what a dominated, addlepated, applepated, mutton-headed dolt . . . Rushing out to find the rusty micrometer in the greenhouse to measure the card's thickness, not attending for a moment to my own thickness. No no no. No measure for that. I felt as I do when my ignorance is exposed, my lack of education laid bare, or when Laura rifled through my chapters all those years ago – *Some may say* . . .

*Some may say, Antony, you've been had, old boy* . . .

My feeble minded son could not have done this, not on his own, anyway. Oh no. There was too much wit, cunning, artistry, accomplishment involved. Why did it hurt so much to think Rachael was behind it?

There's a Neanderthal impulse in our thoughts and feelings that makes us side with others whether we're aware of it or not, whether such allegiance has any meaning or not. Just as we flinch from insects, yelp at mice, duck from shadows, because once upon a time, if we missed it – that rustle of leaves, that snapped twig – we were bitten, poisoned, killed, eaten. It's always there, this need to be on the same side as another: we can no more avoid it than fish in a shoal. Even so, as Alex has become a kind of adversary, I have put myself on the same side as Rachael, however laughable that is. Sharing her impatience with her husband, with his blathering, with his boringness, his drunkenness, sharing her barely hidden scorn, and silently siding with her against my only son, smiling away in tacit agreement that he has amounted to nothing, that he's a numpty, that she married a fool. There are the complications of her attractiveness too, of course, more instinctual stuff, deepening this misplaced allegiance.

But what a plan.

To winkle me out, fly me three thousand five hundred miles to the Middle East – and then what? What on earth came next? A taxi ride into the The Empty Quarter? Food for snakes and buzzards? No consequences in a lawless land, of course. And the website – that is where Alex would have made himself useful, setting that up. But in fact, she could have done that too, these days. Perfectly capable. And it was much more likely that he had nothing at all to do with any of it – he was the foil, the fool, whose part it was to make the ruse so much more convincing, because his responses to the invitation would be perfectly genuine, as mine had been, while hers would all be am-drammed. I hadn't many answers yet but my certainty about the plan, the betrayal, remained unaffected, and solid, immovable, heavy in the gut. Or heavy as a gun, a pistol to kill kill kill. The motive was clear as day. Ever present, in fact.

*Get him out! Get him out! Get him out!*

Details would come clear in due course, whether I wanted them to or not.

My certainty draws its strength from nothing less than mortal combat, from the cockpit, when the sixth sense, intuition, call it what you will, honed and tempered mission by mission, as the odds stacked up against me, saved me so many times, and I learned to trust it implicitly, this other Neanderthal gene, the one that sends a lizard skittering before the leaf has rustled, that speed of anticipation surpassing conscious thought. This was the quality, much more than acrobatic skill, which distinguished the one-in-three survivors, those who long ago had used up their nine lives and who put their faith in something unknowable, inexplicable. We all understood it, we just never talked about it, because there was nothing to say, and it was never in front of us, only behind us.

And – Alas! – the truth be told, my certainty came from a memory that's only too concrete and commonplace, from civilian life, domestic, married life, from an identical moment when I felt the same dismay and disillusionment, even grief, which left a wound in the psyche that has never quite closed.

I knew I was right then, and was proved to be so, and I know I am right now.

When we were first married, Laura liked to flaunt the idea, both privately and in company, that she had had many other suitors, lovers, conquests. She liked to give the impression I had been the lucky contender in a smoky saloon bar, crowded with laughter and good times. In fact, I knew of just one other man, or just one who was in any way serious. A tall, stringy, pipe-smoking fellow named Francis. He was an insurance assessor, which meant he had a company car, when cars were still quite hard to come by, and his job took him the length and breadth of the country. Laura had known him since childhood. He was the son of friends of the family who were so close they were aunt and uncle to her. It was not as if she had been courted by Francis, as she liked to pretend. From what I could piece together, when their hormones came on, Francis had been the safest person to experiment with, that was all. But she always spoke of him as her 'ex'. She was not a virgin when we married, but whether Francis had deflowered her or not I had no idea at the time, and still don't know, in fact; she saved that mystery, making a show of experience and sophistication to keep me on my toes. "My best friend's my ex," was one of her lines back then. "I can tell him anything because he understands how I grew up."

I met him only a couple of times. Once at our wedding, and again about a year later when he came to stay for a weekend at the rectory, which we'd only recently moved into. Of course, I knew the best way to counter Laura's efforts to excite my jealousy was to feign indifference. She was not going to win sovereignty that way! She'd have to do a bit better than that! So when she told me Francis had been in touch and had asked if he might visit, I said, "Of course. Lovely to see him again." She added, as if to flatter and beguile me, and thus make me more suspicious, that he had an interest in old houses and he'd love to talk to me about the rectory and my plans. I hadn't done much at that time because we'd hardly been in the place six months. Still in our first flush of marital bliss.

One thing they'd always loved to do together, it turned out, was cook. Mud pies as infants, cakes and meringues as children, exotic dishes for their parents from trendy cookbooks as adolescents. This left me very much in the cold, as it was meant to. I could hardly sit in the drawing room (my study wasn't finished then) and wait to be called to supper. I would be laughed at as Lord of the Manor or Idle Lackey, and I'd never live it down. So I had to stick around in the kitchen, clearing things away for them, getting them drinks, finding the pestle and mortar, fetching things down from shelves . . . When supper was nearly ready, Laura sent me off to lay the table in the dining room, and there was a burst of laughter back in the kitchen – worse, it was quickly muffled.

I had detected something effeminate about Francis, a quality wrapped up in dainty superiority. In honour of his cooking, I insisted he took the head of the table, and the way he responded was too playfully grand. I'd come across my share of young men of uncertain sexuality in the R.A.F. - public schoolboys who hadn't worked out yet whether they were queer or not. As a trainee pilot officer, I'd had more experience of being courted by men than of courting women, and I was pretty certain of my ground here. Hah! So much for Laura's 'ex' lover, I thought complacently. X summed it up better! His hair was too long and well groomed, and unusually for that time, he used no lacquer or spray to hold it in place; it flopped about in a boyish bundle when he laughed at his own jokes. He also had a habit, as his laughter petered out, of rounding off with some verbal coda - "Delightful, quite delightful", "Splendid, quite splendid", "Brilliant, quite brilliant". Such mannerisms felt terribly second-hand and affected. Poor Francis: this was the late nineteen-fifties, in my lifetime the golden age of social-climbing, but homosexuality would still be illegal for nearly a decade. I couldn't help feeling, as well, that there was some relish, some vindictive spite against my red-blooded heterosexuality, in his enjoyment of my wife's attentions right in front of me, under my very nose. Such gay flamboyance ran into the sand, though, when I looked directly into his eyes, which were small and brown and bedded in dried out, low tide, sallow skin, bruised from insomnia. Nothing boyish there. They were sleepless, cynical, very adult eyes.

"I do love this wine," he announced, carefully pouring us each a glass in the manner of a connoisseur, while Laura served the soup. "But not too sure it travels well."

He had given us two bottles of Sancerre, one of which we were to keep for ourselves. We were very privileged because they were the last of a case he'd brought back from France, after three weeks grape picking, his summer holiday since he was a teenager. Throughout soup and main course we were regaled with stories about the various châteaux he'd visited or revisited in the Loire valley, and how good the whole trip had been for his – I almost offered his next cliché aloud – "schoolboy French".

It was all too much for me, too boring and pretentious, and my token interest brought me under sly attack. We were off north now for some cathedrals, because Francis was a deep Catholic, of course, and he cut me out completely and talked to Laura all the time, and she was lapping it up. Smiling and nodding in all the right places and thoroughly enjoying all this cultured and civilised talk. They'd knocked back a couple of gin and tonics in the kitchen and Laura looked quite flushed. Actually, it became her. She seemed to lose her defensiveness and smiled quite openly to me once or twice between forkfuls. The evening light was also kind: just some stray beams of sunset through the long sash windows, broken up by the wisteria. A soft autumn evening, deep in the English countryside, and, oh dear, the reunited lovers had had too much to drink! Breaking off from the Chartres tour to make a passing remark about the food, Francis slipped in a frisson of innuendo. Something to do with the stuffing they'd made together. I've said how I abhor flirting and drinking, and here they were enjoying both, at my own table, under my own roof.

With the main plates cleared away, we moved on to matters of the numinous, a topic that had to be shared, leaning forward, almost intimately, with Laura alone.

"Do you not find it strange, though, that even in this godless age, all the truly sensitive and intelligent people one meets tend to be of the faith?"

Oh no no no. That was too much by a very long chalk. He knew we'd married in a registry office, at my insistence. I felt quite entitled to stick my oar in now.

"Well," I said, "don't you really mean just educated people? Knowledgeable people? Bourgeois people?"

Laura looked aghast. She sat with her droopy lower lip hanging open.

"Antony," she began, "you must learn – "

"I would go further," I said, cutting her off. "I can well believe that those you are talking about, within your bourgeois circle, are men and women 'of the faith', as you put it, simply because it suits them to be so. Old habits die hard, and all that, with the ancien régime. I defended the country, risked my life, for that lot, just so they could hang on to what they've got, it turns out. One wonders why, sometimes."

Francis's lips were peeled back in a stiff smile. He took another sip of wine and fetched his pipe and pouch from somewhere about him. He put his long, worn leather pouch on the tablecloth. It was decorated with pretty Moroccan beads; it didn't seem quite gentlemanly to lay this slack leather pouch on our white tablecloth; it was too much a part of his long, slack body.

He set about filling his pipe.

Sobered by my attack, Laura turned on me now: "Oh, so it's Quasimodo at the dinner table, is it? We can see the chip on your shoulder quite plainly enough, Antony, without your drawing attention to it!" The drink had thoroughly loosened her tongue. "Most unsightly and unseemly! Francis is *our* guest and *my* intimate friend. You know nothing of *his* friends. *Our* friends. You've never even met any of them, except me. And as it happens, I agree with what he was saying about intelligent and sensitive people.

Only an ignoramus wouldn't!"

"Oh really," I said, and sighed.

"Yes, really."

"No no," Francis dismissed her proffered help with an airy wave and tried to box the triangle. He lit up his pipe, covering the bowl with his Swan Vestas to draw the flame. "Antony is right. I've plainly had too much to drink." He smiled again at me, but more wanly, and any boyish airs sank in his smile, and in his lived-in, dried up eyes, where the tide had ebbed completely now. "Let's take this up in the morning, Antony, when I'm sober and we're on more equal ground." He spoke in a friendly way, with the clear intent that we shouldn't quarrel again at all, any of us. Then he ended the business quite graciously, taking his pipe out of his mouth to say to me –

"If you don't mind, I'm going to carry on drinking and talking nonsense. That all right by you?"

I shrugged. "You're our guest."

I left them to it.

He could only have been around thirty then, I suppose, seven years or so younger than me, same as Laura.

When she came to bed she said nothing further about it and turned to face the wall. She told me she'd had too much to drink and that I was never to let her get into such a state again.

But in the morning I found myself the stern parent to two mischievous children: my attack at dinner had drawn them closer together. Those Neanderthal allegiances again, but rather more to it here. I'd been out early to get some milk and eggs in the village for breakfast, then gone for a walk around the three acres. Still a novelty then, as we hadn't been once through the seasons. When I came in they were enjoying breakfast of toast, eggs and coffee, and were bemoaning their hangovers, which didn't look at all serious to me. Not a word of appreciation for the victuals I'd provided, of course. That was ever Laura's way when she was young: too proud to thank you for anything, and if you pointed it out she'd say she was *awfully* sorry, with a scornful toss of her head, pushing back her chair to go somewhere, she'd no *idea* it was *so* important. Anyway, there they were, either side of the refectory table, Francis facing the window. They were amusing each other now with long-winded accounts of their parents' bridge evenings and cocktail parties, the abandoned mess she and Francis sneaked down to feast on early in the morning: ashets of cucumber sandwiches, water biscuits thick with patum peperium, and all around the feast, those mysterious cut crystal glasses of different shapes and sizes, on which they could play different notes with wetted fingertips, and the empty bottles and soda syphons bestrewn everywhere, the entire upper middle-class milieu in disarray.

I was doing some left over washing up at the sink when Laura said:

"We'll go to Norwich, Francis! This morning! I can show you the cathedral!"

Amid such a spray of exclamations it was impossible to doubt her excitement. I stared into the dirty dish water. When she said, "We'll", she plainly had not included me.

"We can get some things for supper at the Sunday market. And some more wine, of course!"

They laughed about the idea of more wine, and I wondered if they needed me there in order to find this so amusing; such mischievous, flirtatious children.

Francis began, "I'm not sure if Antony - "

"Oh, never mind *him*!" Laura struck out boldly, with more gay laughter. "Can you imagine Antony gazing up at cathedral windows? He's stiff-necked enough as it is! He'd be bored to death. Wouldn't you Antony? Be honest!"

"I will if you will, Laura," I returned, drying my hands on a dish-towel, and I added, before that could lead to anything, "but you two go to town and enjoy yourselves. I've plenty to do here. I have the car if I need anything."

"It's settled!" she declared, staring across the table at Francis, who was sitting with a full cup of coffee raised in both hands, smiling back at her. There was an openness in her face, in her blue eyes, an excitement and delight at the prospect of this Sunday adventure, that had nothing to do with Norwich cathedral. It was something I'd seen before, of course, coming in my direction, at the very start of our life together, but I had not seen it for a while. In just six months I had become the supplicant, full of desire but undesired. A woman's appetite needs to be re-set by other men: that's all there is to it. Such worldly wisdom was embedded in me by those kind, plump, Dutch wives and mothers in Java, before I'd even come of age. As far as that part of human nature goes, you could not conceive of a more hopeless arrangement than yoking male and female together in monogamy. And for the rest? Well, I never found sacrifice and devotion to anyone, or anything, above suspicion.

It was a good job Francis and I did not exchange a glance at that moment – I was still behind him – for if our eyes had met, neither could have hidden that he knew she had gone too far.

They were away in his elderly Humber by half-past ten, in time to catch the market.

It must have been about twelve. High noon.

I was in the drawing room sitting at her father's desk. Some of my first pages were scattered around. I was taking advantage of the quiet and solitude to get something done. In that room the hours were soundless, except for a branch of wisteria scraping a window pane somewhere. The plate glass Georgian sashes killed dead all birdsong and the like, but no matter where you cut the wisteria or tied it back a branch freed itself and scratched at the glass. Nature fidgeting, biding its time.

Ahead, the Sunday morning garden. The grass was cut. Actually, I'd cut it for Francis's arrival, at her suggestion. I'd done the chore willingly enough, to show off the lawn. I'd turned over the rose beds quite recently too, but the roses themselves, that first year, the Harry Wheatcofts, were scanty: the pale yellow ones were wind-blown and de-petalled, but a few pink ones were still in bloom. I was in a state of near mental equilibrium, quietude, a rare moment of guiltless self-absorption, which must have been the preparation needed to admit what I had staved off since Francis had driven away an hour and a half ago, with my wife deep in his red leather passenger seat. Staring at the long, rectangular rose beds, with their dark borders, hearing nothing but the wisteria scraping the glass, seeing nothing but a few blackbirds or starlings stabbing the soil – Ah, the unforgettable details of that scene! – I knew for certain, as if it had been given me in a vision, that they were in a hotel at that very moment.

I knew the hotel too. The Castle Hotel.

The complacent delusion I'd enjoyed the previous night, that Francis was playing at the flirtationship to spite me, came back, opening a few limp capillaries to bring the weakest, most uncomfortable blush to my cheek, sitting alone at her father's desk, amid my hopeless early pages. As if he gave a damn about continuing our quarrel! But what a twisted triumph there was in this *for her*. It was exactly what she wanted. Feeling, as she did, I knew, to be too plain to have made a match on any other terms than marrying socially beneath her, it was her delight to flirt and prove the contrary to herself, that she was irresistibly desirable to other men, that she could have an affair at the drop of a hat, within a year of marriage, before I'd even entertained the idea, being so absorbed in my doubts and debts, plans and walks. And to fool me, gull me in this way – what delight!

I sat back in my chair. Her chair. Everything was hers. This antique captain's chair on its iron swivel, a valuable heirloom given by a fond uncle as a wedding gift, because she'd loved spinning on it as a child. Hers. Hers hers hers! I felt quite faint. The chair rocked, but then offered its support, because in all its creaky, heirloomed joints it knew, as the whole house and all her furniture knew, and the wisteria scraping the sash windows and the scant roses nodding in their creosoted beds all knew, that throughout the rectory and its three acres the taint of disillusionment had spread completely. All my plans and schemes, the redecorating of every room, the re-ordering of the entire three acres to fulfil our great English dream, everything was tainted and undone. The certainty of my new understanding was of such calamitous weight I could not get up from her chair. And I felt terribly old, suddenly, though I'd only turned thirty-seven that winter, and still had eleven years to serve out my commission to queen and country, and countless more to serve on this marvellous rural heap, with its uneven ceilings, fissured walls, its cupboards, rose beds and fruit trees. But in a sense she had suddenly made me old, of a different generation, old and foolish, left behind, the excluded cuckold. While I sat puzzling over my useless, worthless early pages, they rolled around on their hotel bed getting on with life, enjoying themselves. Well, I'd told them to enjoy themselves, hadn't I? I could not bring myself to imagine it properly. The hotel door and its innocent number, closed and locked. Do Not Disturb. Testing the bed. Laughing. Drawing the blinds. Undressing each other.

No. I went no further. The very threat of those images added more weight to my certainty.

It was me she'd taken to the market.

Today's collapse, forty-one years on, was brought about by the same degree of certainty, with the apples slipping out their paper bag and rolling on the floor and under the television; that same weight made it impossible to move out of the recliner, which, on account of some minor shift I must have made unconsciously, opened up on its spring mechanism and laid me out flat in a tragi-comic way.

But whereas, forty-one years ago, the betrayal made me feel like an old man, today I am an old man, who has to bear the weight in the same way I did then, but on this ancient and ridiculous frame.

The confluence of these two great moments, that's what triggered the spring mechanism. I could not help recognizing the exact same feeling and sensing all I'd lost in the interim, that was spoiled, the waste thereof, the regret that I hadn't cut loose when I still had the chance, before we'd had a child. More of her timely planning and outwitting there, no doubt. Even now, trying to set it down, that sense of waste so overwhelms me I'm better off dealing with the actual past, the Francis business, which wasn't over by any means.

When they returned in the late afternoon he didn't come in with her. I'd set the drawing room door ajar so I could hear their arrival. There was something tentative about the porch door opening, and then the surprising silence, no voices. I heard the stealthy closing of the kitchen door. She was alone. She put the kettle on. He must have packed and put his bag in the car before they'd left for Norwich. Then she called out, all innocence, "Tea, Antony?"

So I called back, all innocence, "In a minute!"

I had been sitting in an armchair in the drawing room staring out at the dusk. I'd hardly moved since noon except to take the car out the garage. I had parked it very carefully, where it could be seen from the kitchen window from any angle. Preparation of my own ground. Now I got up and put my pages away (of course I had not looked at them again) and went through to the kitchen.

"Oh! Where's Francis?"

"Had to get on his way," she said, rinsing the teapot, keeping herself busy, avoiding my eye.

"But how rude. Not to come in and say goodbye."

"Oh don't carry on, Antony," she said, scowling into the teapot. "I don't want to come back to your bad temper. I told Francis you'd be all right about it. He was in such a desperate rush by the time we got back, and he has a long drive down to Colchester. Dropping me off was quite a detour. He has to get all the way back to the A12."

"Even so, not to – "

"I thought of calling you to come and pick me up, you know. Please don't make a fuss." She spoke wearily now, but mildly, as if she was prepared to forgive my bad temper. Forgive!

The kettle boiled. She filled the pot, brought it to the table. "I said you'd understand."

"But having enjoyed my hospitality – "

"Our hospitality."

"Well," I said. "It's most odd. Strange manners, I'd say."

She sat and poured the milk, the tea, right way round, perfectly judged, as always.

I sat also. I was already losing ground and very aware of it.

"Nothing from the market?" I said, glancing about.

There was no sign of any shopping, as I knew there wouldn't be.

"Oh, we were too late for all that. The best stuff had gone ages before. Opens at eight. I didn't know, didn't think."

"I see."

From across the table I could smell his pipe tobacco. It was a mellow, oaky, wine-corky smell, quite pleasant, not at all stale or pungent. To me it was the scent of luxurious hotel restaurants. But no, it would be room service, of course.

"And the cathedral?"

"My word," she said, lifting her cup between her fingers, crooking a little finger in mock gentility. "Such an inquisition. What do you care about the cathedral?"

"Well, you said you were going to look at it. It's perfectly reasonable that I should ask."

"What's worrying you? Why all this bad temper?" She narrowed her eyes.

"Nothing," I replied, as blithely as I could. "You said you were going to the cathedral. Naturally I ask about it. If you don't want to talk about it – fine. I've no particular interest in cathedrals, as you quite rightly observed."

*Observed*? I was far more nervous than I thought.

"No no." She shook her head, took the lead again. "There's more to this. To these questions and bad temper. I do believe there's a bit of paranoia, Antony. I do believe you're *jealous*!"

She laughed in my face.

She'd seized the upper hand. It was Francis's departure: I had not foreseen that and it had set me on the back foot. Hands, feet. Feet, hands. Nothing she said convinced me in the least. On the contrary, her performance was exactly as I would have anticipated. Particularly that scornful laugh in my face, judged and timed perfectly, as second-nature to her as pouring milk in the tea cup. If I wasn't careful, she would start enjoying the whole pretence, delighting in her own sleight of hand, not to mention my humiliation. This is what makes women such wonderful liars. Lying makes them feel so powerful, rendering our brute strength useless.

I told her. Came straight out with it. Tried to match her brazenness but in a different way.

"Look," I said, but I spoke down to the table. "I know what happened, Laura."

"What?" she asked.

I looked up. Her tea cup was still raised in both hands, but her brow was now furrowed in concern.

"What happened, Antony?"

"I know, you see."

"But what do you know, you silly gentleman?"

"Everything. I know, since I have to say it, that you cheated on me today."

Her frown deepened, she drew her head back on her neck in a most unbecoming way, a gesture of someone twice her age, and stared at me eyes wide.

"*What*? Antony! Whatever are you saying? Francis is my oldest friend!" As if that made any difference. "He would be horrified to hear you talk this way. He'd never believe it. Horrified." She narrowed her eyes again at me, in pure incredulity. "Really, Antony. If you're going to go mad every time I go out shopping with another man – Well, you've got some growing up to do, is all I can say. It's insufferable. So adolescent."

The next words were quite spontaneous.

"That is one of the shittiest things you can ever do, you know," I told her. "Try to convince someone he's mad when he's found you out, when he knows your secret. Come on. Be honest."

"*Shittiest*? Listen to you! What kind of peasant language is that? *What* secret? What *secret*? Try not to be a bigger fool than God made you, Antony, for goodness' sake. Really. You're out of control."

I knew I was pretty ashen now. She got up and took her tea to the sink.

"I'm really quite insulted," she murmured, with her back to me. She was escaping and I could not let that happen. I thrust my chair back, went to her and span her round. Brute strength not quite so useless, after all. She shrieked of course but I didn't care. We were safe in our own deaf three acres. I had her bent back over the sink and my hand was round her throat. She looked frightened, which was what I wanted.

"I *know* you cheated on me, Laura. I know. Do you understand?" I nodded to the window.

I saw her glance at the car, well in view. "Do you understand now? I only got back half an hour ago."

Her eyes met mine but not in smug control as before.

"You see, now?" I said again but as evenly, as dispassionately as I could.

I let her go and she straightened her clothes, looking down all the while, gathering her composure, finding her way out.

"It's you that have disgraced yourself today," she said. She looked me in the eye and stood straighter, firmer. "Now, I want you to get out of my way and stop being such a stupid brute. Have some maturity, some sophistication."

"I'm not moving until you admit what you have done."

"Oh, you sound so pompous, Antony. Out of my *way*!"

"No."

"What does it matter, now? Hmmn? So you traipsed behind us, hiding away like some dirty little schoolboy. Well done. Bully for you. You got what you deserved."

"At least you admit it, then."

I stepped aside. She made a gesture with her arm as if she were pushing me out the way as she passed.

But before she got to the door I told her that, actually, I had not followed her.

She stopped, arrested. I had fooled her and she didn't like that one bit. She turned.

"But it was not a hunch," I added. "I knew what you would do. It was all obvious to me. And obvious how you would lie about it too. All of it. Obvious."

"Bully for you," she said again, stuck for a better riposte. "The truth is, Antony, since you seem to be so keen on home truths this afternoon – " she opened the door and left it open, stepped back into the kitchen. There was no door spring back then. "The truth is, since you want to hear it – Francis kept going for nearly an hour. A whole *hour*."

I had no reply to that.

"You've surely had your share of me," she added. "Had your chance." She held up an empty hand and smiled a crooked, shaky smile. "Three times with him in an hour. But not once with you – Not once! – in six months!" She shook her head. "Am I not entitled to some pleasure and excitement, now and then, as a married woman?" She lingered on her last words, so that her heavy underlip stayed pouted after them, ushering them out, as it were.

She was gone. I heard her on the stairs. The door stayed wide.

The way that I remember that afternoon, every minute of it, in its every particular, with all its stratagems, its revelations, laid down as it has been for forty-one years in the folds of memory, yet forever fresh and new as if it only happened yesterday, is proof enough she won.

But only that hot little skirmish. Not the long, cold, campaign.

Within a few days he was fool enough to write to her. It arrived, the billet-doux, in a buff envelope with typed address, like a sales circular. Anonymous enough, he must have thought – but not to me. I'd been expecting it. The telephone was out of bounds because I always scrutinized the bills before paying. And inside that innocent buff envelope . . . Hah! What passions! There were hints at a regular rendezvous. My wife was to become his bit of nookie in the sticks.

I lay in wait for the second letter. It took a full fortnight or so, but sure enough it arrived one heavenly Tuesday morning. I let her open it herself, at breakfast.

The colour left her face.

"Oh God," she muttered. "Antony . . ."

There was a pause. She couldn't look up. She half-crumpled the letter, upside down, on the table.

"You must have . . . *opened my mail!* . . ."

Oh, the aggrieved tones! The mortification! How unforgivable! How reprehensible! The end of the world!

"How *could* you?"

I sipped my tea before replying. "Oh," I said lightly, as if just cottoning on. "Is it him again?" I got up and rummaged half-heartedly through a heap of bills and papers on the dresser. "Now . . . where on earth did I put the other one? . . . "

"Just give it to me, Antony!"

I stopped, turned, looked back at her, palms out, empty handed. There was still no colour in her face. She closed her eyes when she spoke again – her sister's trick.

"It's unforgivable."

"What is?"

She snapped. "*Just give it to me!*"

Her heavy lower lip was trembling.

I held out my empty hands again and smiled.

"Can't find it, dear."

She abandoned breakfast.

"I'm late," she said, gathering up her letter, her handbag, regaining control.

She stepped up to me at the dresser, full of defiance. "When I get back from work this evening, I want that letter on the table. Here. Or I will never speak to you again. Is that clear?"

Well, I could only laugh at that.

Long afterwards, when the mood took her, she still searched for it. She knew well enough that part of divorce law. There would be a sudden spring clean of the filing cabinet, of all the outdated warranties, ancient bills and pay slips I let accumulate in there.

"How can we ever find anything in this lot? Really, Antony!"

Even in her late forties, I remember a summer holiday when she attacked the box room, cleared it out from top to bottom, on the pretext of throwing out old junk for charity – one of Alex's schemes. I met her at the bottom of the stairs, taking off her marigolds, hot, angry, exhausted, but covering it up with a wan smile and a look of righteous pride.

"Can you bring the boxes down, dear? Too heavy for me."

"Sure. I'll do it after lunch."

I never bothered. I let Alex bring them down and put them in his car himself.

I showed them the rolled gold invitation shortly after their arrival, watching them closely, ignoring little Joe completely. I'd called Alex and asked them over this Sunday because I had something special to show them that wouldn't keep a fortnight. Some good news. All very odd, most out of character, very secretive – as he remarked – but I wouldn't say more on the phone. When they arrived, self-control was easy because I'd unwittingly dress-rehearsed the scene on Monday, in spilling the beans so stupidly to Natalie.

Needless to say, that particular conversation had become hotly embarrassing to me. All week my smug voice had echoed around the rectory. The way I'd led her on, my finesse, as I called it, when I steered the conversation to my climactic line, but the point is, on account of that spillage on Monday, that excess, I was supremely vigilant now, and in control, with Rachael and Alex six days later. I prepared tea and biscuits for them on arrival, as usual. Following up my hints on the phone, I repeated that I had something "rather special" to disclose to them, but that it was in the study. That caused an amused, and, to me, intriguing exchange of glances in its own right. After tea and biscuits I led all three of them through no-man's-land to the study. Joe trailed some steps behind with a new road-scraping machine he was testing on the hallway carpet. In the study, I led Rachael and Alex to the card table and remained standing with them, very attentive, as I opened the magnolia envelope, removed the gilded invitation, and put it on the baize before them. Rachael reached for it, then stopped herself, looking up at me.

"May I?"

Oh, you're good, I thought. And he's no match for you, just as I was no match for Laura.

"Be my guest."

I held my speckled hands together before my face as if in prayer while I examined her response, at closer quarters than in the kitchen, watching for any unguarded glance, attentive to that moment when the am-dram skills would betray her.

She was frowning as she read through the embossed script. Alex read over her shoulder, stage left.

"But that's perfectly wonderful!" she declared. "How marvellous for you! Of course you'll go? You must go."

I answered her with a controlled and genuine nod, the pipes and wires holding firm.

"Yes. I plan to."

Alex now took the card and read it for himself, on his own slower terms.

"Fantastic news, Dad." He handed the card back to me. "Congratulations. A bit of recognition and all that. Good on the bloody Arabs, what?" he added, in a mock fighter-pilot, jingoistic way. Then, "Who'd have thought?"

I looked down from them to slip the card back in its envelope, and to give them an opportunity to exchange a surreptitious glance, which I could still see, but they did not. No one taking any risks, not at this stage.

"You seem remarkably calm about it," Rachael said, almost with suspicion. "Have you known about it some time? Has there been any other communication?"

"Has anyone called you? Been to see you?" Alex followed up. "You went to one a few years ago, didn't you? Biggin Hill, wasn't it?"

They both seemed so natural that as I stared from one to the other, eyeball to eyeball, I had to blink and pause to keep my own guard, to stop my own incredulity surfacing.

Joe was now holding the door ajar, still on all fours with his road scraping machine, letting the damp cold air in with him, and my dry, expensive, blow-heater warmth out.

"The recognition, Dad," Alex repeated. "That's what really counts, isn't it?"

"Yes." I nodded. "Indeed. But to answer your question – " I glanced at both quickly again – "there was a letter with the invitation, from the base. It goes through all the protocol. And there are further details on a website, which I've explored thoroughly, of course."

Rachael asked: "I presume they'll buy your ticket? I mean, it's all expenses paid, isn't it?"

"Oh yes!" I confirmed. "British Airways. First class. It goes through all that in the letter. We'll go as a group and there'll be someone looking after us. Only a small group now because some won't be fit enough for the journey, of course. Too infirm or doddery, one assumes. Unlike yours truly."

Alex folded his arms and laughed. "First class, eh! Petrodollars!"

I feared for a moment this would lead to one of his boring reflections about something he 'still thought' or 'would always believe' about Arabs, petrodollars, and the Middle East in general, and he seemed to have aroused the same fear in Rachael.

"Well, you must go, Antony," she said, before he got started. "A simply marvellous opportunity. It'll be too hot but you'll deal with that. You'll have to buy some new clothes. Do they cover that too?"

I replied politely to her: "They do, actually. Every effort has been made, as far as I can see, to secure my attendance." I looked from one to the other again, on saying that. "There's a generous clothes allowance in the expenses. One can't quite think of any outfitter in Norwich who'd stock the right thing, but anyway . . ."

"Oh come on, Dad," Alex admonished. "You don't have to go all thobe and ghutra, a la Lawrence of Arabia! Just buy a linen jacket and trousers. The colonial look. Panama hat. You'll love it." He laughed again good-humouredly, without the knowing smugness this time.

"It will all be air-conditioned," Rachael continued. "You'll sit behind some magnificent glass structure in air-conditioned bliss, watching the parades go by." She smiled at me in a kind and open way. Joe was beginning to whine about biscuits. We needed to go back to the kitchen.

"I remember the heat from the kibbutz," she said, folding her own arms too now. I noted these defensive postures, controlled postures, from both of them. "I loved it. Heat that gets right to your bones."

"I remember that too," I said. "Your time at the kibbutz. You came back with a wonderful tan. Very deep. So deep it looked permanent." I was looking at her, then I glanced at Alex, who was staring dreamily at the drizzle beyond the bay window, remembering the kibbutz, his youth, perhaps, or, more likely, composing whatever boring nonsense he had to say about petrodollars. "Both of you. I'll never forget how healthy you both looked when you came back. And happy."

"Well," Alex sighed, still staring at the drizzling Sunday beyond the glass, "you be careful. A tanned skin is a damaged skin, they say these days. Take plenty of cream. Hats on outside at all times, and all that."

It is so much more important to understand people's intentions than their feelings. I had no doubt that if I made the right enquiries I would eventually find there were indeed going to be, or had already been, some commemorations of the Battle of Britain at British Aerospace in Dammam, Jeddah, Riyadh, all over Saudi Arabia, perhaps, all over the Middle East for that matter, fireworks everywhere. They might even be using some refitted Hurricanes that flew in Egypt or Haifa, for all I knew. Or cared. Nothing of a practical nature like that is impossible, given the means, and there were plenty of those, no doubt about that.

The intentions really began to surface weeks ago, with The Grosvenor, with dear old Mr & Mrs Simmonds in their Datsun Cherry, D reg., and I should not have let that pass so lightly, because letting it go had given them confidence. Confidence I was slipping. To remember that they had looked around The Grosvenor, strolled by its willowy trees, escorted by Simmonds, talking things over. How very fortunate Simmonds' opportunism outsped his discretion. *"We'll take care of everything . . . Wonderful place you have here . . . Take the guts out of a million . . ."*

"You'll need your passport renewed, of course," Alex said, as we left the warmth of the study for no-man's-land again.

"Of course."

"Did they say anything about visas?"

"Yes," I told him. "They did, actually, now you mention it."

At the kitchen door I stopped, held the door against its spring, and waited for them to pass, and waited for Alex to follow up his question, maybe give away some of what he already knew – if, that is, he really was in on this, which, from his performance so far, was open to question. I very much hoped he wasn't. Joe slipped through at my baggy tracksuit ankles, pushing his new toy.

"But I only need a visitor's visa," I continued, when Alex had said nothing more. "Which is evidently not so difficult. Lasts thirty days. The forms are all on the website."

"I'll help with that," Alex volunteered. "And the passport. Passport Office is in Peterborough. Couldn't be simpler."

"That would be very kind," I replied civilly. "Thank you, Alex. I'll print out the forms before you leave. I have some photos somewhere from my driving licence renewal.

Remind me."

When we'd settled back around the refectory table with fresh tea and biscuits, I left it to them to pursue the subject, if they wanted to, while I watched.

"Will you extend the stay, then?" Rachael asked. "Explore a bit? If you have thirty days."

"Good question," I said. "I don't know." I poured her more tea, and refilled Alex's cup too. On my very best behaviour today. "Do you think I should stay longer?"

She drank and swallowed, stalling, before going on.

"There are some special things to see out there, if you can get close to them. I always wanted to see Medina. It's meant to be better than Petra. Better preserved. More elaborate."

"I know nothing about it, I'm afraid."

"City hewn out of rock," Alex informed me. The walking encyclopaedia. "Pre-Christian. Fascinating, by all accounts. Perfectly preserved by the desert."

"Why did you never go?"

"Come on, Dad!" He laughed at me. "We were in a kibbutz! If you've got an Israeli stamp in your passport you can never enter places like Saudi! Probably shoot you on sight!"

"Oh," I said. It suited me today to play the innocent abroad. "Is this going to be dangerous, then?"

"No no," Rachael was only too quick to reassure. "Not for you. Of course not. You'll be chaperoned by British Aerospace and Sheikh whatshisname."

I nodded, smiled and knitted my hands.

"I must say," said Rachael. "The prospect of this trip seems to have raised your spirits a bit. I can't remember seeing you so calm and content."

"Well, it has," I admitted, and I smiled at her. "It's

good to have something to look forward to. Plans. Dreams. Important, you know, even at my age."

Alex began again, in his lofty way, "Well, the Battle of Britain is something we damn well should commemorate."

"Now," Rachael reproved, "don't get sententious, Alex." A chink in the armour here, because this was not the way she normally carried on at all. My change in mood seemed to have demanded something different from her, opening up fissures.

"Sententious?" Alex repeated, frowning, arms folded again.

Rachael bent down to Joe to hand him a biscuit, using him as a distraction because she'd taken a wrong turn. Alex seemed the more in control, if it was control.

"What were the instructions about the visa?" he asked me.

I knew them well but frowned and hesitated as if trying to remember, just to see if he could come out with any himself.

"Saudi embassy?" he prompted.

"Yes," I said. "I think that was it. And the passport has to be sent by courier, it said. Or recorded delivery."

Alex nodded, took another biscuit.

Rachael came back in now, trying to repair her earlier slip. "Alex is good at all that bureaucratic stuff," she said. "He'll help you with the officialdom."

Yes, I thought. He'll make sure it's all done properly. He'll see it all works. Just for you. And you'll be nice to him to see he does it right, of course. That's the way, isn't it?

Alex grunted, shrugged off her compliment. "So much of the job is paperwork . . ."

He moved on then to talk about house matters. When had we last checked the internal gutter on the roof?

He meant, of course, when had *he* last checked it, because he won't let me go up there any more. The autumn leaves would need clearing out. This switch of subject signalled he'd moved on, that the visa business would be taken care of, and it didn't interest him much anyway. But he'd not mentioned the website, where he loved to wield expertise and give advice. To resist poking about at it was very much amiss.

He said he'd go up to the roof and sort out the gutter before they started preparing lunch.

The rectory has what is called a butterfly roof: the centre is indented to the same height as the upper ceilings and is a traversable space, each end blocked by the chimney stacks. This creates a sizeable area – some 40' by 4' – covered in lead flashing that runs up the valley gutters to the magnificent apexes. When I painted the place, I made a sling that looped the chimney stacks so that I could work my way round them, and I took my time up there and enjoyed myself. To the front of the house you can see for a mile or so down to the ford and along the shallow valley. It's the same view as from our bedroom, but from a storey higher and in the open air, which makes it completely different – open cockpit, as it were. Behind is the drive and the fir trees, the crows. From my sling, I looked down on it all with the ravening eye of ownership. In those days the stones to keep the church traffic off the verge were freshly Snowcemmed every spring. They guarded a long reach of lawn down to the stream that I mowed in Wimbledon stripes each week with my sit-on mower. A rarity in those days, such a mower. I sold it for a song a couple of years ago to pay an electricity bill. All that grass is now paddock again. The Anglian Water Authority wrote to me last year, ordering me to carry out some clearing work in the stream to prevent winter flooding.

I gave it to Alex and did nothing. Neither did he, I'm quite sure.

Until you've been to the roof and climbed the broad valley gutters that lead to the apexes, or you've painted the chimney stacks all the way round as I did, it's impossible to appreciate the full beauty of the location. I should have dragged Mr & Mrs Simmonds up there to catch a glimpse of what they shall never have.

I've left the roof to Alex because you have to ascend a tiny passage up to a doll's-house door to gain access; the journey makes me stoop and twist more that I should. Too much to ask of a seventy-eight year old frame, whatever its condition. Besides, Alex has forbidden me to go up there in case I get stuck on the roof. I'd be food for the crows, he says. Though he laughs when he says that, and always makes the same joke about Hitchock's 'The Birds', it's something I do fully imagine, something I've even dreamt about, even woken up from. I've seen it, somewhere, on some wildlife programme, I'm sure. A staggering animal, a bear or gorilla or something, old and sick, with birds tormenting it, landing on its head and plucking at its eyes to render it helpless, bring it down. We're just the same, of course, or we were, with our medieval coffin cages suspended in the street, where the victim stood with his arms pinned to his sides so he couldn't defend himself. They set the bars just wide enough for the crows, jackdaws, hawks, rats and whathaveyou to come and feed as they pleased. The highwayman John Whitfield was hung out to die that way – and that was late eighteenth century, just a couple of hundred years ago. I read about him searching up a crossword clue. After a few days someone took mercy on him and shot him with a musket.

The problem with a butterfly roof is that it requires an internal gutter to take the water away. Years ago I replaced the lead drain cover, one hundred and fifty years old but fairly useless, with a roll of chicken wire. This has to be cleaned out periodically, because if it becomes clogged with leaves and lichen the level rises on the flashing and water seeps into the loft space. That's actually only happened once, during the legendary winter of 1963, but since then we've been very vigilant.

In his adolescence Alex took up smoking. He came back from his summer Broads trip with a packet of cork-tips. The roof was where he went to light up in secret. Of course, we could smell the tobacco on him and stopped him immediately. Filthy habit. I'd given it up years before. But what kind of rituals he enjoyed up there, full of hormones and nicotine highs, surrounded by the beautiful views at dusk and the melancholy wind, the sound of the ford, god only knows. Even now I think he loves it up there, and who can blame him. He always spends so long inspecting and cleaning the drain, and I'm sure it's because he can't resist climbing the valley gutters to stare out in solitude down to the ford, listening for the rush of water down there, and remembering his virgin days, his boating trips and campsite sing-a-longs – *Michael, row the boat ashore!* – when life was just a question of dealing with moods and daydreams, not work and bills, and an irascible, ageing, paranoid parent, and a clever, discontented wife, and a spoilt-rotten six year old.

Rachael started busying herself with lunch once Alex had gone and I slunk back to the study to browse the papers. If I'd stayed I would have been given Joe duties, which she never tires of foisting on me. She won't give up the forlorn hope that if she just persists I will eventually, through virtue of Joe's charm alone, start to regard him with more affection.

Whenever I'm confronted with this point of view – here, in real life, or on tv soaps, or in sentimental moments in the papers or books – involuntarily I think of the war. After we'd ditched Command's attack plans – *From the rear in flights of three, etc.* – I went in just under head-on, offside, like the mad Poles, low enough to keep out the way of the Messerschmitt's engine cannon, level enough to shoot out the cockpit, pilot or engine when I chose my moment to come up. The Poles had no time for tactics. They'd break loose once we'd made enough height, sometimes claiming not to understand the radio – 'Cannot hear! Cannot understan'!' – and sign off – 'Attacking enemy!' Eventually Command shoved them all together in their own mad squadron. But whatever they were doing, it worked. Glowacki was an ace-in-a-day, with five kills in twenty-four hours, and there were precious few of those, and Witold, whom I met a couple of times but whose surname I forget, was one of the top six overall in the entire battle. Pilots explained the Poles' recklessness with talk of their country being overrun, their insatiable thirst for vengeance, but that was just the old romance of war again, a story that suited morale. I never believed it. That was our way of giving them licence to be wildcards, which was what we all wanted to be, and what the more experienced of us were, as the sorties rolled on, and the pilots – the less experienced ones first, of course – dropped out the sky faster than they could be replaced. It was fatal to follow those Command attack plans. The third in a flight of three was a lame target by the time he came into play, and he was always the greenest and least able to defend himself. In pairs we were far more effective, which is how the Germans always came down on us, a tactic they'd learned from the Spanish Civil War, and that we learned from them too late. But within seconds of the attack starting, none of that mattered, not when you have a fifth of a second between burning alive in your own cockpit or roasting the enemy in his. Would any of the Poles have enjoyed putting a blow-torch to a stranger's face, or ramming a bayonet through his ribs, just because his compatriots had invaded their homeland? I don't think so. I'm killer enough, but no degree of patriotism could have made that pleasurable to me. The exact equivalent, though – setting his cockpit alight, or putting a machine gun bullet through his chest – from where I was, throwing around this marvellous, 1300 horsepower, V-12 racing machine all over the sky – well, this was the sport of kings. And when the prey was easy I revelled in it. The Stuka dive-bombers were so slow you had to throttle back in pursuit. We took them out like skittles. The Luftwaffe gave them up because the losses were unsustainable.

Having enjoyed that degree of excitement, exhilaration, power and terror, what room is left in my psyche for what Rachael wants me to feel, which just doesn't make sense to someone who fought a war like mine. I do not see children, infants, or tender babes as she does: I see Joe entire, with the nature I know he has inside. A parent's view is too narrow, short term, too purblind and involved. In China, women shed children in the paddy fields. It is no special thing to have and to rear a child. And here so many of them are unwanted anyway, just a means to an end: marriage or a council flat. Yet I am called upon to give the infant some sacred status, as if it were my duty, and to forget its own nature: that Joe will be thrilled, in just twelve years' time, to have the chance to kill another of his kind, just as I did, to burn off another face that was kissed, nurtured and tended fondly, just as his was, ever since its arrival in the world. Joes at eighteen, nineteen are our scourge, with their murderous toys, their bloodlust, rape-lust and tribal pride. For so many young men life has no purpose without an enemy. They'll divide against each other for whatever cause. In fact, most of the time, the cause hardly matters, they don't even need it. Cane and Abel – teams, gangs, sects, factions, armies, squadrons . . . That's not a way of apologising for what I did or what I was. I recognize my nature because I have met it head-on. Of course, I have my disguises as well, the lies I tell everyone, from the historians manqué to family and friends, to well-intentioned strangers like Natalie, but that is a very different thing, not hormone-driven at all. What I was talking about in my own youth was the delight and satisfaction of killing, given these beautiful weapons, which made combat something playful and creative, and artistic in its expertise. I'm sure the same thrill existed in the amphitheatre, or at jousts in the middle-ages, and there must be something similar at bullfights, but in the dogfights of 1940 that thrill was intensified a thousandfold by the mechanised violence, the roaring Merlin in your hands, your 350 m.p.h. tearaway escape from the mess, the splintered bone, the burnt-off face, the blown out groin and severed hips.

That exact image of a joust came to mind when I first tried the oblique head-on with a 109 or 110 – I've never been sure which because the kill was unconfirmed – but from that kill onwards that is how I thought of it, and the idea gave me the recklessness of the Poles, because if I couldn't come down out of the sun (and you seldom could) I copied their tactic. I saw it, and saw it work. Attack speed was doubled – 700 m.p.h. – something that shocked me the first time, having attacked until then only from the rear, flank or below, following Command's useless tactics. When that first one tried to pull out above me I raked his underbelly then used the turn of the Hurricane like a slingshot – because nothing could turn like that aeroplane – to roll and come up behind him and he was finished. Thereafter I picked my prey. The easy ones. The less experienced pilots misunderstood or pulled up out of the joust when their only real option was to dive, and you could identify them from their squadron position, from their dithering, their reluctance to break loose to find aggressive positioning. So I went for the youngest, the weakest, and revelled in it, in their slaughter.

Well, that was some of it. Not the kind of thing I rant about to the puppies who come for their "research" into their glossy books, coffee-table tomes that no one buys. With them I'm in control and playing along with it all.

So why can't I play along with it all when it comes to caring for my grandson? Go through the motions, at least. Then something might naturally arise, as Rachael forlornly imagines. But no. It just does not interest me. I will not do it. Will not get involved. I'm not going to lie on the carpet with his road-scraping machine and make silly noises, or help him with *Donkey Kong* or *Fighter Pilot*. They brought him onto this dying planet and they must pay the bill, not share the bill, because sure as eggs he will be as much a monster as me someday.

Back in my study on my own, with Rachael busy in the kitchen and Alex on the roof, I had time to reflect at leisure on what had happened so far. The middle pages of the Sunday Times, more about our second Industrial Revolution, were in front of me, but I was not reading a word. I had the paper there for protection, lest anyone came in. What I was actually doing was poring over my pilot's-log memory, examining every detail of what had happened. The way Rachael had taken up the card from the baize. "May I?" The way Alex had responded: "The recognition, Dad. That's the main thing." How he'd stood there with his arms folded, staring at the autumn rain. Well, could I have got it all wrong? I had to ask myself. They had been so pleasant to me about it over tea and biscuits back in the kitchen, so full of goodwill, and those thoughts softened me. But surely there should have been at least a trace of churlishness from Alex, some jibe or other, that was in his nature, rooted there since his mother's death, and yet there had been none I could detect, playing back the memory, nothing at all like that. And his lack of interest in the website was entirely out of character too. But then, perhaps, he was just being more sensitive than usual. Perhaps he did not want to ask in case it seemed he was trying to take the occasion over, in that way he has, which makes him so boring, that way of trying to own or appropriate anything that surprises him. Then again, he had shown real surprise, and such warm surprise, at my astonishing news, which didn't fit very well either.

So how would they respond if I confronted them with my conviction that it was all a fraud?

*Oh my God!*

*Dad!!??*

*How ridiculous!*

*How absurd!*

*How paranoid!*

In fact, I realized, shifting uneasily in the recliner, turning the unread pages to the sports coverage, an action shot of some brilliant cover-drive the other side of the world, in sunny Melbourne, any such challenge actually made my position so much weaker. Had they done something more down to earth, exposing it would pose no risk, but in trying to bring down something as elaborate as an attempt to actually *get me out of the country!*, all the way to the Middle East, my paranoia ballooned out from the very scope and stature of their own plans. How crazy to even imagine anyone would go to those lengths!

Without either of them in the room to defend themselves with their innocent smiles and wiles, without Rachael there with her arms folded beneath her lovely breasts, lifting them slightly into view, and without Alex standing there staring at the rain, they both became darker, deeper, and disquiet blackened to anxiety. I felt outmanoeuvred by my own conjecture. Alone and unvisited, the swelling idea of being subtly manipulated by them, or by her at least, busying herself in the kitchen with her own secret thoughts, brought on an acute sense of helplessness.

The confusion intensified over lunch, after lunch, because during the ritual they seemed so unusually calm and kind and good-naturedly inquisitive, not only about the trip but also about other aspects of one's current lifestyle. The swimming, for example. I told Rachael about the sauna, which I have never mentioned to her before. She was immediately very approving, on health grounds, but not so amused about Mark and Aaron, whom she saw as eminently reportable. I passed them off lightly as a pair of oafs and mumsy boys.

Then it broke – Alex's boring lecture about petrodollars. It had been threatening all day, since he stood staring out the rainy study window: another louring cloud of drivel. As soon as he started Rachael began clearing away, so I was left alone to learn about the U.S. masterplan: how they would gobble up all the Middle East reserves before exploiting Alaska and the Gulf of Mexico, then into shale gas . . . on and on he droned, *I still think this and I always say that and I suppose the next thing will be* . . . the Minervois slipping down to wet the threads of conspiracy. He didn't sound like one of the less deceived at all, more a dupe of shoddy journalism.

He paused to lift the empty Sainsbury's bottle to the

light.

"Crikey!" he laughed. "Where's all that gone?"

"Down your gullet, Alex," I replied, a touch too harshly, and stood to take my plate to the sink.

"Suppose so," he replied ruefully, and laughed again, at himself now, and shook his befuddled head.

"Don't bother with all this," I told Rachael at the sink. She was struggling with a baking dish of roast potato skins. "Let it soak. I'll do it later. You're not dressed for this sort of thing." It was true: I was concerned for her smart grey suit and her square, tight black blouse, her modern Sunday dress.

"All right." She flicked the water off her fingers and reached for a dishtowel. "Let's have some tea in the study," she said, smiling again, drying her hands. "A bit warmer too."

And things continued to warm up pleasantly once we were through in the study. Rachael was sitting opposite me, across the baize of the card table, on the old kitchen chair I use for the IBM. She'd been reading an obituary in The Sunday Times. She often reads them after me and we chat about them. I flatter myself she finds these conversations interesting because naturally I tend to know more about the subjects than she does, if they've been much in public life. So we fell to chatting about dear old Alastair Hetherington, because I knew quite a bit about him, as it happened. I wanted to dump The Times when he turned The Guardian into a genuine national in the seventies, but Laura wouldn't hear of it. It had to be The Times for her snobbery's sake, though she only read it on Saturdays. Even after Murdoch had got hold of it we still had to have The Times, and now I can't switch because of the crossword. There was all this and more to chat about over Hetherington, who'd been shipped off his beloved Isle of Arran to die of Alzheimer's in Bannockburn. Seventy-nine. My senior by a few months. Maybe that's what did it. That thought. That he was only a few months ahead, and now dead and gone, reminded me that it would be Alzheimer's or something worse for me pretty soon, and yet here I was fighting underhand skirmishes with kith and kin not just about electricity bills but about the very roof over my head. The rural poverty of living in this place now, the thought of which chokes me with anger, with no help from Alex for the bloody bills, rates and so on. Hetherington had it warm and snug on the Isle of Arran, I'll be bound, with sheep-skin jackets and Aga heaters, but three hundred miles south I'm freezing in November, with four of the worst months still to come. Some run of thoughts like that must have made me bring things to a head, because when she picked up the gilded invitation again, from the green baize, it lost its lustre entirely and just looked silly and fake, like part of a Christmas decoration, or a bit of packing left over from a box of confectionery.

"Oh. By the bye," I remarked, "I won't be going."

I studied their responses carefully. Both frowned, perplexed. To be fair, there was no fleeting glance from one to the other, as I had expected from my shock tactic.

Rachael broke first. One of her rare exclamations.

"But you must go!"

Oh, indeed I must!

*Get out! Get out! Get out!*

Alex was on the floor helping Joe with the land-scraping machine, trying to adjust the blade that was leaving nasty marks on the carpet, scraping up dirt the Hoover never reached. But at least this toy made no noises. Sound chips would have upset the drama of the moment.

"Of course you must go, Dad," Alex said from the

floor, landscraper in hand. "Why on earth would you not go? Don't be daft."

I didn't answer that but stared across at Rachael, trying to detect some flaw in her performance. Hedda Gabler. Nora Helmer. She was still frowning, still confused.

"Didn't you say it was all expenses paid?" she asked.

"Yes." I answered crisply. "That's what it says."

She repeated Alex's line: "So why on earth wouldn't you go?"

The Sunday rain had cleared and weak afternoon light was falling across her lovely ringlets and her heart-shaped face, the shape I have always associated with slyness and treachery. The light exposed the imperceptible down on her cheek. I sat back in the shadows, semi-reclined.

"You tell me," I said.

Now they both looked at me together, and Joe had to reach up and prise the yellow landscraper from his dad's hand.

"But we don't know!" Rachael laughed in astonishment. Oh, the sheer absurdity of our conversation!

"You'd be crazy to pass up a chance like that, Dad. If you're really worried about the money we can always - "

I cut him off – "But I'm not worried about the money, Alex. It says it's all expenses paid."

Rachael offered another little laugh of total bemusement, and encouragement. "Then what's the matter? Why so cryptic? . . . Is it a health problem? Waterworks or something?"

I shunted the recliner upright, too violently, perhaps. I looked hard at the pair of them, going from one to the other, trying to hold both in the line of fire without going wall-eyed.

"I won't be going," I told them, glancing from one

to the other very quickly, "because there's nothing *to go to*!"

Rachael was still frowning deeply: she'd give herself a migraine before long.

"Whatever do you mean?"

"I mean," I said, savouring the moment of revelation and confrontation, "that it is a con. The invitation is a con. The event doesn't exist!"

Silence.

"*What*?" Rachael stroked a set of her lovely ringlets behind her ear, leaving more of her face in the light. "A con? How can it be a con? What do you mean? How do you know?" The card was in her hands. She studied it, flipped it over, looked at the back of it, turned it round again. "Why would anyone do that? Make up something like this?" She laughed helplessly at the absurdity of my claim. Oh, you're awfully good, I said to myself. Just like Laura. Just like all your sex. Interesting that she took the lead like this, leaving Alex on the floor in support role, while she dealt with the old man head on. Proof, if any were needed, that she was the brains behind it all, just as I'd suspected. But traitors both, kith and kin, whatever his role. The excitement, as we closed in on the confrontation, was too much for the old pipes and wires and I'd begun my terrible nodding.

"You're not making any sense, Dad," Alex threw in, adjusting his kneeling position. "And you don't look too good. Are you having a turn or something?"

I left Rachael a moment to glance down at him. He looked back quizzically at me, cocking his head, concerned. "Are you all right?"

The nodding was giving me away, weakening my position. They could treat me as infirm from here and be sympathetic – slip into that role, that manner. He's having a turn, that's all.

"Have you ever known me have turns, Alex?" I asked, but the question was too sharp, too vexed and sarcastic. "Hmmn?"

"Well," Rachael said, "you're having one now. Why so irritated and hot under the collar suddenly? Why so excited? What's all this about?"

Any moment now she could pull the rug from under my feet, just as Laura had done forty-one years ago – "I do believe there's a bit of paranoia, Antony!" She was about to do that. I could sense it coming but I didn't know how to pre-empt it without declaring my hand, which I couldn't do just yet, not until there had been some sign from one or the other or both of them, some breaking-down, some movement or eye-contact or remark that would give them away.

"Antony," she said patiently, holding the gilded, magnolia card between her fingertips. She repeated her question. "How can this be a con, a scam?" She smiled bemusedly, shrugged her lovely shoulders in their grey jacket. "Tell us what you mean, for goodness' sake." She threw out that laugh again. "You're sounding a little paranoid, Antony."

And there it was. She'd pulled the rug. She only ever used my name when she wanted to patronise me, or when she was annoyed with me.

"Antony, who on earth would want to con you by inviting you to a flypast - in your honour! - in godforsaken Saudi Arabia? It's just absurd! What you're saying. I'm sorry, but you're not making any sense."

"I think you're having your first paranoid delusion, Dad," Alex lobbed in lightly, fiddling with the landscraper blade. "Let's hope it's your last."

That did it.

"Who on earth would want to con me?" I mimicked

viciously, head nodding wildly now, totally betrayed by the pipes and wires, which must have been doubled up all over the place, leaking and short-circuiting everywhere. "Who?" I whined. "Who would want to con me?" I stabbed at her chest across the baize with such violence I shunted forward in the recliner – "You would!" Then at him, my only begotten son: "And you would!"

The shouts were so fierce Joe burst into tears.

Alex stood up and took his hand and led him out the room.

Rachael stood to follow them but stopped herself and stayed there, leaning on the card table, bearing down on me.

"You've been on your own too long," she said. "You know what's happening to you, don't you?" she added.

"Oh, yes," I answered her. "I know what's happening, all right."

I let my shaky gaze drop from her face. I must have looked uncomfortable or embarrassed somehow to her, as if I'd suddenly realized I'd gone too far or awoken from my delusion, and realized it was just that, a delusion, because her voice, though upset – I'd made Joe cry, after all – was not without gentleness and sympathy.

"Well, if you know, then . . ." She didn't finish.

My gaze had come down to her breasts. The way she leant against the card table left them three-quarters exposed to the warm air of my study. My gaze fell to her hands, spread on the edge of the card table, her left with its thin gold wedding ring on the green baize, her right splayed across the invitation and its envelope. But then my nodding head, involuntarily it seemed, lifted once more, responding to some greedy impulse within that I could not control. It seemed just then that there had never been so much of her flesh on show, on offer, as it were, not even when I'd stared down in the cupboard with my whisky advertisement, and I became – head nodding, hands shaking – overwhelmed by the single impulse to touch, to feel at last – for the first time in 25 years, ¼ of a century, 1/3$^{rd}$ of my godforsaken existence! – the blessed softness and smoothness of female flesh that so tormented me, that mild tissue, to cup her flesh in my ancient speckled hands, draw her breasts out entire from that token restraint of her tight black blouse, and suddenly I had to seize this chance, this flesh, because I knew again with a certainty that passeth all understanding that I would never have such a chance again, because these relationships were finished now, after what I'd just said and done. My arm was heavy with reluctance but I brought it up as quickly as I could and reached out my crumpled, trembling, speckled hand and was nearly there before she dashed it aside, aghast, disgusted, as if it were an amputated stump, and ran from the room.

"Ye gods!" she cried out in the chilly hallway.

They left.

There was another note on the refectory table, in Alex's hand, this time.

*Dad – you've upset Rachael dreadfully and we're going home. I'll call during the week to see what's what. You don't seem quite yourself today. For goodness' sake think again about that trip! You need a break of some kind. (I can't*

*take what you said seriously, I'm afraid. I hope when you wake up tomorrow you find that's a relief!)*
*Alex*

Alex. Dear Alex.

You are an innocent, dear boy. A gull, a foil, your innocence and trust used against you, and against me.

Mid-week, after my swim and sauna and my leisurely crawl home, I was boiling an egg for brunch when something caught my eye out the porch window. Bandits at 11 o'clock. The paddock to the stream is clear and there are no trees until the other side where a strip of woodland obscures the road, or rather the lane, with all the usual blind-spots and encroachments from trees, tumbledown gateways and grassy verges, not a place to stop at all. And yet, this morning, there was the glint of a stationary car, a chrome wing-mirror and door frame, glinting through the trees.

And the car was red.

Oh the pipes and wires, how they rose to the occasion, a-trembling and a-nodding and a-drawing tight until I felt an uncomfortable pain across the shoulders, premonition of a heart attack or angina at the very least. I turned off the egg and left the kitchen for the living room. Instinct shuffled me along there and instinct was good.

Striding along the end of the garden towards the stream, following the perimeter of the property, was the Simmonds fellow. On the previous visit I had been stricken with outrage. Now I only watched in anxious fascination, nodding away at the French doors in the living room. They open onto the garden, and the overgrown pits that once were my rose beds, my pride and joy. He stopped, glanced up at the house, and shadowed his eyes with his hand, even though the November skies were cast-iron as always, as if looking up to inspect the attic windows. That was an automatic thought on my part because they look so shabby and derelict and I am so ashamed of them. The sills have lost their paint and they lend the place an air of abandonment that haunts me always. Guilt. Shame. Impotence. Nothing I can do about the place falling apart. Like the wisteria scraping against one window or another, or several windows at once these days, since it hasn't been tended properly in years; the sight of those three derelict attic windows brings on the sense of inexorable decline, more intimations of mortality; the sense that the place will soon be empty, full of my death.

No such thoughts disturbed Simmonds. *Take the guts out of a million* was all that reverberated in that skull. And if weatherproofed, restored, centrally heated, properly decorated, subjected to the Long Cottage treatment, who knows what price it might command. It would be in the cash millionaires' market, without a doubt.

When he heard the rattle of the handle and the creak of the antique mechanism and saw me coming out, I imagined Simmonds would skip nimbly to the stream and flee across some stepping stones, like some middle-aged sprite. In fact, he did not move an inch. He had his hands in his pockets now and just stared at the doors while I fiddled there, because the damn things wouldn't open. After a couple more tries I returned to the kitchen, grabbed my coat and went out the back door. I crossed the sodden, overgrown lawn almost at a trot – my goodness! – but soon slowed. He made no move to shorten the distance between us, just waited there while I soaked my tracksuit bottoms and Hush Puppies wading out to him through the plantains and dandelions, that clung to my ankles and held me back like seaweed.

His face was impassive, unconcerned. There again was the nicotine fringe, and beneath it the wrinkly pits of insincerity. However, there was no ingratiating manner about him this morning. That had gone without trace.

"Morning, Colonel!"

I stopped about ten paces from him. "What?" I asked, pointlessly, then hurried on to face him.

"Just what the hell do you think you're doing on my property! Get off! Get out! Get away with you!"

He blinked slowly, then spoke slowly.

"No more yours than mine, Major."

That confounded me a bit, I must say. I was not towering over him in the kitchen with a dish-towel over my arm, as before. I was out in the garden, in the wild and overgrown and desolate garden, under a leaden November sky, and feeling quite undermined, quite vulnerable, if the truth be known.

"What?" I said again. "I'm not going to stand here and bandy words with you! Just get out of here! Get off the grass! Away with you!"

"Awful sorry, Cap'n."

He laughed at this little trick of demoting me each time, and in the wrong service too. How witty.

He cleared his throat. "I have been, shall we say, set straight on a few things."

"You're trespassing!" I accused, rather feebly. "Now, get out of here before I – "

"But on whose land, Private Rose?" he interrupted, raising his voice, asserting himself now. "Not yours. And as it happens, I'm not trespassing. I have permission to be here. From the owner."

Hearing that made Alex so distant it quite severed our filial bond, such as it was. Well, wasn't that severance all of my making? And hadn't Alex tried, god knows, to be at least dutiful, despite me, coming by each month with the

Sunday roast, that bloody offering in its Sainsbury's bag, and his Minervois, or Corbieres? Hadn't poor Alex tried to protect me from myself, stopping me from tending the roof gutter, forewarning me about farmer Steggles? Wasn't Simmonds just what I deserved?

So many guilty thoughts and memories of that kind washed over me there, standing at the end of the garden in confrontation with this ghastly man, that I stood silently, nodding away, and I must have looked quite gormless to him. Very close to departure itself.

Simmonds shook his head.

"I see a lot like that all day," he told me, nodding back at me, his eyes moving up and down my face. "Too many. Seven days a week." He looked around a moment at the skies, the paddock, the overgrown lawns and woodland, the derelict attic windows. "That's why I came out. Quiet drive is what you need, the missus said. You have to get away from them sometimes."

There was nothing I could do or say to him. I could not threaten him physically, after all.

"I'll call the police," I told him.

He took a deep breath of rectory air and exhaled. "Last thing I wanted was to find another one in front of me right now, out here in the wilds, in this beautiful spot." He took his hand from the pocket of his corduroys – new, expensive, thick and warm, olive-green corduroys – and looked at his watch. "They'll be starting lunch now. Greedy buggers." My eyes remained fixed on his new trousers. It must have looked as if I were concentrating on something.

"Hey! Don't shit yourself! Spare me that."

I thought of Aaron, Mark, for no discernible reason.

He started to walk away, towards the stream.

"Good day to you, Private Rose!" He called back

over his shoulder, "Have a nice day! . . . Not many left, you know! . . . Not many of you either! . . . Last of The Few! . . ."

I watched his short figure descend the bank of the stream without difficulty, and saw his yellowish head bob across between the banks as he stepped from stone to stone. He pulled himself up the other side by an overhanging branch, quite nimbly, it must be said, as if it were the most natural thing in the world, and disappeared among the trees.

My boiled egg, I thought, I must get back to my boiled egg, my routine. I needed to put routine back in place quickly. To make a dam against the alienation that was flooding in all around me, the de-familiarization of all that had been only too familiar for the last forty-something years. But I could not go back in just yet. I must face this out somehow and reconcile myself to the reality of the visit, come to terms with it. Too cowardly to slink back inside, put the egg back on, and pretend this had no deeper significance. I started walking around the lawn perimeter. At least it was a line to follow, and it felt like a duty of sorts, to follow the border, after Simmonds' invasion, to retrace his steps, reclaim them from him. I continued up the slope towards the churchyard wall. The trees and vegetation are thicker here but there is a path still and there are visible, here and there along the edge, the remains of glazed, violet tiles, put in when the place was built, circa 1825. Georgian, don't you know. Tiles to prettify the walk for the rector and his family, his guests; for the young couples who'd come to arrange their marriage banns; for the middle-aged to discuss last rites for an ageing parent . . .

What a totally shattering visit this had been. After the calamitous weekend, the afternoon of the long knives, I had slipped back into my habitual world as swiftly as I could. Turning up at the pool before it opened, having my swim and sauna, coming home at 11 o'clock for a late breakfast, or brunch, I liked to think. After that weekend there had been a need to return to habit and order, and I had responded to said need. But this visit had put all that pretence and defence in perspective. Well done, Simmonds, if that was part of the desired effect. His visit had knocked me for six! But the overgrown path smelt heavenly. Cow parsley. Wet ferns. Why did I not come up here more often? Appreciate it. Deserve it. Travel the circuit of the property, as Simmonds had done. State the claim. Leave a scent.

*Don't shit yourself! Spare me that.*

The path follows the churchyard wall, the graveyard wall, though you can hardly see the brick through the undergrowth and saplings, and comes down at the corner to our own blue latticed door, the private exit the rector would have used as his shortcut a century ago. The study window is at the bottom of the bank here. I passed the blue door in the wall. It hasn't been used in years and is immovable and rotten, but still serves as a barrier. Laura and Alex used to walk down the drive and round to the church entrance that way, during those moribund months before sickness stopped her going out at all. But there is another way to the churchyard. I could not go past the house. I would be drawn in and I was not ready for that. The sameness of the kitchen lino and the dirty walls. The semi-boiled egg yet to be re-boiled, hard boiled.

I doubled back up the bank and along the path and retraced my steps briskly to the end, where an electric fence, not operating at the moment, is mounted to keep animals in the glebe field. Local farmers lease the field from the parish for a peppercorn rent and graze cows and calves in there, or unruly animals that need to be on their own awhile. Sometimes there's a horse – there was a few weeks ago, I remember. Two summers past a teenager from the village used the glebe for her pony and came riding at weekends and on Wednesday evenings, which cheered things up a bit. I watched her from my bedroom windows. With her father's help she set up garish obstacles for a miniature gymkhana. But that was a tragic family. The girl was killed on the Norwich road in an accident her parents survived. Head-on smash with a drunk in a van. She was in the back yet she alone was killed – no seat belt, was the rumour – leaving the parents childless again when they woke up disfigured in hospital. The swindling grocer told me about it, I think. No. It was Eric, the ancient librarian. "Makes you wonder," he remarked, looking down, straightening the returns on his trolley, pushing them to the first shelves, "why any God would do that, and leave us here, Mr Rose."

Speak for yourself, Eric, you old electricity-bill-swindler, crossword-chiseller, crossword-hog!

Her pony trotted about on its own for a couple of weeks till a dealer came and took it away in one of those closed, grey, corrugated horse wagons. He took away the colourful obstacles for her gymkhana too. Pinched them. Stowed them in his Land Rover. I saw it all go from the bedroom.

Where the fence ends there is a proper wicket gate before the graveyard, with a shelter for the churchgoers of yesteryear, who might pause there at the top of the glebe field if it were raining. These days everyone arrives by car using our drive, whose maintenance costs I'm obliged to share with the church, which leads to endless friction. I have pointed out a thousand times that my car cannot do any damage to the road. It is only the church traffic, including hearses, wedding congregations and heavy equipment for repairs that damage the drive. Not me. But they want me to pay for half the maintenance. I asked Alex to take this up with his commissioner hypocrites, but if he tries he never gets anywhere, and he won't contribute to the bill at all.

In the shelter of the wicket gate I couldn't help but pause to look down across the glebe to the ford, unusually full for this time of year. I held my breath and stood completely still so that I could hear it, hear the water swirling across the road and snagging on a tree stump down there, my side. The sun was beginning to break through the cast-iron skies in the east, a hot puddle of light, quite low even though it was a little before noon. A red Post Office van came down the hill the other side of the valley and gently splashed through the ford. There's a postbox the other side. I watched the postman unlock the box and collect the mail – Who on earth uses that postbox! – and go back to his van. But he didn't drive off. Not him. Of course not. He'll sit awhile down there enjoying the countryside and the sound of the ford behind him. Maybe reading a paper or eating a sandwich, or opening some child's birthday mail, looking for cash. What an enviable job! The sort of thing I should have liked to have done after quitting the R.A.F., but anything like that was too lowly for Laura. Married to a postman? I don't think so, Antony!

Onward through the covered wicket into the churchyard itself.

The church is always open now. They used to keep the enormous key dangling behind the door of my greenhouse, the other side of the church wall but still on my land. Some brass-rubber stole it and the door has been open ever since. My greenhouse is another well-made thing from the son of a painter & decorator. Empty now, of course. The winter after Laura died I used it for slave-labour, pressing brickettes for the fire. The press was one of those Sunday Times swindles specially invented for poor, cold, lonely widowers, mugs like me. A Swedish steel lever squashed sodden newspapers and cardboard into flammable brickettes. They burned in minutes and emitted no heat whatever. In the advertisement it had talked about running your central heating off them. There is no weekly service any more. The priest has the care of three other parishes, so he only comes by once a month. Or rather twice a month, half the time, I suppose. The church is never heated. Hardly anyone comes. The paraffin heaters they used are now deemed too dangerous and never lit.

So.

Inside the hallowed place itself, at last. I pushed the door to gently behind me and was rewarded with an eerie creak and clunk.

Nothing could be more empty. A swift, swallow or house martin, impossible to distinguish in the dull light, but not a bat, soared about the nave, the vaulted rafters, drawing black lines through the grey emptiness, as if trying to measure it from chancel to belfry.

Oh you Saxons, what did you have in mind here, with your mighty flint and crude cement? There's the dark, stubborn altar with its fastened candlesticks. And that pulpit, all miniature studs and newels and carvings of faces aghast. The wooden apparatus of Faith and Fear, long fallen into disuse. Right on cue a shaft of sunlight penetrated the high eastern window, ineffably beautiful in this stillness, with just the bird for company, the light squinting through the stained glass blues and reds of Gethsemane and falling refractorily across the empty pews, across the palm-size psalm books, lettered in gothic black, all blue with cold and shrivelled and sorrowful. Nothing easier, nothing more wonderful or awe-inspiring, to believe that a moment like this is a sign of some numen or numina. But no spirits, no souls, no epiphanies now. That is all over. Those things took shape from marvellous aesthetic experiences like that shaft of light, when the mind is overwhelmed for a moment and we live as that swift or swallow or house martin lives, without language, time, money-worries and all the rest of it, detached for a second from all ratiocinative powers. Then the cloud passes and the window glass you're staring at is rippled grey and concave in its lead filaments, its stained-glass colours are dull again, and the bird continues its bored and meaningless rounds of nave, chancel, belfry and rafter, until it drops out of the emptiness and lies fluttering under a pew or choir stall, food for mice and beetles.

And Lo and Behold, amidst such reflections, there came the sound of mighty iron movement and the door being shoved open, and I turned to see Natalie at the entrance, the grey afternoon behind her, coming in with a basket of bright yellow flowers. Not daffodils at this time of year, surely.

"Hello there," she whispered aloud. "You old agnostic, you!"

"Good morning!" I returned, not quite self-possessed.

She was wearing a beige coat, camel hair perhaps, a rather manly and unchurchly coat. She approached on tiptoes, beaming a smile worthy of the bright flowers in her wicker basket.

What to do? I felt very caught out. Quite non-plussed. I had to rake around to remember how I'd left things with this woman. Why did she feel so very at ease, and so very pleased, encountering me like this, and, furthermore, prepared to show her pleasure so openly, as if it weren't a surprise at all? As if she knew I was in here. Our last meeting – how had it gone? It had been a week and a half since I'd last seen her. When we'd met for tea to discuss her bridge idea, and when I'd casually spilt the beans about the commemorative trip, whose prospects were now in tatters, whose spell was now quite broken. And of course I'd talked about that with such pride then, handled it with such finesse, I'd thought. And afterwards I'd congratulated myself with such pomposity about trumping everything with my war record. "Were you in that?" "Up to the hilt." Up to the hilt! I all but tittered aloud in church to remember that. Why could I not resist that kind of self-aggrandizement? Ye gods, as poor Rachael had exclaimed, what an impossible old bugger, pushing eighty and still blowing his trumpet.

All such thoughts had their sweet flypast at this surprise encounter with Natalie Stein in church, and left me speechless with shame.

"Well?" she teased, stepping closer, touching my Crombied arm. "What on earth are you doing here?" She cocked her head. "Having a gander? Having second thoughts?" She looked me up and down. "What a get-up for church, Antony! Overcoat and tracksuit! Just look at you – those Hush Puppies and tracksuit bottoms! – you've got half the rectory plantains there! All most irreverent, I'd say. Cracking up or what, ole fella?"

"Hah," I said. "Not me! Not after I . . ."

But there I had to stop myself, because just in those few words, in their quacky tone, reverberating in the hollows of the church, I had conveyed, to myself, at least, that life had taught me lessons too severe to make the comforts of this place accessible. Immediately, the self-aggrandizement again. It's what conversation is for, as far as I'm concerned.

"Oh, dear oh dear," she said, at my speechlessness, and she hooked me through the arm and began marching me up the aisle. "You'd better help me change the flowers. Do something useful with the day."

Being marched along like that, her camel-hair

coated arm through my Crombied arm, was the most sensual experience I'd had for – for what? – more than a decade, or more like two decades, nearly a quarter of a century. Even with all that compacted hair and lambs wool between us, I imagined I felt her warmth, her humanity. The absence, the sheer indignity, of living without any kind of physical contact with another person, is one thing I have never deluded myself about. To hold and be held by another is a simple human need, a basic human need. For most of my life that need has not been fulfilled. Full stop. Look how uncomfortable I was with poor little Joe. I could not even put my arms around him. It felt too presumptuous. I might enjoy the sense of his young body close to me in some bear-like way, but he could get no reciprocal satisfaction from sitting with me. Just as I had never enjoyed the intimacy of parenthood with Alex. These failures lead to the current plight, where the closest I come to sensual experience is a visit to the dentist, doctor or hairdresser. In a memory that made me falter halfway down the aisle and nearly cry out in pain, I was suddenly at Alex and Rachael's wedding party, walking up this very aisle next to the overbearing step-dad with his hands folded behind his back, in his light charcoal morning dress – I shut it down. No mercy. What a curse involuntary memory has become, gatecrashing the delightful party of the present whenever it pleases, bringing along any unsavoury guest or hanger-on it fancies. I suppose, in a distant way, the heat of the sauna at The Leisure Pool is a surrogate, a reaching out for sensual warmth or satisfaction, but that is spoiled every time by the presence of Mark or the dreaded Aaron, in all his naked glory. With Laura there had never been much hugging, and a frigidity stiffened between us as soon as intercourse died, sometime in her early fifties. That part of our lives came to a miserable and bathetic end when I broke wind while on top of her. "Oh, keep your gases inside you, for God's sake!" she cried, pushing me off. Unforgettable moment of dissolution.

That stinking memory, with the residua of the wedding memory, clung to my discomfort and self-consciousness as Natalie steered me to the end, towards the chancel, in mock-matrimonial fashion.

"Well? Explain yourself!" she pressed, letting me go at the choir stalls, where there was a heavy brown vase containing a few browner, naked stalks. "What are you doing here? Looks a bit wacky, you know. Particularly in that get-up."

She took out the dead stalks and set them neatly at one end of her basket, and replaced them with the fresh yellow flowers, whose ends were sealed with crumpled silver foil. Flowers from her garden, I supposed.

"I don't really know."

She lowered her head to the vase.

"Oh dear . . ." she said again.

She sighed. "Dry as a bone. Can you get some water from the font? There's a jug on the pedestal."

I was grateful for the demand to do rather than say something. There was a small, red, plastic jug, a miniature watering can without a rose, seated on the pedestal out of sight of the congregation. The font was covered by a lid with a polished brass handle, around which the wood was dark and waxy from years of Brasso spills. I lifted the lid and was confronted with something I hadn't expected: an extraordinary depth of darkness, blackness, bleakness. Cut out in a circle and caught, trapped under the lid. The same unfathomable darkness the submariner must stare into in his water tower, during aptitude tests. It was a maximum of three feet deep but the vessel was so full, to the very brim, and so absolutely still, and reflected no light but absorbed all light, it was fathomless. And not a drip fell from the ancient lid. To baptize a child over this! Little wonder they yelled! It was such a disconcerting feeling, to sink the red jug into that blackness, that it actually required courage. For a moment I couldn't do it.

"Why is it so black?" I asked aloud, to myself. "So terribly black?"

She answered me from behind but from somewhere else, looking in another direction, it seemed. She had moved on to a different vase.

"It's pitch," she said. "The original seal. Hundreds of years old. Never been allowed to dry out."

"I've lived next door most of my life and I didn't know that. You've only been here a few months."

"I know all about churches, me," she said. "I like churches. You need to top this one up as well."

The vase she was talking about was another clay object but larger than the first. It sat on the altar, obscuring the rather mean brass cross that was screwed down like the candlesticks.

"Such dull vases."

"They are not dull, but modest," she corrected. "Ostentation has no place here. The Anglo-Saxons were very reverent." She left me to go and sit on the organ bench. "Now," she directed, undoing and settling her coat. "Take a seat in the choir and listen to what I have to play. It's so nice to have an audience."

Ostentation has no place . . .

So this is why she was really here. From behind, sitting dumpily on the organ bench, her ageing floss of hair atop the camel coat, she looked incongruent. What a silly, pretentious old woman, I thought, staring at her curved back.

And what new departure was this, playing the church organ. After the house-warming and the bridge, there would follow an invite to, A Musical Evening at Home. I glanced at the choir stalls but found them altogether too small. They were for children, or for the smaller Saxon folk of nine hundred years ago. I went back up the nave and took my seat in the first pew.

She turned round on the bench altarwards, scanned the empty choir stalls, then rotated the other way and found me in the front pew.

"It has to puff itself up!" she declared, massaging her cold hands and smiling. As indeed do you, I thought. There was an electrical whirring from the organ. This was not a modern Japanese substitute but a genuine pipe organ, scaled down, installed between the wars. That much I did know because Alex had told me. He used to try to play it.

She pulled out a couple of stops, and was away.

The piece she played was one I knew, as it happened, because it had been part of Alex's repertoire as an adolescent. It was a very simple Bach Prelude: No. 1 in C Major. Few sharps or flats to speak of. The sun broke through the eastern windows again and there should have been that marvellous aesthetic experience to bring on the tired old sense of the numinous, but there wasn't. She played the piece in a ponderous way, slowing for the more difficult transitions as if she were interpreting the music, when she was merely fumbling. And anyway, the organ was unsuited to that prelude. So the experience was ugly, jarring, and I felt embarrassed by her presumption that she, a newcomer, could offer her impromptu recital without permission from anyone in the village, from any warden or sexton, if there were any left. I hoped she would not offer more. Some busybody might arrive at any moment and make his or her disapproval known. Music-making for the hell of it, indeed!

"I didn't know you could play," I said quickly, in neutral fashion, after the last major chord was struck.

"Did you like it?" she asked, blinking, and forcing the issue with another broad smile.

"It was lovely. But I'm worried the villagers may not approve. That rather spoilt my enjoyment."

To my relief I heard the fan dying.

"But you don't know any villagers, Antony," she said, rising from the bench and picking up her basket with a nonchalance that suggested I had given insufficient praise. "So how would you know if they approved or not?" There was a sudden coldness that did not fit with what had just happened at all. Totally out of proportion.

I stood also and we walked together back down the aisle, separately this time. The mood of five minutes ago, of pleasant surprise, even adventure, had passed. We were on our way out, into the grey midday, separately. I left her question as rhetorical.

She was on her way to Norwich to buy some towels, she told me outside. Couldn't get anything of the right quality locally, so she was off to Jarrolds'. She had a book to pick up from there too, some gardening tome she'd ordered by Lady Awfully-Important, whom she greatly admired. She didn't call her a gardener, of course, but a horticulturalist. She spoke like this about gardening, trying to turn it into her science, which then afforded her so many opportunities for showing off; after all, the flowers and shrubs were all about us, unavoidable, and who knew what they were called, let alone their Latinate names. I had the war and the Battle of Britain. She had her haughticulture. What wonderful conversations lay in store for us between cucumber sandwiches, the snort of soda syphons, and our first rubber of bridge with Mr &

Mrs Steggles -

NO NO NO NO NO NEVER NEVER NEVER NEVER NEVER!

Back in the kitchen, staring once more at the film of dusty water about my dirty egg, the first of Natalie's free-range eggs, dear old Simmonds came to mind from not an hour ago, strolling through my garden, soaking his patent leather slip-ons, filling the turn-ups of his new olive corduroys with dandelion and plantain seeds. To think again of that lizard of the temperate climes, precipitated a darkness so severe it made me lower my head and close my eyes. When I opened them again on the dirty egg, sitting there in its film of dusty water, too little water, actually, darkness seemed to gather at the corners of my pilot's vision, blurring and obscuring the kitchen, my territory, my home ground for over forty wretched years. The tiny black saucepan I use for boiling eggs, chosen to burn the minimum of electricity, which I never fill for the same reason, only enough to cover three-quarters of the egg – How has my life come down to such measurements, I should like to know! – that tiny black saucepan, on my ancient, inefficient, grubby yellow cooker, was suddenly a miniature of the font in the church, that perfect circle of pitch, and the egg within it, my sustenance today, my binding of body to soul, just an irrelevance. Darkness at the edge of things and at the core of things. And with that unification came another binding of thought, connecting the ghastly Simmonds with flower-toting Natalie.

When I could pass weeks, months, without any chance encounters, how come both these persons crossed my path in a single morning? And this morning, of all mornings, just the Wednesday following the Sunday of the long knives? I tried to remember the conversation, such as it was, with Simmonds. To remember exactly what Alex and

Rachael had told him, or rather, what he had told me they had said, or she had said. From his presence in the grounds I was meant to draw the inference that she was indeed using Simmonds as some kind of messenger or threat, some harbinger of doom.

Maybe she'd told him some lie, perhaps along the lines of putting the property in hock to Simmonds to cover my as yet undefined expenses at The Grosvenor. Just hinting at such a prospect would put the hissing Simmonds into such a feeding frenzy he would do whatever she asked. For Alex to be so cunning, deceitful and insidious was just unimaginable. Impossible. Even I could not believe that of my son. No. Simmonds was being used, sent on a mission, but not by Alex. The lead had such a slippery feel of truth about it, slippery as her lovely dark ringlets, that I had to distract myself. I took the egg to the sink to add more water, start again.

The cold water cracked the egg and a foul stink filled the kitchen. It was a fertilized egg. A rotten egg. Even from where I stood in the dim kitchen, though the crack was not great, not more than quarter of an inch, I could discern brown foetal elements of chick between the jagged shell, and something like a miniscule crumpled limb or wing protruded, reaching for the drain.

Messages, signs, portents, all balled up in the stink of rotten egg, and the egg had come from Long Cottage.

From her friendly overtures, her recent invitation to the bridge soirées, her kind assumption that we should be partners, no less, and from her marching me up the aisle arm in arm, Natalie was still apparently unaware of my status here as destitute tenant in situ. Apparently, to me, to muggins, but I'd underestimated her in the first place, at her house-warming. Maybe I was still doing so. What if she had known my situation from the very start?

"I'm a miniaturist, don't you know!" she'd said. That cluster of paintings in the living room, in a squadron, each painted onto the same gold-beaded card.

No no no! That surely made no sense at all!

I scooped the egg up with a serving spoon, took it outside and slung it deep into the paddock beyond the drive.

Away with all paranoid nonsense of that kind, Antony! For goodness' sake – that way madness lies, and your bed at The Grosvenor, and a bedtime story from Frank or Fanny Simmonds!

Back indoors I did not put on another egg but went directly to my study to search high and low for the invitation. It was not there. Then I remembered Rachael had taken it with her when she'd stormed off. Of course she had. I hurried back through no-man's-land to the kitchen and searched the dresser, the drawers, all surfaces where envelopes, notes, reminders, bills accumulate. It was not there. She'd taken it away with her, slipped it into her bag out of sight because it was useless now, or it had served its purpose. Her performance at the card table had been simply that, done to distract, so I wouldn't notice her taking the invitation when she stormed off in high dudgeon. Oh, she knew me too well! One step ahead at the very least, all the bloody way.

"You know what's happening to you. Don't you?"

Now I was on the right scent. I was beginning to unravel the whole scheme right enough. With triumphant certainty I returned to the study, wheeled out the IBM from its cupboard and plugged it in. I stood apart, in the chilly bay window, overlooking the unkempt garden, up to the strip of woodland and the church wall, trying to calm myself as the machine whirred and clicked to life. There should have been a grave. Something I could look up to accusingly and at which I could mutter my curses – *Look at her now, your precious daughter-in-law! Behold how she's carrying on now!*

They were ahead of me, though, for certain, or rather she was, and Simmonds – and Natalie, for goodness' sake? Not such a good egg after all? And such a coincidence that –

"You're having your first paranoid delusion, Dad."

There was no internet connection. Infallible since its installation, the system was now broken. The dish was on the roof. Alex: up there on Sunday, taking so long. And his lack of interest in seeing the website on the computer.

He too, then, after all. My beloved son.

They would drive me mad, or prove me mad.

Either way suits their gain.

I made myself go up and look.

It's quite an ascent to the attic rooms, two high floors. I hadn't visited for more than a year.

Always above us is that heap of things undone, unsaid, the irreducible and indissoluble heap that grows with the years and crushes the spirit. After nigh on eighty years, it crushes pretty deep. Simple physics.

The signs that this shelter of mine is becoming unweatherproof, a wrecktory, as Rachael calls it sometimes, are too much in evidence in the attic rooms. The repairs remind me of all that I will never do, because I haven't the physical strength any more (even if I had the will) despite my twenty-one widths twice weekly, deep in the beet fields

The attic windows are the worst. Rotten sills falling away from the flashing into their own gutters. Frames have parted in places, leaving the glass fixed only by the ancient putty, tough as cement. Look away from the windows to the low, blotchy, baggy ceilings, weighted with damp, and from which emanate scents of straw and rotten plaster. The kind of surface you dare not reach up and touch. The sense of decay, of moribundity, despite all my efforts from our early years here, laughable though they might seem today.

Worse is the accumulated memorabilia in what Laura pretentiously called The Box Room, though I suppose such rooms do exist in houses like this. I didn't go in, but the door was open at the top of the stairs and I turned left and stood there on the threshold for a full minute, because it is quite impossible for me to deal with the feelings this room evokes. So much better off downstairs, with the television, newspaper, current affairs, obituaries, the distractions of the factual world without, rather than the emotional world within.

The cold water tank, a galvanised monstrosity on a roughly hewn builder's trestle, squats in this room. Why doesn't it fall through the ceilings to my study and bring an end to everything? Its oversize lid is something I knocked together after Alex discovered a dead bird in there. He was only five or six years old but he wasn't frightened of the great tank or its dead bird secret, or of the stop-cock that has always made a loud, sinister, continuous hiss.

You had no business, Alex, clambering around in here at five or six years old. None at all. Good job you found that bird, though.

Good job, Alex.

Around the tank are various boxes of worthless paintings and hardback books, and Alex's exercise books from school; then an ancient high-chair with faded floral covers, tall and proud and erect, still awaiting a grandchild for my dead wife; then some obsolete electrical paraphernalia. The usual waste of family life. Detritus, as Alex would have it. A couple of suitcases that belong to me are buried at the very bottom of it all, from the R.A.F., filled with god knows what memorabilia, and stencilled A.R. I will never, ever open them. But the saddest thing for me in this room is a home-made desk, the one I made for Alex when he was eight or nine years old, a year or two after we'd sent him away to school. We were disappointed with his reports and wanted to encourage more studious habits. Still in perfect condition, never scratched or doodled on, the desk stands very low, in mellowed yellow and turquoise, near the door. The chemistry set is on top of it (with the foldaway hood), but underneath that I'm sure the paint on the desk lid is unfaded and pristine. I didn't move anything to look because I never touch anything in this room. Box Room Law. If I touch any part of it the beaten up brocade of my life will turn to dust, offer no pattern at all; there will be just the hiss of the tank in the silence, the pitch dark under the tank lid.

The top of the desk is hidden, as I say, but I know I painted it turquoise, and Laura painted *Alexander* in magenta italics in the top right hand corner, in the old-fashioned place for an ink well. She actually painted his name quite beautifully. Against the turquoise, it looked like a name painted on a boat, the work of a professional signwriter. And I fitted the top of the desk with a ratchet hinge, so he couldn't trap his fingers fetching out his books. There was care then, all right, and not only in the craft of the thing.

Enough.

I turned away from The Box Room.

Instead of carpet or linoleum, I covered the landing up here with cheap and noisy hardboard, hammered down with carpet tacks. This drew derision from Laura, and then her sister, months later, when they came up together to see the finished labour. "Are you thinking of opening a dance studio?" Sylvia sneered. Well, I'd had my fill of her by then.

I let her have it. "You bloody well do better!" I told her, and turned away and snubbed them both, descending the stairs without them. They sniggered softly when I reached the landing.

Opposite The Box Room is Alex's old bedroom. He painted it himself, as a teenager, in black and white. Stark, adolescent thoughts.

I turned away to get on with what I had come here for. A doorway mid-landing, fastened by a cheap chrome snib, leads up to the butterfly roof. With some apprehension I pulled back the snib, opened the door and stared inwards and upwards. There's no light for the narrow stairway, apart from the daylight on the landing. The passage is hardly fit for a chimney sweep! Cobwebs in deep whorls all over the place. A large, sluggish beetle was patrolling the second tread, where there's a brick Alex uses to stop the door for the light.

There are only eight steps to the top but one must go up in a crouched, defenceless position. A thin door of scantlings, no more than three foot square, opens onto the roof itself on the right. It's fastened from the inside by a wooden lozenge on a screw. Crude but enduring. The door opens outward with theatrical creaks and whines and then you literally have to crawl through onto the lead surface.

The ascent into this marvellously windy open roof space, and the sudden memories that being up here brought to the fore, after the gloom and guilt of the attic landing, quite blew away my purpose. Instead, I looked first at the internal guttering drain. The chicken wire was free. Nothing at the bottom either. Not a single leaf. I could see the marks where Alex had swept away any leaves or moss from the flashing round the drain with a dustpan and brush.

Good job, Alex.

The internet dish was no longer there, as anticipated. It should have been fastened to the left hand chimney. The clips for the cabling and the bolt holes were still there, but not the dish. However, what they had in mind – my precious son now back in the frame again – was for a moment irrelevant. My immediate and most pressing concern was to mount the valley gutter to the apex at the front of the roof, and enjoy again that view down to the ford and the ancient elm with its bees' nest, the same as from my bedroom but here a full storey higher, not bound in by glass; that cockpit view I'd had from my sling when painting the chimney stacks. The grip of the damp Hush-Puppies wasn't ideal but it was good enough, and keeping my balance with both hands on the tiles at either side I nimbly drew myself up to the apex, where I clung to the ridge tile, perfectly safe. How impossible it is, though, to enjoy anything contemplative if one is in a state of physical discomfort or anxiety or both. I had no sooner got myself up there in a secure crouch, left foot braced on the tiles of the valley gutter, right leg drawn up beneath me, knee in the curve of the roof tiles, than there was a loud bang behind me – the roof door had blown shut and it had not whined open again, which suggested the wooden fastener had slipped around with the impact.

How could I enjoy that blustery view with the worry of that door shut behind me, from the inside? For a few moments, gripped fast to the ridge-tiles, I stared down towards the ford, and I could see the grey water there on the greyer road, but it was quite soundless from up here, with the wind around my ears, tousling my hair. I managed a slow retreat, one Hush Puppy at a time, bracing myself to the edges of the valley gutter. It wouldn't do to have an accident now, not with the door shut.

It was fast. There were gaps at the top of the

scantlings where I could get my fingers in to prise it back a fraction but it held firm.

Should it rain, I didn't fancy slipping about up here in the butterfly roof calling for help. Nobody would hear above the caw of the crows anyway.

If the wooden lozenge the other side had slipped around, it could surely only be a matter of pressing the door and banging it with sufficient force to allow the lozenge to slip to the open position.

After the fourth such bang I'd had enough. Filling in crosswords does not prepare one's hands for such treatment.

I left the door to scour the roof space for something I could use to lever the door or smash it apart if need be. There was no sense of panic about this search. If all else failed I could dislodge a tile and use that. The door was not substantial and I knew I could free it or break it open somehow. But halfway along the lead flashing, just as I passed the internal gutter with its chicken-wire chimney, I stopped dead and froze.

Music!

Strains of music. The wind, funnelled in the butterfly roof, still tousled my hair about my ears but I could definitely hear music. Lyrics too. Only my study gramophone had the power to reverberate all the way up through the house, and it must have been at full volume, enough to shatter the ancient speakers. I never played it at full volume for that very reason. I went back to the roof door and bent down. There it was. Unmistakable.

*The Desert Song*. Gordon MacRae. One of my ancient 78s. The sentimental rubbish of the fifties, of which I am so ashamed these days. I should have thrown it all out years ago, made a vinyl and shellac bonfire of it all. But there was Gordon all right, as if he were alive:

*My desert is waiting;*
*Dear, come there with me!*
*I'm longing to teach you*
*Love's sweet melody!*

Strangely, again it did not alarm me in any way or cause any panic. With my back to the door I heeled the scantlings with my Hush Puppy as hard as I dared, striking three times in quick succession. It didn't matter what happened to the door – it could fall off for all I cared – I was only worried I might do my heel or foot some mischief and lay myself up for weeks, months, and then how would I drive to the shops, the baths? On the fourth bang the door freed. The wooden lozenge must have worked round. I pulled it wide and crawled back through without further incident.

Melodrama – with or without musical accompaniment – over!

Tra la la!

This is what I half-muttered to myself as I closed and fastened the door behind me, but then I froze again in my tracks, kneeling there on the musty miniature staircase, because the music below had stopped. Musical chairs, then, of a certain kind? But what kind? Without further incident, I had said – but what incident, exactly, had been intended? What resonance that phrase had as I gingerly made my descent to the attic landing. I replaced Alex's brick on the first tread of the stair, closed the door, and drew across the cheap snib that held rain, cold, crows, and all mortal perils of Nature at bay a dozen feet or so above. Those perils to which, it appeared, I had been knowingly exposed, as some kind of test, warning or punishment. Quite a trap, the butterfly roof. I couldn't very well slide down the pantiles to the attic windows and force re-entry. But for me the visit had achieved its objective, a success that someone did not like, it seemed: Alex had removed the dish. He hadn't cut the wire, or pushed the dish out of position, or left things in such a state that they might be reparable; he had actually removed the dish itself, and the cabling, and cut me off completely, so that major work and expense, quite beyond me, had to be undertaken to reconnect.

I stood still on the hardboard landing, allowing myself to recover.

"Anybody there?" I called. An affable, unworried, quite gentle call.

I stood perfectly still, at ease, and drew a deep breath.

Called again. Louder.

"Anybody there?"

Nothing. Only the wind in the shaky attic windows. I started my descent, a hand on the banister. On the first floor landing I stopped and waited. I was going to call again but refrained. Pointless. Still using the banister, I made my way slowly down to the ground floor hallway, to no-man's-land, and then towards the study. The door was not completely closed, not drawn to the jamb and fastened to keep in the precious heat, as was my habit. Well, nothing in that: I left it open myself often enough, in absent-minded moods, and cursed myself on return to find it thus.

Rather than fear itself, I felt a strange premonition of fear.

What if the music were to start again, at full volume, as I stood out here by the door?

What would I feel? What would I do? Still no alarm? No panic?

I thought I could hear the crackle of the needle on the

shellac. It was about to begin. Full volume. Full mockery:

> *My desert is waiting;*
> *Dear, come there with me!*

But inside the study there was no one, of course.

First, the computer cupboard. I jerked the door wide fearlessly, as if I were going to uncover the boy Alex playing hide-and-seek. *Alex! Enough of these silly games! Grow up!* That was easy. But courage faltered a moment at the gramophone cupboard. My most recent, vivid, intense memory of this special space, was of sharing it with Rachael. I could not help imagining her behind the door, and in some perverse extension of that autumnal moment, I imagined her in a state of undress, with her blouse open, pulled back or torn back, and her lovely white breasts rudely exposed. On opening the door, she'd cry out in shock, and bring Alex running to rescue her from his demented father, that ghastly, dirty old dad, who should be indicted as a danger to his family, and the public at large, and who should be banged up forthwith in The Grosvenor, under the good care of Messrs Frank and Jane Simmonds.

The music was to draw me down here to the cupboard, for that very scene. She knew how I had behaved in there.

"Is that all?" she'd asked, her arms folded beneath her breasts.

I hooked my speckled fingers to the handle. Nothing to turn. These cupboard doors were fixed with magnetic catches, my handiwork from decades past. I could still unhook, let go, pull back, no damage done.

But I did not.

I pulled the handle. Drew the door wide.

The light from the study bathed the shadowy, dusty,

cluttered space. The gramophone light was out, switched off. I lifted the wooden lid. The turntable was empty.

Had I imagined *The Desert Song*? I had heard the whole of the first verse. True, I knew it by heart anyway. A delusion, then? Or was that just what I was meant to believe, to doubt? And perpetually to believe or doubt, until such ambivalence undid my reason completely.

One thing they may have overlooked, which could give me the advantage here. In terms of electronics, this Fidelity gramophone was a 1950's, state-of-the-art masterpiece, a beautiful antique. The valves took a full minute to warm up and hum. I lifted the whole unit with one hand and felt its underbelly with the other.

Still warm.

"Very funny, Alex."

"Hi Dad. How's things? What's funny?"

"I don't remember you as a practical joker. This is something new."

"Dad . . ." A weary pause. "What are you talking about?"

"What have you done with the dish?"

"What dish?"

"From the roof. You took it down on Sunday, when you were up there clearing the drain."

"Is this a crossword clue?"

"You're awfully funny, Alex."

"Who ran away with the spoon? The dish?"

"You're awfully funny these days, Alex. Perhaps it's

the booze."

"Don't get sarcastic, Dad. Doesn't suit. Tell me what you're calling about so I can get back to Joe's supper. Have you been up to the roof? I told you never to go up there. It's too dangerous for you now."

"Internet wasn't working so I went up to check. You took the dish. Last Sunday. When you were up there clearing the gutter."

"You should never go up there, Dad! *Never*!" He actually sounded quite angry. "I told you I'd go up when we need to. You break your hip and what happens? No one would know."

"That's my business."

"Food for the crows, Dad. Hitchcock. Remember? Think about it. Never again. Promise me that. I don't want to worry about you going up there. It's a death-trap."

"The dish. It's gone."

"Dad, it hasn't gone. Unless it's fallen off. Promise me that."

"It wasn't there."

"You can't see it. It's on the right hand chimney, the other side. You have to climb up round the chimney stack – and you are not, repeat *NOT*, to do that! Don't go up there again. I'll put a lock on the door this weekend. You're not to be trusted any more. I can't *trust* you any more."

"The drill holes are still there. Left hand chimney. That's where it was fitted. I saw the holes. But the cabling and dish have gone. You took them."

"Dad . . ." A laugh. Another weary pause, and then a far wearier, or perhaps sadder tone. "They moved it when they set it up. First they put it in the easiest place possible but reception was no good so they had to move it. To the other chimney stack, on the outside. Can't you remember any of this?"

I didn't answer. I didn't remember.

"When they installed it. Three years ago, or whenever it was. They came back after you told me it wasn't working properly and they moved it for you. You said it was only working on and off. Intermittent signal, you said. Kept breaking up, you said."

I could remember no such thing, but did not say so. He sounded too reasonable and patient for it to be untrue. Patient with me and my failing memory, and my endless suspicions.

"Then why doesn't it work now?"

"I haven't the foggiest idea. Try switching it off and on. Check the cables. Check mice haven't eaten through them. Perhaps Mason has come back from that farm you gave him to and ripped the cabling to shreds because he's so mad at you – but don't go up to the roof again! Do you hear? Promise me that now. Do you promise? . . . I don't want to worry about this. I've enough on my plate. My dish."

"I'll try switching it on and off."

"Do you promise? Not to go up there?"

"Yes."

"Good. I have to sort out Joe's supper. See you at the weekend. I'm coming to see what's up with you."

Looking for some petty triumph, I put the phone down before he did.

I did what he said. The ethernet lead into the computer had come adrift, or had not been inserted properly. Quite impossible not to do it right if you have half a mind on what you're doing, and I'm always very particular about that when I wheel the thing into the study.

But once I'd fired up the internet there was no longer room for doubt. Same result. The site had gone. Nowhere to be found. I went into the Favourites and History pages. Nothing. Erased. Both records. When I first started using the internet I had a notebook where I wrote down all the addresses, copying them off the top of the screen with a pencil so that I could rub out mistakes, because some addresses were so long and difficult. Alex laughed at me, but how I wish I'd kept at it, that old system, like a pilot's log, showing where I'd been and for how long. With nothing in the Favourites or History pages, and with no invitation card any more, and not even the envelope in which it came, I had a pretty good idea what was going to happen next.

There was still Natalie, though. Kind, friendly, flirtatious, church-visiting, flower-toting, organ-playing Natalie. I would go there, see her. Make sure of her before the weekend and the next round of ploys and ruses.

But first I had to feel all of her blasted towels! They were in outsize Jarrold's bags on a work surface in the kitchen. She unfolded them on top of their bags. I could hardly contain my impatience, which it seemed she wanted to tease. Yes yes, such lovely damn towels! Oh, you've no idea the price, she said, but worth every penny for something so soft to the touch! She kept holding them to her face and smiling, for goodness' sake, as if posing for a detergent ad. Such lovely pastel shades! She told me to feel and stroke them. Go on, go on! But I didn't want to see my speckled hand caress her lovely new towels. They were towels for young bodies, for young lovers, drying their own and each other's bodies, or they were towels for young mothers and babies. Everything is for the bloody young, can't you see that, old woman? You shouldn't have bought them, I wanted to tell her. You should have bought something thin, white, cheap and disposable, such as you'd find in a hospice, to suit your age, our age.

I needed to get on. To establish what had happened, before they descended on the weekend. Or just Alex – it could well be one of his solitary visits this time, because for her that would make a good stratagem. Let me set about cursing and accusing the innocent, compounding all my other misdeeds. I left the towels, without by-your-leave, and led the way into her living room, because out the corner of my eye I'd spotted a change. Already. The tight squadron of miniature paintings had gone. "I'm a miniaturist, don't you know!" Not any more, it seemed. In place of the seasonal masterpieces was a single, very large, very oily and very gauche canvas; a seriously awkward and self-conscious work, something that looked as if it had been hung in a rush to cover a stain in her immaculate and tasteful living room. It was a painting of the ford, viewed from the glebe field, including the violently red post-office box, which stuck out from the cow parsley looking rather lopsided, sore-thumbish, bloody-minded. The day she'd painted this bucolic treasure was a good deal brighter than our usual Norfolk weather. Sunny East Anglia, indeed. And the colours were all so new and fresh. Cow parsley in clots of starchy white. I was sure I could smell the paint it was so new.

"Well? Do you like it?"

She laughed to let me know it was not a serious question. She stood close behind me now. "I know one should never ask, but . . ."

"Very striking. I like it very much," I told her. "You're very talented."

"Oh, rubbish!" She snorted in contempt. "I learnt to paint by numbers, Antony!" She was so boldly dismissive, I felt she was not only exposing my ignorant manners but my ignorance about art as well. "I enjoy it, that's all. Gets rid of some of the creative juices. And I had to catch the ford before it goes."

"Goes? Where's it going?"

"Lord, don't you know?" She sounded quite astonished. "They're going to put a humpback bridge there, dear!"

Humpback. Quasimodo. At the dinner table. At the soirée.

I said nothing. I blinked. This was genuinely disturbing.

Lord, don't you know?

Ignoramus. The world changing so fast all around, cranking me into a spin, a nosedive.

"Do keep up, Antony!" She was so familiar with me here, in her living room, on her territory, bossing me about in this good-humoured way, and laughing at me and telling me off. Of course, there was something pleasant and kind in all that too, because underneath the teasing she seemed to give a damn, one way or another. "There have been endless meetings about it, dear," she continued. "Parish Council. Local Council. We were so surprised you weren't there. Everyone asked after you. We assumed you knew best, somehow, or just didn't care any more." She nodded at the canvas. "It'll change your view. Not much, perhaps, but it will change it. It's more than just the view, though, isn't it? It's the nature of it." Her tone became more serious. "A ford is such a beautiful thing, don't you think? The sound of it. The way it changes with the seasons. Such a reminder of things past. It'll be more noticeable from the glebe field, coming down from the church. And it'll change the view of the rectory from the road down there, because the ford makes such a pretty foreground."

"It does," I said. I felt helpless after her explanation. *Gone: The Ford.* Another for my private collection. Helpless. Hopeless. "It does."

She paused and looked at me, concerned. "Do you want to sit down? Has it all been a bit of a shock?" She laughed again, but mildly, without mockery now, concerned. I knew I could have sat down, and I knew she'd have brought me some tea or brandy or something. But I didn't want that. I dismissed her concern.

"No, no. You're right, though. It is a shock. It'll be horrible if they're building down there. Diggers and so forth."

"That's the least of it." I seemed to have missed the point again. "Three weeks, they reckon. They'll start December, before it gets too frosty or there's any flooding from snow and thaws."

I looked back at her painting.

"What happened to all your miniatures?" This is what I really wanted, nay, needed, to know, for her sake, for my sake.

She stared back at the canvas too, frowning critically at it now, as if, in my company, she saw it through fresh eyes. For a moment I thought she wasn't going to answer, and that would have been very difficult because I had no way of returning to the question without it seeming forced. But she did answer, after some reflection.

"Got fed up with them, dear." She looked at me and smiled. "One decided one wasn't a miniaturist, after all!" I sensed any further talk about her painting was going to be too uncomfortable. She'd been modest enough about it already.

"Cup of tea? Something stronger? Not too early, is it?"

I shook my head. "That's very kind, but I only dropped by about the bridge business."

"Antony!" She all but scowled in perplexity. "Wacky, or what? You said you knew nothing about it. Just a minute ago." She lowered her head discreetly. "Know what that's a sign of, don't you?"

I looked sharply at her.

"No no no." I looked down at the carpet to concentrate. "I meant bridge with Lord and Lady Steggles."

"Oh!" She laughed. "I'm sorry." Suddenly she was grave. "Look – you're not pulling out, are you? Don't tell me that. Can't bear that kind of thing. Won't have it. Very bad taste."

"But Natalie – "

"Twenty-eighth. Which reminds me. Why didn't I see you at Guy Fawkes, Winterton's Farm?" She splayed the *Fawkes* in her upper class way, and held her chin up. Her manner had actually turned quite brusque, quite cold and crisp and accusatory, reminding me of her sudden chilliness in the church after her organ recital. And with that another memory crowded in. The image of the sun in the eastern stained glass window, and the cloud passing and the sharp colour dying.

She stood stiffly, chin still raised, as if preparing herself for some momentous treachery on my part, with which she would not up put – all very stalwart and Churchillian. Attack is the best defence, and all that.

"But you remember, Natalie. I told you about my trip."

She put her head on one side. Her soft brows

furrowed in the middle, mildly curious. I saw for the first time the powder in those soft brows. It made her seem so vulnerable suddenly.

"Antony," she said very calmly, rather patronizingly. "What are you talking about?"

"The flypast."

"Fly past? Fly past what? Fly-sticky? Could do with some in the kitchen."

Oh, no. No no no.

Not you as well, after all. Not you as well.

Please, not you as well. Kind, friendly, flirtatious, church-visiting, aisle-marching, flower-toting, organ-playing, ford-painting Natalie.

I stayed calm. "You remember," I told her firmly. "You invited me to tea to talk about the plans for the bridge soirées. We were to be partners against the ghastly Steggles."

"No." She shook her head resolutely on this point. "Not so. You're partnering Mrs Steggles."

"Well, never mind that," I said with some relief: at least we were talking about the same conversation. "I explained to you that I'd been invited to Saudi Arabia by the Crown Prince – "

"The Crown Prince!"

"His excellency, Sheikh - "

"*What?*" It was too forceful an interjection to ride over, this time. "What Sheikh? Sheikh what? What on earth are you talking about, Antony? If this is some rigmarole to get out of our bridge arrangement, you can just forget it! You're coming and that's that. It's all arranged. You're not letting me down now. I don't put up with that kind of thing. Not me. Never have done. Won't have it. Pit of bad manners, poor taste, breeding, all the rest of it, in my view."

I proceeded breathlessly, and the dreadful nodding

had started too. The ancien régime could not take yet another revolution against sense and memory. However, my voice stayed under control, quite calm and matter of fact. "I told you I was going to Saudi Arabia, Natalie," I explained again, "as a guest of BAE systems, British Aerospace Electronics Systems, that is, for the memorial Battle of Britain flypast. The fifty-ninth anniversary. In November. And you were thrilled for me when I told you about it. You congratulated me. You didn't know, until that conversation, that I was one of The Few."

She burst out laughing.

"One of the Phew!" she mocked in cockney. Eliza Doolittle. Pygmalion. At this, my mind raced. Audrey Hepburn. Rex Harrison. Marni Nixon dubbing Hepburn. The posturing, the accent, the class, the education, all of it. Once my favourite, when I was still a fool for sentimental things. *"Oim gettin' married in the mornin'!"* Walking me up the aisle. Puffing up the organ. Keep your gases inside you, for God's sake. The lovely picture of Hepburn as flower-girl on the cover, with yellow flowers, in a wicker basket. *"Ding-dong the bells are gonna choime!/Pull out the stopper! Let's have a whopper! . . ."* Am I not entitled to some pleasure and excitement, now and then, as a married woman?

Natalie was shaking her moonish head at me in solemn reproof. She mimicked Eliza's cockney - "So who's puttin' on airs and comin' on all hoity-toity!"

I didn't respond and she smiled again. I stared at her, holding my own, my poise and equanimity, and she replied by fixing her expression, very deliberately, a touch to one side, as if posing like an actress for a studio shot, wearing this puzzled, tolerant, yet still warm and friendly smile.

"Antony, I don't know about your Sheikh, if he ever existed beyond The Empty Quarter of your addled old brain, but someone needs to give you a good shake coz you're not making a great deal of – "

I smashed her across the face.

With my right hand, flat across her moon-face and thick smile. It was a swipe to wipe away her deceit, all the decks of it she'd stacked up in her mind, way into the future – every finesse, trump and dirty little trick of it. Oh, the way she'd clapped her hands in triumph, and laughed with delight, eyes tearing up, when I'd told her about the invitation. She'd called me round so soon, too soon, the very day, before I'd had time to think, because she couldn't wait to see the effect, and her absolute delight to see what a gull I was, how I'd swallowed it hook, line and sinker. Then at her door, on my way out - "Here. Have some eggs, Squadron Leader." Have some eggs, Antony. Every one of them rotten, specially selected from Steggles' pale of water - *'Steggles! Look here, I need some rotten eggs. I want to create a proper stink!'* Every one a portent, a maddening message. Like Benson's apples. Like Aaron. *Fuck off!*

*Get out! Get out! Get out! Get out of the way! Get out of everyone's way!*

That invitation. Ha. How I'd rushed to the greenhouse and scrambled around in there to find the rusty micrometer to measure it. The respect, indeed. 3/16ths deep.

My life, my life, my life.

3/16ths deep. 1/16th left.

When I hit her all I felt was the fat of her face, the old, powdered fat of her cheek, nothing hard at all, and her head jolted to the left and was covered in a fan of hair that flipped around with the impact, so for a moment her face, her eyes, were all totally obscured, and her ear protruded obscenely from between strands of hair, reminding me for a second, with some revulsion, of my earlier lust for her.

As I made for the door she called after me –

"You're barking mad! Don't you ever, *ever* come back!"

Though I knew it was futile, at home in the kitchen I could not resist another look through those nests of negligence, the stacks of notes and bills and circulars that I leave on the dresser, shelves, any horizontal surface. It was a struggle to keep focused on what I was looking for – the card, the envelope – yet there was a terrible urgency about this search now. Card, or envelope. Envelope or card. Either would do, neither could I find. Then, in a smaller heap that included the note from Alex, at the far end of the dresser, next to the toaster that no longer works, for which I was hoping a replacement would be forthcoming last Christmas – no such bloody luck! – among these papers was a torn off sheet of A4 on which was printed, in the same italics as my very own dot-matrix printer, a short verse, or quatrain, I believe. As contrived as the note about the Madeira cake they'd never eaten and left in the fridge, or Rachael's line to Alex about being so 'dreadfully upset'. They knew I'd search high and low and stumble on this:

*The Beloved . . .*
*Good God, but he's more loathsome than I thought!*
*His wizened heart can n'er be caught nor bought!*
*Let him fiddle on the roof till he finds his way!*
*Born under a wandering star, <u>some may say</u>!*

I was still taking this in, re-reading it for the umpteenth time, wholly unamused, when out the corner of my eye I spied the navy blue corner of my chequebook poking from the nest of papers, flyers, village 'newsletters' and receipts. Something made me frightened to even touch it. Some omen took hold. But once action is reduced to a question of courage, I can deal with it well enough. I took the book by the corner and pulled, as if pulling at the wing of a dead bird, or the tail of a dead rat. Across the cover of the chequebook, in crude red felt tip, but recognizably my own hand, was the message, with ellipsis – *I love you, Natalie . . .*

I took the remaining eggs across the paddock, lobbed them one by one into the stream, and watched them bob to the surface, every rotten one, and float down to the bridge.

"Here. Have some eggs, Squadron Leader."

But the sequence baffled me, remained random and meaningless as the pattern of eggs in the water. When should I have discovered her verse, or verses, or notes? Was there another tucked into my recliner? Beneath my pillow in the bathroom? Under the phone in the freezing cupboard? Hand written love notes, perhaps, from me, that I was supposed to have given her. Written evidence that I'd lost it completely. What games, what larks! But when? Back at the weekend? *When?* What was the sequence? After they'd gone? Then, verse in hand to incriminate myself, I was meant to storm down to Natalie, through the brimming ford, maybe stall in the ford and walk soaking in my tracksuit and Hush Puppies down to Long Cottage to demand her explanation, whereupon she would look bemused and bewildered, just as she had this afternoon, and demand of me *why* I was doing this to her, dressed like that, in my wacky outfit, why I was pursuing her in this way, stalking her like a horrible, wizen-hearted, dirty old man, blundering in with these barking mad accusations, making up these crazy notes and stories. Cranky, loopy, wacky, love-sick, paranoid, or what? Who did I think I was? That is what was meant to have happened, or something very like it. Instead, I'd gone down there on an entirely different pretext, but to exactly the same effect. Either way, I'd been expected, I'd arrived, and delivered. I took the note from my pocket and reread it by the stream. There was a slyness in all this that pertained to the women alone. Even Laura was there, for only she could have told Rachael about that closing phrase, which had been underlined by hand, in blue biro, not by the printer. I destroyed very other scrap of evidence years ago. And only the women had the wit to inflect those lines with a parody of my musical lyricists of yesteryear, reminding me of my shameful, peasantish, ignoramus tastes. With a twist and stretch this could have been some scene-filling verse from a walk-on actor on the set of *Paint Your Wagon, The Music Man, Oklahoma, Fiddler on the Roof* or *The Desert Song*, but never, of course, *My Fair Lady.*

Thursday, it must have been, when I saw her again, because it followed a pool and sauna day, and it certainly wasn't Tuesday. I was on my way into town to do some shopping when I noticed the driver of the oncoming car wildly shaking her fist at me. The car was Natalie's silver Lexus. She was all but unrecognisable. She wore an ugly surgical collar. My swipe had caused some whiplash, it seemed. Her face was puffy and discoloured on the left hand side and her eye was black. There must have been rather more force in my hand than I'd imagined. But most distinct, as our cars passed, was the anger and hatred blazing in her right eye; the left being too puffy and dark, and too static, somehow, to express much feeling. Quite unmistakable, the emotion there. I'd temporarily disfigured her, and that had aroused some passion, no doubt about it.

Anxious but unmoved, I kept to a steady 40 m.p.h. all the way into town.

My anxiety was twofold. Firstly, I had not foreseen at all that she would have to see a doctor about that slap in the face. I didn't think I'd hit her that hard, not to give her whiplash, anyway. Could she have exaggerated this to the doctor? Faked the need for that horrible collar? Secondly, which was my deeper worry – I had done that without premeditation or restraint. I had, literally, lashed out. Now, when someone lashes out we all know that someone has lost control. Rather more troubling for a military man.

Parking the Allegro, I began to anticipate the repercussions. What had she told the doctor? And if she had said she had been the victim of a vicious and unprovoked assault, what would the doctor do? Given the sluggishness of our tweedy GPs, there might be no consequence at all, but if she'd said that she intended to press charges against me, that her next stop was the police station or a solicitor's office, then no matter how wearisome or exaggerated our good doctor might find her complaint, she or he would be obliged to make a proper report – perhaps shoving her off to an orthopaedic specialist to mitigate responsibility – but a clear and factual diagnosis and prognosis would be the order of the day, no doubt about that.

Such anxiety made for a gloomy shopping trip – exchanged no pleasantry with Benson at all – and on my return to the rectory, it was almost with relief that I saw things had come to a head already. Two cars were parked in the turning space. The first, which had completed its circle and faced back down the drive, was one of those stately, bulbous Rovers, invariably some shade of burgundy, and distinctive enough in town as the property of Dr Lyvich, or Loveitch. He's a figure of ridicule and notoriety. Girls always have to strip for his examination, no matter what their age or complaint. His Rover's polished radiator grille carried on one side steely badges for the RAC and AA, and on the other, several green and silver memberships for Golf clubs, country clubs or whatever. An imposing vehicle, indeed. The second car belonged to my only begotten son: his puny Micra had not completed its circle and stood panicked and shamefaced, staring across the paddock.

Alex and the good doctor were in my kitchen. I only lock the house at night.

That strange combination of dread and relief, as if it were time at last for some momentous showdown, invoked the warrior in me. Natalie's injuries were a result of my own: I was the victim here. I was also desperately keen to find out more, and with only Alex on guard, without Rachael spinning her fanciful yarn like a fairy-tale damsel, something might come to light. Why should I let these people push me around, after all? The last time I had kowtowed to doctors and professionals the results had been pretty disastrous. I would remind Alex of that during the scrap.

Starting out with a cheery, "Good morrow, gentlemen!", quite uncharacteristically hail-fellow-well-met, and taking on each pair of eyes in turn, as I might have done had they been in enemy cockpits fifty-nine years ago, I strafed them with questions – "To what do I owe the pleasure? Alex, have you offered Doctor Lyvich a cup of tea? Do either of you want the heater on? Is it on already?

Can you check, Alex?" – all of these, while I went about unloading my humble groceries and lending myself an air of such insouciance, because my guests had to keep moving out the way to allow me to reach this cupboard or that, then the fridge, and across again to tuck a bottle of bleach under the sink, and lastly to the refectory table to put my apples in a bowl, my Golden Delicious, inspecting each and every one from Benson's brown paper bag as I did so. Not a single bruise.

To finish, confident already of victory, I blew up Benson's bag and popped it with a bang, as I used to do when Alex was a child. And I laughed, just as he did back then.

Lyvich, tall and stooping, his self-importance all trussed up in a crisp white shirt, red bow tie and three piece flannel suit, kept his eyes on Alex while Alex explained why they were here. Throughout the first half of the visit Lyvich stood like this, with his hands behind his back, in the manner of some admonishing headmaster of yesteryear, the kind of figure who might be caricatured twixt the pages of a Dickens novel – how indebted we remain to that era for our pretences, posturing and snobbery, even now - while Alex, rather gingerly, picked his way through the thickets of my neighbour's complaint.

"Gentlemen," I said, looking from one to the other while rubbing an apple to a shine on my tracksuit, as if preparing to bowl a googly, "I am quite as shocked and disturbed by this news as you are." I took a bite from the apple, chewed, swallowed, and gave my side of the story: "Perfectly true I went over there and we quarrelled. Perfectly true. She thought I had reneged on a social engagement she'd organized – which emphatically I had not – and she was rather upset about that, about the principle involved, she said, quite unreasonably upset, but that is all. There was nothing physical about our little altercation." With a full-dentured smile to Lyvich, I added: "I'm rather too old for fisticuffs and all of that, you see."

"Doctor Lyvich examined Mrs Stein," Alex resumed sententiously, "and he's of the opinion that her injury is compatible with a blow to the face, as if she had been struck very forcefully with the flat of the hand."

"Well, there's nothing I can say that will help you with any of that, I'm afraid," I replied. "I'm as clueless as you are. Did she really say I did this to her? I can't believe that. I thought we got on rather well."

"Yes."

The first word from the good doctor, and very resonant too. I faced him and smiled.

"Well, that's really rather mischievous, and I can't imagine why she's going about telling such tales. Unless she's still upset about the social engagement. But I find that difficult to imagine too."

"What was this social engagement?" Alex asked.

"None of your business," I replied tartly, still looking and smiling at Lyvich.

"Dad."

I looked back at Alex then. His look of seriousness, even sadness, made him older. I'm not good at birthdays but he must have tipped forty now. This morning he looked, in the full daylight of the dirty window, standing to the side of the refectory table with one hand supporting him as if he were sick, more like a man in his mid-fifties. His forelock, that dry cone of hair with which he will not part, was sandy in the light and flecked with grey. In the study he is always in the shade. Here, in the kitchen, his tired eyes were baggy with humanity and self-doubt.

"Dad. This is very serious. Mrs Stein is accusing you of assault."

"Well," I told Alex, blinking slowly, patiently, as Sylvia used to do, "quite apart from the spuriousness of her accusation, against which I might consider a counter-suit for slander or defamation of character – and you two are now my witnesses to that, don't forget – her accusation would never come to court, because it's simply her word against mine."

"Which is why I'm here, Mr Rose," said Lyvich, with some gravitas. Funny how only people further up the social scale drop my rank.

"But," I said, levelling my pilot's eyes at him, getting him in my sights. "You're not a lawyer as well as a doctor, are you?"

"Indeed not." Lyvich sighed. "But as you are both patients on our list I am obliged to look into – "

"Whether or not I'm telling the truth? Under Hippocratic oath?"

"No. If there's a possibility – "

"I'm demented? Is that it?"

"If you're in complete control."

"And what about her? Have you looked into the possibility of whether or not she is in complete control? She's always struck me as a bit of a cracked egg, you know. A bit of a wacky old thing. Lift doesn't quite get to the top floor. You know?"

"There is no reason as yet – "

"And you have no reason as yet to suspect my sanity either." I interrupted firmly. I was enjoying my interruptions, staying ahead of the pompous old fool, but I could feel the nodding coming on and that made me want to finish the interview as quickly as I could.

"Get out of my house," I told Lyvich. "You are a disgrace to your profession."

"Dad!"

I rounded on Alex now. "Don't you 'Dad' me, Alex. Your coming in here – aiding and abetting this, since we like our legalese today – shows the very worst of your filial negligence and ingratitude. You get out too. The pair of you. Get out and leave me alone."

"Dad, it's not as simple as that, and you're not doing yourself any favours here. This is just the kind of thing that'll land you in even more trouble."

"Except I am not in any trouble."

"Not yet," agreed Lyvich calmly. "You are quite right. But there could be trouble and none of us wants that. You mistake what's going on here, Mr Rose. I can go away now, if you want, but that won't be the end of it. If you just let me do what I came here to do, there may well be an end to it right here and now. This morning. In fact, I'm all but certain there would be, having listened to what you have said so far."

Alex slid Lyvich a glance that went unreturned.

"So what on earth is it that you have come here to do?"

The apple was still in my hand, with its single, dentured bite removed. I could not bite it again, that would be going too far, so I set it aside on the table.

"I want to give you a very straightforward test," Lyvich replied, his best bedside manner returning, "which I am perfectly confident, having spoken with you face to face this morning, you will pass with flying colours." At which there was another unanswered, sidelong glance from Alex. "There is no clinical procedure, no examination is necessary. I'll be completely open with you."

"I should jolly well hope so," I said, for good measure.

"The questions establish whether or not you have any of the symptoms of dementia. Nothing more than that. I'm more than confident your answers will defeat that idea completely. That is all."

"Fair enough." Then I did take up the apple and have another bite. "Fire away. Let's have your questions," I said with my mouth full, "and let's get this bloody nonsense over with."

"You've no objection to your son being present?"

"Every objection, but let him remain."

"Very well. No witness is necessary but it can do no harm. I should first advise that both your neighbour and your son have brought to my attention some features of your recent behaviour that have troubled them, and which do suggest some of these symptoms."

I looked stonily at Alex, then back at Lyvich, but said nothing to either.

The paranoid, as I have learned, and to such cost, is the last one in possession of all the facts. What had he told old Loveitch? And, more to the point, what had his lovely wife said, or told him to say, or corroborated.

Ye Gods, indeed.

Now it became clear why Loveitch had his hands behind his back. He produced a small black clipboard, from which he unclipped a ballpoint pen.

"Please don't be embarrassed by the simplicity of some of these questions. They are part of a formula."

"Oh, just get on with it and go away."

"Very well. What is the day and the date, Mr Rose?"

"Friday twenty-sixth November nineteen ninety-nine." I glanced again at my son. "Twenty-one shopping days till Christmas."

"What newspapers are delivered here?"

"Just The Times. I complete the crossword regularly, if not daily."

"What is the name of your grandson?"

"Joseph."

"When is his birthday?"

"No idea. Sometime in the spring, I think."

"Your son's birthday?"

"Unknown. Best forgotten."

"Your own birthday?"

"Oh, for goodness' sake. January twentieth, nineteen twenty-one. Can we leave birthdays now?"

Lyvich read from the questionnaire. "'Does the individual become easily and unexpectedly irritable, agitated or suspicious, or has he started doing things or imagining things – seeing, hearing or believing things – that are out of the ordinary or unreal?' Both your son and Mrs Stein have answered this in the affirmative."

"Well, they would, wouldn't they? Certainly I'm irritable, agitated and suspicious. Who wouldn't be, when subjected to this kind of thing?"

"Actually, that's not the part of the question I wish to dwell on."

At that I felt I'd jumped the gun, put him in control; certainly his manner became more authoritative. Perhaps he wasn't such a fool.

"I'm told you've recently been up on your roof, Mr Rose. Despite your son's very serious and reasonable concerns about your going up there. It can't be very safe, can it, for someone your age?"

I shook my head. Oh. Was that all?

"That's easily explained."

"Very well," Lyvich replied, and I saw that it was not his main idea at all. I knew exactly what was coming next – my pilot's infallible sixth sense – and they were ahead, true, but only momentarily, because I also knew exactly how to deal with what was coming, head-on. I'd already worked out how to turn their own invention against them.

"There is also this. Three persons – that is, your son, your daughter-in-law and Mrs Stein, all tell me that you have talked recently about going abroad. Your daughter-in-law and Mrs Stein say you have told them, on separate occasions, more than once, that you have been invited to a commemorative event in the Middle East. They say you told them most emphatically that you would be flying out to attend said event, that you had a first class ticket, and all expenses were paid. But your passport expired some decades ago."

I frowned at the good doctor, then looked at Alex, utterly perplexed. Who was Lord of am-dram now?

"*What?*" I shook my head again, in utter disbelief. "*What?*" I was so pleased to use Natalie's and Rachael's favourite repetitions *agin* them. "I don't know what you're *talking* about! I've never said any such thing, heard of any such thing. What on earth is this nonsense? Where is this invitation? Let me see it."

"It's not quite as Doctor Lyvich said, Dad, but – "

Loveitch interrupted, reading from his clipboard: "Mrs Stein said you told her that you had a personal invitation from the Crown Prince of Saudi Arabia, and when she said she didn't believe you, or words to that effect, you struck her across the face."

I looked confounded, bewildered.

"That would be barmy indeed, and I could quite understand her point of view, if it were true, but I have no idea what any of them is talking about. This is quite ridiculous. They're making it all up. It's most bizarre, doctor. Where is this invitation? Let's see it. Let's see what they're talking about. The evidence. The ocular proof."

"Now, why would they do that? Make it all up?"

"Aha!" I wagged a finger at Lyvich. "Not so fast. I can see where you're heading. It's a trap. No matter what I say now, what explanation I give for why they're making all this up, I have paranoid delusions. Just by saying – It's a trap – I fall foul of that, don't I?"

"Not necessarily."

"Yes, necessarily, because you already believe their fantastical stories. Commemorative events in the Middle East, indeed! For goodness' sake! What if *they* are making it all up, and not me? What if *they* invented such an event? Such a story? Ever thought of that?"

"But why would they do that, Mr Rose?"

This mock-respectful use of my name brought out a reciprocal contempt in me.

"Dear oh dear, doctor. Isn't it obvious? Does it really demand such perspicacity, from a medical man?"

Lyvich lowered his head, and I knew I should not have answered him, certainly not like that. I should have bitten my tongue. There was no answer I could give that wouldn't have led to the same place. He believed them. That was the long and short of it. I was nearly seventy-nine years old. To the good doctor, there lay the essential medical evidence.

"Let's leave that," he said, suddenly conciliatory, all scientific fair-mindedness. "Your daughter-in-law has told me that on two occasions in the last few months, you have behaved in an aggressively sexual way towards her."

"Excuse me!" I was beginning to enjoy my feigned

outrage. I hoped Alex appreciated it too. "I'm nearly seventy-nine years old, Doctor Lyvich!"

"Most recently, you tried to – "

"I'm not listening to this!" I declared, standing erect, bracing myself on the table edge. "I don't want to hear any more of this. I don't know what she's talking about but it's just disgusting and ridiculous and very low to make accusations of that kind, against someone my age." I turned on Alex. "I never want to see you or your wretched wife and son in my house again, Alex. Do you hear me?" We were past the point of no return. Long past. "And never forget that it is my house, to all legal intents and purposes, until I choose to leave it, or bloody well die in it." I wagged a finger at him too. "Never forget that." I repeated. Then I looked back to Lyvich. "You can go now. Both of you. This interview is over. You're on my property and you've outstayed your welcome. Now *go*!"

Alex sighed. "Dad – "

"Don't you 'Dad' me, I tell you! Your behaviour is beneath my contempt. You and your ghastly wife. You are no son of mine. I disown you!"

Saying so, I pushed myself off the refectory table and moved towards the kitchen door to the hallway, to no-man's-land. I pulled the door open on its spring, but then stopped, waiting for them to depart through the porch.

"Well?"

There was a gloomy silence.

"Off you go, the pair of you!" I treated them as children. "See yourselves out."

Lyvich nodded at Alex and they left in single file. I actually waited at the kitchen door, letting out the precious Belling heat, and kept waiting there, listening for the Rover to start up. There was a delay. They were having a confab out there on the drive. But then the motor came to life and I heard the heavy old car crunch the gravel, then saw it slip into view and glide down the drive, its burgundy bulk and polished windows caught by a break of sunshine through the trees, followed by Alex's sad little Micra. I watched the convoy go down the drive, then indicate right and pull out onto the lane.

Then I returned to my study, my papers, my playing cards, my radio, my television, and my solitude, which I now felt, with some sense of inevitability and relief, was at last complete.

Unless it's raining, I always park the Allegro at the very top of the multi-storey, so that I can walk to the perimeter wall and stare down awestruck over Norwich below. Ah, the madding crowd! Up here, one's halfway to heaven already. It's market day. Christmas shopping day. The tents and makeshift shacks of yesteryear, which we used to walk among on our monthly trips to town, coats buttoned up to the throat, are now the stuff of postcards you can buy in polythene slips, clothes-pegged to union-jack ribbons, strung between the very stalls where they once stood. Where we once stood. Today everything is permanent, anodised aluminium, secured to the granite setts and rented from the council. Downmarket they sell sweets, burgers, and shoddy tools; upmarket it's CDs, jewellery, computer bits, and more miscellanea from Korea, Japan and China. A year from the millennium and the only thing anyone actually makes down there is a picture frame, from a kit, to be filled with your gypsy portrait for £25, no less.

There's the monumental church, useless, forlorn, shoulders slumped, and the whitewashed, Elizabethan lanes. Down those lanes, past the delicatessen and a shop selling electric guitars, I used to have my hair cut every fortnight at Ridley & Livock, once the *Gentlemen's Hairdressers* but now *The Coffee Rooms*. When coming to town on my own I used to dress up in casual tweeds – the country squire. After the haircut I'd drift around, window shopping, perhaps try to find a tool or a special varnish or paint, choose my red and gold wallpaper from the rolls in Sandersons . . . Then the drive home in the Hillman to show Laura what I'd bought, and to talk about it, a shiny tool on the refectory table, some swatches from Sandersons, and to make more plans, and to assume such drives and skives would go on to the end of bloody time.

I need to bring him back, that gentleman in tweeds with his airs and graces and his projects reaching way into the future. Now that I'm actually in it, his future, taking the concrete stairs down from the multi-storey rather than using the grubby lift – keeping fit again, staying strong – taking the stairs that reek of fags and urine, now that I'm in his future I feel he's rather let me down, that middle-aged chap in tweeds. I feel he's got some questions to answer. I am not here to buy anything any more. Just here to walk, stare, go back home.

As December bites I'm spending longer in the sauna, dallying there, shilly-shallying, charging up the body heat like a reptile, like Aaron. I outlasted him on Monday, and Mark on Wednesday. Of course they don't like it but in a sense I purify the place for them, de-sexualize it: with me in there the sauna is no longer haven for their steamy fantasies. Silence is the rule now: not a word, not even a good morning, to either of them, from either of them. When time's up, and duty calls, each slips away sulkily to Mumsy's cooked breakfast.

Outside the sauna I towel down under the fierce white tiles and dress completely – Crombie over tracksuit – before taking leave of Male Changing; such a crassitude, that sign.

Still stop at the receptionist's booth and stand there with my stub of orange towel under my arm and my dentured smile, but I no longer rap my car keys. Life has moved on here.

She has lost her virginity, and this depresses me beyond measure.

There are various tell-tale signs: an 'I'm-a-woman-now' confidence, and what I can only describe as the beginnings of slovenliness, as if she is no longer quite so worried about how she presents herself to the world. Sometimes she has no make-up, and looks the better for it, in my view. More often than not she wears her hair up so she doesn't have to fuss with it all day. (The nape of her neck is covered in soft dark hair.) She didn't lose her virginity to Aaron or Mark, despite Aaron's renown as "virgin-buster". I'm quite certain of that. Neither of them hang around the booth drooling any more. With her new confidence she's given both the cold shoulder. She might even have said something to the supervisor, the Welsh termagant with cropped hair, always in her shell suit, same as me in my tracksuit. Our Mediterranean lovely might have told her the lifeguards had been "harassing" her. That would do it – that word. Harassment. Shell suit would have put them in their place firmly enough, no doubt, and would have loved it too.

But why should this lower the spirit, the receptionist's coming of age, as it were? It's not just other lives changing while mine stays one-tracked, terminus in view. Nor is it any sense of exclusion, a reminder that I don't belong any more to the world in that way. It could be that, but it isn't. The entire future of the receptionist, even before this change, always filled me with sorrow. I tried to ignore it, her youth in a booth, tried to treat it like some pretty flower I walked past twice a week on my way to the car park. As she was before, virginal, sitting there reading her horoscopes and doing her wordsearches, she had become to me like some character in one of her own magazine stories, or agony aunt letters, and being so, remained complete and flat and two-dimensional, without background or address, without a home to go to – and, here is the point, without a regular boyfriend nagging her to have intercourse all the time, just because, among peers, he could only talk of the petting proscribed in the swimming pool diagrams. In the end he had his way, and the urgent mystery is no more. Before long, if not already, she and boyfriend will uninhibitedly cup each other's genitals, fondle, lick and suck each other's genitals, and he her arse (but never vice versa; such is the difference in hormonal charges) and all of that will be part of her life for several years, with this mate and others – different hands, different cocks – until by accident or design she swells up with pregnancy, gives birth, and the woeful business starts all over again for some other poor creature. None of the intervening phases of being the loved or unloved infant, toddler, child, adolescent, adult, have the slightest interest or are in any sense enviable to me. The dark is in the red light of the sauna, in the aching white light of the changing room tiles, in the church font, the car park, in the silent grey sky before I insert the key and turn the ignition. Behind my right ear, my pulse beats the countdown to aneurysm, heart attack, stroke and death. Dark is in the hallway, inside the very cold itself. So I want to say to her – "Stroke, lick, suck, fuck, fornicate all you will - but DO NOT procreate. Don't fall for nature's tricks. Don't do it. Amen. You have no right. It leads nowhere. Only to this."

Part of her new maturity is of course an air of disillusionment. The gloss and froth of the magazine and make-up world has gone, leaving the stark realization that, yes, she has sex now right enough, but sex in a dead-end job, which means sex with mates who are virtually certain to have similar prospects, or worse, and therefore, long-term, life can only go downhill. Until she wins the Lottery, of course.

She has asked me to stop tapping on the glass with my car keys when I leave the building.

"Could you stop doing that? Please?"

That was on Monday, near enough through gritted teeth, and the lead weight of her "Please?" sank right to the bottom of the deep end. Quite uncalled for. It isn't my fault she's fed up with her lot, with all the fuss that was made about sex, which distracted her from her studies at school, and used to distract her from her job, from the unfolding misery of bills bills bills – we live, we earn, we die – and from the old sod who comes on Mondays and Wednesdays, every wanking Monday and every wanking Wednesday, who just won't do the decent thing and go away and die, and from those quirks of his that grind her nose in the dirt of her new realism: his tapping, his dentured smile, his damp stub of orange towel, his Crombie over his grubby tracksuit. It depresses her beyond measure too, that she has this obligation twice a week even to speak to him, this member of the walking dead, let alone smile at him, and that this is what she is paid so little for. Her time on earth, her youth and joy, has such a low premium it is worthless stuff. Tosh. Throwaway. Two a penny. Rubbish.

Once again, I tap the glass.

"Could you stop doing that, *please*? I told you *Monday*!"

"Sorry," I said, tapping my head with the knuckled ring and smiling apologetically – such a sweet old man. "Forgot. Getting on a bit!"

"You're scratching the glass, look."

Still smiling I added, "Senile."

"You're scratching the glass, I said."

"Demented. Hahaha."

I left her. I walked over to the automatic doors. They opened, and the freezing December air poured through, squeezing out the paltry heat I'd stored from the sauna, flushing away the clammy chlorinated heat of the pool building, paid for by the good burghers of the town who never come here, who book holidays in sunnier climes on the internet, without ever leaving their central heating, and take warm taxis long distance to the airport. I waited while behind me the hissing cold writhed about and squeezed and penetrated her cosy booth, her nest, her place in the world.

"Can you let the doors close, please?" she called out. And then, when I didn't respond. "Let the doors close! . . . Is something the matter there? *Let the doors close!*"

When I heard her opening her booth, I passed through the automatic doors and they shut behind me.

Again the bright Allegro lozenge is the only car in the car park, under the grey dead belly of the December sky. I need a radio in the car, so I don't have to face that silence when I close the door, and the dark in the fields ahead, and the sky above, and the pulse behind my ear, all the way back. But I bought the base model. No frills, no thrills, no bloody money.

I'd just returned from a morning drive to Norwich to see the Christmas lights, but they only put them on at dusk these days.

Locked out.

Good. Jolly good.

So. The endgame, at Yuletide.

Why not?

The porch door sticks hard in winter, and I'm a year older and weaker, but it just wouldn't move. Definitely locked.

I wheeled the dustbin round to stand on. The key was there, exactly where I'd left it this morning, where I leave it every morning, after unlocking front and back doors, on the frame of the window above the porch door, behind the glass. Unless I discovered a forced exit, someone had locked the house with a copy of the key, or, if nothing had been forced, someone was still in there, watching and waiting, having locked it again from inside.

Calmly – oh, so calmly! – I went around the great ruin, peering in at my own ground floor rooms, which looked so alien and bereft of my habitual world already. Laura's dusty dining table. Alex's dusty, worthless piano. I could discover no damage whatever. Front door locked, of course, though I opened it as usual before breakfast, and that door is more secure because there is no glass. All around the house no evidence of any latch left open. They must have checked all those, driven every latch home, to be certain I couldn't rattle a sash free.

No.

The house had been locked up as if no one lived there. As if it were for sale.

I went back to the car, started the engine for the sake of the heater, and tried to organize my thoughts. There has been nothing and no one for nearly three weeks, apart from a call from Alex that I swiftly aborted. But of all the manoeuvres thus far, locking up the house was actually the most aggressive, the most overt, blatant. The endgame. Not a shot across the bows, like the Simmonds' visit a while back, or the pillar-of-the-establishment visit of Dr Lyvich. No. An invasion. An expulsion.

Had they taken the key away, my mind would have swarmed with suspicion and self-doubt. I would have asked myself, in a panic – Had I mislaid the key? Had I left it deliberately in some out-of-the-way place or pocket? Oh no. The key had been left there to show me that someone had decided to lock me out. Not a mistake of any kind.

How predictable would my behaviour be now, was the question. Was I meant to fly into a rage and smash the window to get it? The windows are all plate glass, even above the door. I would do damage I was in no condition to repair. And breaking into my own home offered further evidence, clinching evidence, perhaps. Or did they think I might do something manic and rash? Set fire to the place?

In which case I must be taken away forthwith, as a danger to myself and to others' property.

The idea gained purchase that someone was actually watching the house, watching me, to see what would happen, as I sat perfectly still in the Allegro, engine running, smoke dribbling from the exhaust. With a sudden movement I opened the door, and, leaving it open in my haste, quickly stepped to the centre point of the turning circle, so that I could look up directly at the church tower. Nothing. No movement against the even, grey sky. My eyes followed the line of the butterfly roof of the rectory. No one. I turned sharply on my heel and looked to the belt of woodland across the stream. No glinting wing-mirror. No Datsun. No traffic at all. The long sound of the ford filtered through the caws of the crows. There had been rain in the night and the stream was filling up, the ford broadening its proud sweep.

Still no work on that bridge, Natalie. That humpback bridge.

The key would not be an easy thing to copy. A job for a Norwich locksmith rather than the local hardware store or ironmonger. Specialist work. Only one or two places would do it. Should I return to Norwich? I had plenty of fuel -

The speculation sank my spirits – and I had to stop that, the sinking of spirits – had to stay above that, or, I sensed, there could be a far worse subsidence. As I stood there, examining the three acres high and low, quadrant by quadrant, a memory bubbled up from my youth, when I lived in London studying for my wireless operator's licence. One of my landlords, a Jewish cab-driver in Stamford Hill, accidentally woke me up at 4 a.m. one morning, returning from a shift that should have finished at midnight. Something had gone wrong with the steering of his cab, he explained, so that he could only make right turns. He knew, he physically sensed through the vibrations of the steering column and the lurching movement of his cab, that if he turned to the left the cab would be immobilized. Some wishbone or ball-joint would shear and the vehicle would be wrecked in the middle of the road, on a corner. So he spent four hours finding his way back from the West End to Stamford Hill, taking only right turns. In the same way, I sensed physically that I had to keep taking right turns, to keep thinking, moving, reacting in that way, and that if I allowed my spirits to sink for just a moment I would be utterly immobilized. I swivelled on my heel to the right again and stared down the drive. Nothing. No movement or human sound anywhere. Just the concatenation of the cawing crows. I turned sharply through the last quadrant to come full circle and stared up at the church tower once more. Nothing. But there is room enough to duck behind its stubby castellations.

Back in the car I waited a further five minutes. I made myself time it by the digital clock in the dashboard. Plenty of fuel to run the engine for a few hours yet and keep warm until dark if need be. Dusk at three-thirtyish, quarter to four.

When the five minutes had elapsed, with a modest spurt of gravel, I drove round into the church car park by my greenhouse and stopped there, close to the steps that ascend to the graveyard.

Inside the church I made straight for the belfry.

Narrow metal wall-ladder to a first storey platform. I ascended cautiously, resting both feet on each rung before each step. The bell ropes pass through the same aperture at the top and I had to push them aside, but otherwise it was a slow, grim, determined, uneventful ascent, as if to the gallows. Much darker beyond the platform, of course. The only light came through the slits in the tower walls. From the platform, a spiral stairway led up to the roof of the tower, encircling the bell and clock mechanism. I had to stop on the platform to catch my breath and listen to my heart before the next exertion. I needed energy. I needed to eat and drink. I needed lunch. Anger and resentment that I should be put to such lengths drove me on to the spiral staircase, and I sustained a steady pace to halfway up, then stopped to catch my breath and listen again, and to stare and marvel at the massive gears and ratchets, the noise of which, combined with my own heavy breaths, drowned out the thickened pulse behind my ear and any other sound. It was impossible to listen for furtive movements above or below, so I carried on to the very top, where, in the corner, a transparent convex trapdoor – some recent refurbishment – led onto the roof itself. The lid was light, made of fibreglass, but only just movable because its hinges had already rusted. Once over halfway it flapped down easily enough with a dull thud. Bright grey poured in upon me, fell all around on the open, rusty clock mechanism and the dead bell below. I could hear nothing. No one was there. Nonetheless I took another couple of steps upward so that I could raise my head above the trapdoor and take in the emptiness of the roof space.

The Saxon or Norman battlements, that had always looked so proud and strong from below, were actually in advanced decay. Some were so worn at the base they looked as if they might topple down in the next storm and do mortal injury to some passing worshipper or brass-rubber. Another couple of steps and I could climb out without difficulty. The roof did not afford, as I had supposed, standing space behind the battlements. It was shallow, some three feet deep, and gently pitched from each side to an apex. At the base an internal gutter fed the rainwater to the gargoyles at each corner. But of course the gutter was blocked and the water ran out between the battlements, and over hundreds of years that had rotted their sturdy bases.

Everywhere I am, everywhere I go, everywhere I climb, these relativities stick out, extrude, jut out, abut, cantilever, these constant reminders of my own time left, which can no longer be vaguely stacked up in decades, years, or even months, as if towards the end the mad thing accelerated or telescoped out of control.

To hide up here would be impossible. How could I even think of such a thing?

It was windy and the sloping surface was awkward to walk on, and the battlements were too low for support. The additional height of the tower gave some advantage to the view, but only to the church car park and the back of the rectory. The rectory gardens, glebe field and ford were cut off by graveyard trees. Yews. Centuries old. Perhaps five hundred years, just after the discovery of America. The height of the tower enabled an oblique look into the butterfly roof, but not enough to be conclusive.

I couldn't flip the fibreglass lid back. There was a canvas strap but it had perished. I left it open. The additional light was useful for the descent. Let the rain pour onto the clock mechanism and rot the belfry ropes. Let it pour in as it may, of what concern was it to anyone but Natalie and her brass-rubbing, brass-grubbing kind. Instead of returning to the car I walked in stealth through the graveyard to the wicket gate at the glebe field. From there, once over the electric fence, I came down the path by the churchyard wall. Through the scant trees I saw the study light was on. Could I have left it on? With my electricity bills, I think not. There was a chance I had not noticed it was on, because the light was still bright even on this eastern side, but again that was more something I wanted to believe than could believe.

All around the house, a complete circuit, as I'd done

before going up to the church, but twice this time. On the second circuit I stopped at the front door and attacked the handle as if taking it by surprise. Still fast. But – What games! – when it came to the back door to the kitchen porch, I now had access.

Thanks so much, friends.

I slipped inside. The key had been returned to the exact spot I'd noted twenty minutes before. I was about to take it from the frame above the door when my mind misgave and I froze.

Voices . . .

At some distance, but from inside the house, definitely. Gentle, female voices. A run of open laughter too.

I took the key, pocketed it, entered, and crossed the ancient lino on tiptoe. To avoid the whine of the closer, I drew the door open only a fraction, and felt the quick draught from no-man's-land.

"Flesh pink, methinks . . ."

At some distance.

Flesh pink, methinks . . .

With those three, irrelevant, incidental, harmless words, with their playful, intimate tone, I understood everything.

So obvious! Once one knows.

But I couldn't blame myself too much on that account. I had done my best. Fought my corner. Sent Simmonds packing. Seen off Lyvich. Cut off poor Alex. But now they let me know what a gull I am, the true extent of it. Now they rub my nose in it.

"It would have to be faint."

In the dining room or drawing room.

Drawing room. More distant, but near the entrance, with door ajar.

"Faint would be too cold! Everything's quite cold enough as it is! Let me call it *Rose* and you'll agree, darling!"

Another run of gentle laughter.

"Am I right?"

Upstairs, possibly. Their words dropping down from the landing, heavy, frozen, into no-man's-land.

"Yes. You're right, of course. Picture rail?"

"Lily white gloss. Nothing else. Has to be lily white. Has to be gloss. No alternative. No decision. None of his eggshell blue nonsense."

I pulled the door wide, the closer whined, and the conversation stopped. Halfway through no-man's-land I peered into the drawing room. No one in view. I entered. The room was empty. Terribly empty. For a moment I stopped to wonder, to doubt, to get my bearings, but then there were steps on the stairs. They had been on the landing above, after all. I came out and stood at the foot of the staircase, hand on the newel post. The stairs are in three flights, rather broad and grandiose. They stopped together, side by side, on the lower landing. Natalie slipped her arm through Rachael's. Both were dressed up warm. Jumpers. Scarves. Thick trousers. Green, wet, wellington boots.

Rachael's smile was one I had not seen for twenty years. Not since the Lowestoft jetty that wonderful July day, the day she'd met Alex, and for a moment her smile brought that weather with her, that blustery but intermittently warm July day, into my cold, inhospitable hallway. Open, amiable, trusting, and full of optimism, honesty, youth. Carefree again, but with the peace of mind only money, not youth, can bring. Her hair, in its dark and slippery ringlets, was not the same, of course, and the look in her lovely grey eyes was not quite as it had been twenty years ago. I had been right all along about her heart-shaped face.

"There he is!" she declared. "And did you see any bats in the belfry?"

Natalie's bruising had subsided but not enough to leave her expression undistorted, so that her smile was something like a leer. Her left eye was darker, but more open, less shocking, less static than it had seemed before. The surgical collar had gone. She was on the mend.

That angry mix of excitement and loathing, such as I had felt when I'd discovered Simmonds trespassing in the garden, made me tighten my grip on the newel, triggering another severe pain across the shoulders, and from there, of course, the grotesque nodding.

"Oh Lord, he's off again!" Rachael said, resuming her descent, but taking care, looking down at the treads, as if she'd been drinking. Yet she hardly ever had a glass with Alex.

Natalie stayed with her, arm in arm, but said not a word until they were near the foot of the stairs, almost in reach. Her smile might have been genuinely squiffy because I could smell drink from both of them on the chilly air. Gin & tonics, or white ladies perhaps, as they'd sat by the fire at Long Cottage before popping round.

Without thinking – a reflex, a distress signal – I asked, "Where's Alex?"

Rachael glanced at her watch. "Tending to Joe's lunch, I hope," she replied. Then she looked up at me: "Joe always minds your son when I'm out and about . . . "

"My son," I repeated to her, and to myself, my voice heavy now, with a remembrance of my wife's words from years and years ago – "I just feel so sorry for my son, that's all" – and heavy with a lifetime's regret for how I had treated him. My son. Innocent, after all.

I looked as steadily as I could at Natalie.

"Your daughter."

"I told you to stay sharp," Rachael said, still smiling, but in her tone there was just a trace of pity now; at least, I thought there was.

Natalie wagged a finger at me: "Don't you even think about getting violent again, d'you hear? Frank's around somewhere. He'll deal with you, right enough!"

Saying so, on her lead, they turned away from me together, towards the kitchen. Natalie pushed the door wide against the closer. I was suddenly out of breath, too out of breath to follow.

"Horrible mess," she said, entering. "Wouldn't know where to start. Leave it to Carter's."

The door closed on its spring behind them.

I heard the clink of a glass against the kitchen tap. A run of water. Another run of laughter. Natalie's. The back door and the porch door opened and closed, and they were gone. I went back to the drawing room and stood by the French doors to wait for them. They took longer to appear than they should have done because they'd crossed the paddock to walk along the bank of the stream. They stopped and chatted at various points along the bank, Natalie pointing at trees, plants, clumps of reeds. At the end of the paddock they turned to follow the perimeter next to the glebe field, retracing Simmonds' trespass, but stopped about halfway to help each other over the fence into the field. I watched them walk through the pasture in their Wellington boots, following the route of that dead girl's gymkhana from two summers past, and up to the gate, and the ford, in the greying light, and they never once looked back.

Boxing Day, and there were still the crackers and hats, Butterball Turkeys, plum pud etcetera, and the smells all gathering in a warm sandwich – low piss rising from the underfloor heating, sage & onion high on its way down, and the jammy scents of vaporizers in between. I strode past it all after my walk. Crumpled mouths in crumpled heads under pink and green crumpled crowns. No talk, just eating. Forks and faces. They have become what they eat: broiler fowl, kept in their cages by the orderlies, who are just floral, fatter, far less jolly versions of Mumsy at The Leisure Pool. No men.

When I strutted past, chin up, head high, dentures clenched, an orderly called out:

"You'll get nowt unless you join a table and pull a cracker with me!"

Ha ha *ha*!

To be fair, the room is perfectly adequate. And, at last – at last! – it is warm. The struggle to keep warm that has dogged my whole life is over. I don't have to worry about how much it costs either. Nor what anything costs, for that matter.

There are certain no-go areas. There's a 'TV Room' where fifteen chairs surround a heavy set on a trolley. The tv is so old it's pre remote control. Each chair is occupied by a bewigged revenant, mainly female, incontinent without exception. At nine o'clock this morning one of them died again. The easy chairs stink not only of a thousand meaty Sunday dinners but of the excrement of such. They have casters fitted to the back legs. Two orderlies wheeled her out the room and took her body down a strip-lighted corridor to the 'Clinic'. That's another no-go area: entrance to the

'Clinic', even for an aspirin, is proscribed by old fanny Simmonds, who does most of the work of managing the place, as far as I can see. Frank sits in his counting house and 'meets and greets'. I can't help putting inverted commas around everything because words do not denote their customary meanings here. In the TV Room they only doze and die, their sleep induced by the sedatives fanny Simmonds slips into the drinks and food. Everything is drugged. Since arrival I have eaten nothing but bananas and McVities courtesy biscuits, that sit everywhere in bowls; the biscuits in sealed packets of three only. My room stinks of bananas. My dentures and breath stink of bananas. There was a short row yesterday because I'd taken The Daily Express to my room. Some ancient biddy wanted it back and tracked it down to me. She hissed at me in broad Norfolk:

"Yer breath stinks loike oald banaaaaaaana skins!"

Charmed, I'm sure. An orderly took her away, but with the Express.

Funny how seeing only the tacky MFI furniture around my room, which creates an undulating flow of pale beech veneer, and how hearing only these vague, linking sounds, of wheelchairs in the corridors scuffing the skirting boards, of heavy key rings, of cupboard mortice locks being locked or unlocked, of scrabbled voices on walkie-talkies, of occasional wails or shrieks – though those are rare, to be honest – funny how being surrounded by all of this, and being without all the paraphernalia of home, the caw of the crows, the still and empty drive, the kitchen door on its closer, and freezing no-man's-land beyond – funny how this change, this sudden swap, has led to a desuetude of memory, and what I can only describe as a sublime detachment.

Almost peace of mind.

The war, for goodness' sake! Laura! Oh yes, indeed!

All that. Alex as a child. His birth. Laura's death. Family life. His school. All ancient history to me now, like something about primitive peoples I might have read about in hard cover from one of Alex's book clubs. He might have sold me downriver for it in exchange for a case of Minervois and a dozen rotten eggs! Even the very, very recent past – Rachael and Natalie on the stairs – connects to nothing: they hover on the dirty landing in a thin grey film. None of it has currency in my new, warm room, surrounded by the beech MFI. Memory has no purchase on these antiseptic surfaces. As for peripheral stuff such as The Leisure Pool, the sauna, I can hardly believe they exist from here, only a few miles away on the edge of town, t'other side to The Grosvenor, and Aaron and Mark are but phantasmagoric figures in a moist red light – but no, not true: they are entirely without colour, feature, interest, consequence. They arouse no feeling whatever. Best forgotten, not dwelt upon. The Mediterranean lovely – gone. Sunk. Drowned. Disappeared without a trace. Ah, but how relieved she'll be that I no longer tap at her booth Mondays and Wednesdays. Thank god he's dead, she'll think.

Live for the present! Value every precious minute!

All Boxing Day. In this stink. Even Alex and Joe together – nothing. No one has visited and I can't think why anyone would, except Alex, perhaps. I think I should like him to come just once. I've said as much to fanny Simmonds, but she says visits are not advised for the first week or so. Later, then. It is not even a matter of curiosity to me what has happened at home. The dusty piano. Overgrown rose beds. Rotten attic windowsills. All of that . . . Good heavens! Good riddance! Carter's will be in there now, putting it all to rights, making it weatherproof, installing central heating just so they can work in the warm, and dry it all out for the decorators in the spring. A summer/autumn sale, perhaps.

Two residents, both male, tried to make my acquaintance, shall we say, on arrival. One of them is a simpleton: a tall, broad, loose, white human sack, that hangs upright somehow, as if from a coat hanger; a long sum that comes to nothing, a meaningless cipher of a fellow. Never found out his name. He has a theatrical shock of white hair, like a mad scientist from yesteryear's cartoons, and wears a pair of skew-whiff tortoiseshell glasses. He came to my room and just stood there in the doorway, taking up the whole space up to the architrave, watching me unpack, saying nothing.

"Hello?" I said. "And who on earth are you? . . . What can I do for you?"

He looked at me and frowned, but said not a word. I waited but nothing happened. I smiled as best I could and went back to my unpacking. After a few minutes an orderly came and led him away. Drugged to the eyeballs.

The other gentleman is Charles, who is a queer fish indeed. He is only fifty-five years old! Young enough to be my child! Alex's elder brother! I know his age because I asked him – big mistake, it turned out. At first I thought he worked in the place. He was sitting in the winter sun early this morning, just outside the dining room, where there's a patio area before a belt of lawn that ends in a high, Victorian garden wall. Come into the garden, Maud! A lofty and rather beautiful red brick wall. Margaret, are you grieving? Over Goldengrove unleaving? Because I thought he worked in the place, I asked Charles if he would move my bed for me. I want to arrange it so that when I lie down I can look at the sky, rather than just the car park beyond the net curtains. Then I learned that he too was a resident. "Good grief!" I exclaimed, and laughed. "But you're just a chicken! What are you doing here?" He told me his story in three or four simple sentences. He'd worked on his father's farm all his life. Then father died. He lived on with his mother, still working on the farm, till she died. He found he couldn't 'coape'. "What do you mean? Couldn't *coape*?" I queried. It seemed an extraordinarily feeble excuse for settling for life and death at The Grosvenor. "Couldn't coape with the cooken an' cleanen and tha'," he told me, as if it were the most natural thing in the world. He spoke in a slow, empty, very boring Norfolk drawl. I gave him an equally slow but very severe looking over, by way of an answer. His head is pointed, brainless, and his hair very thin all around and far too long. His shoulders slope down so unmanfully to his broad, sedentary base, that he has exactly the shape of a chess piece. A pawn or bishop. Talking to him, I felt like Alice in Wonderland. He's the most unlikely farm labourer you could ever imagine. "Good grief!" I said again. "But that's ridiculous!" I told him. "You're ridiculous!" I walked off and left him in the sun, which had gone in anyway. I didn't know what I'd started. When I returned from my walk around the beautiful garden wall, looking for a real gardener to help me with my bed, he retold, without prompting, the very same story he'd told me five minutes before, in those three or four simple sentences. I left without reply before he'd got halfway through. Then he started again, when I passed him by after lunch. "Oh shut up, Charles!" I told him. "Put on the B side, for goodness' sake!" He stared back open-mouthed. Now I have to avoid that exit altogether, and take a circuitous route through all the bodged extensions that leads me past the ghastly TV Room and the Clinic corridor, to a fire door at the rear. I get to the nether end of the garden wall via the kitchens and dustbins, then follow the circuit round, across the car park and back to the fire door, which

I have to leave ajar for re-entry. If the orderlies see me exit, they call out – "Mr Rose! Mr Rose! Mr Rose! Mr Rose!" – and then come and shut the door so I can't come back in that way. But they don't lock it because it's a fire door, and I've timed it to perfection a dozen times already. Nip and tuck all the way, of course – hamster on the wheel.

In the end I had my bed moved without Charles' assistance by going to see Frank in his counting house. He was most polite, couldn't have been more obliging, and saw to it straightaway. "No problem, Colonel!" He fetched a proper gardener, a big burly type in overalls, and lent a hand himself.

A strange arrangement because this side of the room is entirely taken up by two vast, white sliding doors, made of plastic, which should lead out to the car park but don't, because they're permanently locked with some kind of allen key. So it doesn't matter that my bed is now shunted next to them, leaving a foot or so for the passage of the beige curtains and the nets behind. With both drawn I can at last lie down and stare at the sky, which is very overcast as usual, but there is still some fascination in watching the changing clouds, the light and dark billowing about, changing shape, though at times it's much the same as watching the bodily stuff, the twists and straggles – broken blood vessels? – floating across the lens like amoebae, and that's all I do, no lingering reminiscence about the hours, not so many in total anyway, if I remember the log right, that I spent up there above it all, in the brilliant blue, behind the roaring Merlin, roller-coasting in the sky, as Alex used to say, my beloved son.